MURDER AT THE AUCTION

Growing increasingly frustrated with the situation, she checked the time. Bryce had been outside for almost twenty minutes. If he didn't show up soon, she'd give up and just mail his check. On the other hand, there was always an outside chance he'd stopped to talk to someone else on their way out. If she hurried, she might just catch him.

As soon as she reached the parking lot, she realized chasing after him was a stupid idea. She had no idea what kind of car he drove, so there was no way to know whether or not he'd already left.

As she made her way back to the door, she heard a faint beeping noise, the kind a car made when the door was left open. If that was the problem, she'd just close it so the battery didn't die. If there was something else wrong, she would memorize the license plate number and make an announcement once she got back inside.

Naturally, the car was parked all the way at the distant end of the lot. As she drew closer, it was clear that the driver's door was still open even though the beeping noise had finally stopped. Odd that someone would've walked away and left it like that, but there was no one in sight. But as she rounded the end of the car, she realized it wasn't only the battery that was dead.

The owner was, too. . . .

Books by Alexis Morgan

DEATH BY COMMITTEE
DEATH BY JACK-O'-LANTERN
DEATH BY AUCTION

Published by Kensington Publishing Corporation

DEATH BY AUCTION

Alexis Morgan

KENSINGTON BOOKS
www.kensingtonbooks.com

KENSINGTON BOOKS are published by

Kensington Publishing Corp.
119 West 40th Street
New York, NY 10018

All Kensington titles, imprints, and distributed lines are available at special quantity discounts for bulk purchases for sales promotion, premiums, fund-raising, and educational or institutional use.

Special book excerpts or customized printings can also be created to fit specific needs. For details, write or phone the office of the Kensington Sales Manager: Kensington Publishing Corp., 119 West 40th Street, New York, NY 10018. Attn. Sales Department. Phone: 1-800-221-2647.

First Kensington Books Mass Market Paperback Printing: June 2020
ISBN-13: 978-1-4967-1955-3
ISBN-10: 1-4967-1955-7

ISBN-13: 978-1-4967-1958-4 (ebook)
ISBN-10: 1-4967-1958-1 (ebook)

10 9 8 7 6 5 4 3 2 1

Printed in the United States of America

This book is dedicated to the wonderful ladies in my book club. Thank you for all the great discussions, the laughter, the amazing refreshments, and, most of all, your friendship!

I also want to thank my agent, Michelle Grajkowski, for her constant support. Having her in my life has made all the difference in my journey as a writer. As well, I am really grateful for everything my editor, John Scognamiglio, and everyone at Kensington have done to help me polish the Abby McCree Mysteries to the shiny bright best they can be.

Chapter One

"I'm pretty sure I hate you for making me do this."

Abby McCree prayed for patience and kept driving. "No, you don't."

Tripp Blackston, her tenant and usually her friend, didn't back off his stance on the upcoming event. The former Special Forces soldier took up far more than his fair share of the front seat as he sat there with his arms crossed over his chest and wearing a take-no-prisoners expression on his handsome face. "For the record, these days I don't appreciate being volunteered for missions without being asked first."

Okay, enough was enough. She couldn't believe he'd gone there. Rather than punch the man, which would've been childish, she tightened her grip on the steering wheel. "Um, I assume you do realize the reason I ended up organizing this fund-raiser for your veterans group in the first place was that someone volunteered me. Let's see now, who could that have been?"

Tapping her chin with her forefinger as if struggling to remember, she finally shot him a narrow-eyed look. "Oh, yeah, that would be you."

Before he could launch another salvo, Abby staged a preemptive strike of her own. "The original deal was that you and I were supposed to be co-chairs on the event, but somehow I ended up flying solo ninety percent of the time, maybe even ninety-five."

She paused long enough to make a left turn across what constituted heavy traffic in Snowberry Creek, which meant shooting between the only two oncoming cars on Main Street.

Driving into the parking lot on the other side of the road, Abby picked up the discussion where she'd left off. "I do realize that was because you'd gotten behind in your classes at the college and had to get caught up or risk falling behind a year in your studies. Of course, that was because you'd gotten yourself thrown into jail right when we were supposed to be brainstorming ideas together."

"I was protecting—"

"I know, I know. You were protecting your friend, but your decision to do that had consequences. One of them is that you're going to be strutting your stuff up there on that stage tonight for a good cause."

By that point, she'd run out of fresh ammunition in their ongoing battle over the bachelor/bachelorette auction she'd arranged to kick off the two-part fundraising event for his veterans group. The close-knit organization had big plans, ones that could really help other veterans in the area. But to carry out those plans, their budget needed a huge boost.

Tripp had asked her to take on the project as a personal favor. Well, actually, he'd guilted her into doing it. Something about him having helped her deal with a dead body in her backyard a few months back. Fine, so she'd owed him big-time. The least he could do was let her honor the debt without giving her constant grief about it.

She pulled into a parking spot near the entrance of the hall they'd rented for the auction, as well as the dance that would follow in two weeks. After shutting off the engine, she made no move to get out of the car.

"Look, I'm sorry you hate this so much, but it was the best idea I came up with. The whole board liked the concept and approved it immediately."

Nothing but silence from the other side of the car.

"The good news is that two weeks from now, it will all be over."

Tripp wasn't the only one who couldn't wait to put all of this behind them. There was nothing but stubborn silence coming from her companion, so she gave up and reached to open her door. He could come inside the building and be helpful, or sit out in the car and mope. His choice. She refrained from pointing out sulking wasn't a good image for a soldier, even a retired one.

At least he got out of the car and even helped her carry in the last three baskets of goodies that had been donated by local businesses. She had volunteers lined up to sell chances on the baskets, which she hoped would help get the evening off to a great start. Some of the businesses had shown a lot of creativity when it came to putting their offerings together. In fact, she had her eye on a couple that she wouldn't mind taking back home with her.

Tripp followed her over to the row of tables arranged across the back of the hall, where the baskets were displayed. "You can set those two down there."

He did as she asked but continued to trail along in her wake, crowding her just a little. Finally, she set her own basket down and turned to face him.

"Did you have something else you wanted to say, Tripp? If so, spit it out. I've got work to do before the doors open."

He no longer looked angry. In fact, if she had to guess, Tripp looked . . . embarrassed? What was going on in that head of his? All of her irritation with him morphed into concern.

"Tripp, what's wrong?"

He glanced around the big room as if to make sure they were still alone before zeroing in his attention back on her. "Don't let her buy me, Abby. Bid whatever you have to and I'll pay you back. I promise."

"Don't let who buy you?"

"Jean." His broad shoulders slumped in defeat. "Don't get me wrong. She's a really nice lady, but taking her to the dance would be like dating my best friend's grandmother."

Abby bit back the urge to laugh. Clearly he didn't find anything about the situation funny. "What makes you think she's planning on bidding on you?"

"Let's just say she strongly hinted at the possibility and more than once."

Abby wasn't privy to all the details about the elderly woman's finances, but she'd always had the impression that Jean lived on a pretty limited income. If so, she certainly shouldn't blow a wad of cash on a one-time outing with Tripp, not even for a good cause.

On the other hand, judging by how often Jean showed up at Tripp's door with one of her infamous tuna casseroles, she definitely had a thing for the man. So did at least two other members of the quilting guild that Abby headed up. She'd somehow inherited the position on the guild board along with the house she now lived in when her aunt Sybil passed away. Tripp lived in the small mother-in-law house on the back of the property and attended classes at the local college. In return for a reduction in his rent, he did a lot of work on the yard and small repairs on both houses.

Jean, along with her best friends Glenda and Louise, loved to watch him work, especially on hot days when he took off his shirt.

Okay, maybe she did owe him a little something for putting him through this. That didn't mean she couldn't give him a little grief along the way. "I'm sorry, but you can't pay for a date with yourself, Tripp. That wouldn't be right. I'm sure it would be against the rules."

He took another step closer. "What rules, Abby? You set up this whole event. That means you can do things however you want."

True enough. Even though she hadn't said so, she'd planned all along to bid on him. It was just too much fun watching him squirm to let him off the hook too easily.

"Regardless, I can't stop her from bidding."

And they both knew it would hurt her feelings if they tried.

"Look, forget I asked. I'm just not into this kind of thing, and it's weirding me out on so many fronts."

She didn't need the reminder that he was a pretty private person. Heck, she'd known him for over a year now and still had no idea what degree he was working toward at the college. On the other hand, she knew for a fact he'd risk his own life to keep her safe.

"This is a new experience for all of us, but at least you won't be alone up there on the stage. Gage even volunteered to lead things off."

She'd been pleasantly surprised by that, although it was a huge relief that she didn't have to beg someone to take that first step down the runway. Gage was the local chief of police and an army veteran. He and Tripp had actually served together at some point in the past, the details of which neither man had ever seemed eager to share with her.

That was a discussion for another day. Right now, she had a long checklist she needed to finish up before the auction was due to start.

"I promise I'll do my best to make all of this as painless for you as possible. Right now, though, I've got to finish up a few things before the onrushing hordes start arriving."

Tripp snickered. "And what happens if these hordes you're planning on don't actually show up?"

The last thing she needed was for him to mention her worst fear out loud. What would happen if no one came? She'd lost enough sleep the past few weeks over that very idea. "Don't say that. You'll jinx everything!"

The big jerk actually looked happy for the first time all day. "What's the matter, Abs? You're not superstitious, are you?"

"I am when it comes to stuff like this. It's a lot of responsibility. We can't give even the idea of failure a chance to get a toehold in our thinking. Your group has already paid out a lot of money in advance of these events, money they can't afford to lose."

Not to mention she'd feel obligated to pay them back if her idea fell flat on its face. She'd done everything she could to keep the overhead to a minimum, but the expense would definitely put a crimp in her lifestyle for a while.

To derail any more discussion along that line, she pointed Tripp toward the tables shoved up against the wall. "Would you start dragging those out and arrange them in rows? The rest of the crew should be arriving soon to help finish setting up."

"And here I thought I was only here as part of the evening's entertainment. No one said anything about having to do a bunch of grunt work, too. How disappointing."

Despite his complaint, he headed off toward the tables. She left him to it and moved on to the next item on her list.

Ninety minutes later, Abby stood against the back wall and surveyed her surroundings. The hall was pleasantly crowded, far more so than she'd expected it to be even in her wildest dreams. So far everyone seemed to be having a good time. For sure, the caterers had outdone themselves, serving a wide variety of hors d'oeuvres coupled with wines from local vineyards, along with coffee, tea, and soft drinks.

The evening was rolling along smoothly, at least so far. There was only one problem. The actual auction was scheduled to start in fifteen minutes, and there was still no sign of Bryce Cadigan, the man Abby had hired to run the whole shebang. Bryce was a Seattle radio personality, but he'd grown up right here in Snowberry Creek. She'd checked his references, and he'd come highly recommended.

Traffic in the Puget Sound area was problematic at times, and he'd texted to let her know that he'd gotten caught in the backup caused by an accident. While she understood that had been out of his control, he'd promised to arrive an hour before the auction was supposed to begin. Judging from where he'd been when he texted her, there was no way he'd left when he should have.

Unless the crowd got super restless, she would delay the start of the festivities up to an extra half hour and then step in and do the best she could on her own. While she really didn't want to emcee the actual bachelor auction, picking the winners for the baskets wouldn't be all that hard to do.

A distinguished looking man with a scattering of silver in his dark hair stepped out of the crowd to head right for her. She'd first met Pastor Jack Haliday the day she'd presented her ideas about the fund-raiser to the veterans group. Just like Gage, he'd volunteered to be another one of her "victims," as they'd taken to calling everyone who had agreed to be auctioned off tonight. When she'd asked him if he was really sure he wanted to do it, he'd stared into the distance for several seconds before responding.

"I can't lead from behind, Abby. Helping those who served our country is important to me. I'll do whatever it takes for our mission to succeed."

As he spoke, he had the same shadows in his eyes that she sometimes saw in Tripp's and even Gage's. None of them talked much about their time in combat, but it had definitely left its mark on all three men. The power in his answer had helped carry her through all the hassles involved in getting something like this up and running.

Jack scanned the room. "I'm thrilled with the turnout tonight."

Relieved was more like it, but thrilled also worked. "I am, too. I finally feel like I can breathe again."

His smile turned sympathetic. "We never meant for you to feel that all of this was on your shoulders."

She put on a brave face. "I really didn't."

Okay, they both knew that was a lie. "Well, not all the time. One of the positives Tripp told me when he asked me to help out was that your group was used to working as a team and taking orders. He was right about that. Whenever I posted a job description that needed to be filled, there was someone ready and willing to step up to get it done. No nagging necessary. I can't tell you how refreshing that was."

"Yeah, we have a good bunch of people in the group."

He dropped his voice. "I actually came over because I noticed you keep checking the time and watching the door. Is something wrong?"

"Our guest of honor for tonight hasn't arrived. He texted to say he'd gotten stuck in a backup on I-5, but I thought he'd be here by now. If he doesn't show up soon, I'll start the evening's festivities myself by picking the winners for all the baskets."

"Good plan. Let me know if I can do anything to help."

Before she could answer, the door that led out to the parking lot opened and a tall man wearing a tuxedo walked into the room. Although she'd never met Bryce Cadigan in person, she recognized him from the pictures on his website. Well, except he'd been smiling in all the photos he'd posted there. He wasn't now.

"Whew! There he is."

She and the pastor made their way across the room to where the newcomer stood waiting for someone to notice him. Abby stopped right in front of him and stuck out her right hand. "Mr. Cadigan, I'm so glad you finally made it."

His gaze did another slow sweep of the room before he finally tipped his head down enough to look at her. When he didn't immediately speak, she launched into the necessary introductions. "We've spoken on the phone. I'm Abby McCree, and this is Pastor Haliday, the head of our local veterans group."

A slick smile slid into place on Bryce's handsome face as he gave her hand a quick shake and then offered his to Jack. "If you'll point me in the right direction, I'll get started."

He directed the comment to Jack, looking over Abby's head as if she were invisible. Jack immediately deferred to her. "Abby organized this whole thing. If you have any questions about what comes next, you should ask her."

Jack turned to face Abby more directly. The sly twinkle in his eyes made it clear he sensed her irritation and understood. "I'll go join my fellow 'auctionees' and let them know we're about to start."

He walked away without saying another word to Bryce, leaving Abby to deal with the emcee for the evening. She pulled out the crib sheets she'd typed up for him. "Here is the lineup for tonight's festivities. I'd penciled in approximate times for everything, but we're already a little behind."

"The traffic—"

She cut him off. "No need to apologize, Mr. Cadigan. I'm sure you got here as quickly as you could."

She'd meant to come across as friendly and professional, but his eyes narrowed just a touch in response. Maybe he'd picked up the hint of irritation she'd been trying to hide. "Let's head over to the stage."

A ripple of recognition followed in their footsteps as they made their way over to the door that led backstage. A few people called out Bryce's name as he passed by, but he simply offered them a quick wave and kept walking. Then one man planted himself right in front of them and blocked their path. For the first time, Bryce's smile looked genuine, and he slowed down. "Coach, I'm so glad to see you, but if I stop to talk now, we'll never get things started. I promise to find you as soon as I finish up onstage."

"Sounds good, Bryce. I just wanted to make sure you knew I was here."

They made it the rest of the way without interruption. Once they were clear of all the hubbub, Bryce stopped to read over the notes she'd given him. "This all looks pretty easy. I'll warm up the crowd a little first. After that, it's baskets and then the auction itself. Will you be close by if I do have any questions?"

"I'll be seated at the front table on this side. When you're ready for the baskets, give me a nod. I have volunteers lined up to carry them up to you. They will hold out the bag that contains the tickets for each one. After you choose the winner, the volunteer will deliver the basket to that person before returning to pick up another basket if there are any left."

Then she handed him the final printout she'd put together. "Here is the list of our 'auctionees' for the evening, otherwise known as my victims. I had each of them give you a brief bio and some interesting facts about themselves."

He glanced through the pages and actually looked genuinely impressed. "You've thought of everything, Ms. McCree. That will make everything flow more smoothly for everyone involved. Thanks for all the work you put into making my job easier."

Pleased that he'd noticed, she injected more warmth into her voice. "You're welcome." Then she pointed across the stage. "I set a small table over there with bottled water for you. I figured auctioneering is probably thirsty work."

"It is that."

"Well, if you're ready, I'll read the introduction you gave me, and then we're off and running."

For the duration of that brief conversation, Bryce seemed real and more genuine somehow. Then he shot the cuffs of his snowy-white shirt, drew a deep breath, and closed his eyes for a few seconds. When he opened them, it was as if he'd slipped on a totally different persona, and the overly polished slick charm was back in full force.

Bryce was undeniably handsome, but for some reason he left her completely cold. Crossing her fingers the audience didn't react that way, she walked out to center stage and picked up the microphone.

"If I can have everyone's attention, I'd like to introduce Snowberry Creek's very own Bryce Cadigan!"

Forty-five minutes later, Abby had dollar signs dancing in her eyes. Zoe had reported in that the ticket sales for the baskets had far exceeded everyone's expectations. Considering all of the goodies had been donated, the money taken in was pure profit. Abby had even won one of the baskets herself that she was excited about. It had come from a local bookstore and contained a wide variety of autographed books by Pacific Northwest writers.

She gave Bryce credit for keeping everyone's attention riveted on him. His opening monologue had been funny, even if it contained a few barbed comments about some of the people in the audience. She suspected a couple of the folks he'd singled out for attention didn't enjoy the experience as much as they pretended to, but they hid it pretty well.

As promised, Gage Logan had been the first victim to walk up onstage to be auctioned off. He'd quickly gotten into the spirit of the thing and made a second

trip down the runway, encouraging the bidders to up
the ante. After a brief flurry of bids, his price was up to
almost four digits. To everyone's surprise, it was Mayor
McKay who jumped to her feet and offered an even
thousand dollars. Bryce immediately declared Gage
sold.

The next man up was Pastor Haliday. He lacked a
little of Gage's panache, but he quickly garnered his
own share of bids. No one, him especially, expected
Connie Pohler to counter every other bid that was offered. She was the mayor's executive assistant and had
perhaps taken her cue from her boss to go big or go
home. Once the bids slowed down, she stood up and
offered a thousand and one dollars. Bryce's hammer
came down before anyone else could say a word.

Abby was pretty sure she wasn't the only one who
was staring at Connie as if they'd never really seen her
before. Jack looked a little shell-shocked as he stepped
down off the stage to where Connie stood waiting for
him. Luckily for the them, Bryce had already announced the next candidate and the attention shifted
back to the stage to see what happened next.

They were nearing the end of the auction, and
Tripp would be stepping up to bat right after the
woman who was up onstage now. As soon as he came
into sight, Jean and her two friends sat up straighter,
confirming Tripp's worst fears. That was all right.
Abby would let them have fun bidding, but then she
would jump in with a sniper bid high enough to shut
them down.

While they might be disappointed, they'd forgive
her. All three women were romantics at heart, and
they all thought it was time Abby put her divorce behind her and started dating again. They'd be thrilled

if she and Tripp actually got together for something more exciting than coffee and cookies at her kitchen table.

Bryce announced the man in question's name. "And finally, here we have Tripp Blackston. He is a former master sergeant in the Special Forces. After twenty years in the army, he's now living here in Snowberry Creek and attending college."

Tripp looked good in his dark green dress shirt and gray slacks, a dramatic change from his usual jeans and T-shirt. Strutting to the end of the runway, he did a three-sixty turn and smiled down at the audience. To no one's surprise, the ladies went crazy.

As soon as Bryce opened the bidding, numbers came flying in from all over the room. Not to shortchange Tripp's good looks, but Abby suspected the high interest might have had a lot to do with the amount of wine that had been consumed over the course of the evening. Regardless, Abby kept an eye on Jean and company, who were her most serious competition. To give Tripp credit, despite his earlier reservations about being up there in the first place, he really worked the crowd. When Jean upped her bid for the third time, he gave her a long, lingering look and winked. Abby was pretty sure the elderly woman swooned.

Crazy man, didn't he know the lady had a heart condition?

The bidding had already reached four digits, already bypassing the previous high bid by more than a hundred dollars. It was time to swoop in for the kill. Bryce raised his gavel in preparation to end the bidding. Abby stood up to catch his eye.

"I bid—"

But before she could finish, another voice rang out

over the room. "I bid five thousand dollars for Tripp Blackston."

For the length of a heartbeat the room went completely quiet. The shocking amount of money left even Bryce momentarily speechless, but then he slammed the gavel down. "Sold to the lady in the back for five grand!"

Abby sank back down onto her chair. Tripp looked as if he'd just been hit with a sledgehammer as he made his way down off the stage, where a stunning blonde stood waiting for him. As soon as he reached her side, she threw her arms around his neck and kissed him as if she'd been lost in the desert and he was a glass of water. It seemed unlikely that he'd let a total stranger do something like that, which meant the two of them had a past.

Even after he broke off the embrace, the woman clung to him like a barnacle. A gorgeous, tall barnacle with depressingly long legs and wearing a dress that cost more than Abby's entire wardrobe. When Tripp finally glanced in Abby's direction, she mouthed a single word: "Who?"

When he answered, she really, really wished she hadn't asked. His reply was only two simple words, but they turned their whole relationship inside out and upside down.

There was a lot of guilt in his dark eyes as he answered, "My wife."

Chapter Two

Abby had been sitting with several of the board members, but they had all drifted off to spend time with other friends now that the formal part of the evening's activities was over. She should probably do some schmoozing, too, but she wasn't in the mood.

Unfortunately, she was about to get some unwelcome company. Jean was headed straight for her, slamming her walker down on the floor with each step she took. Glenda and Louise trailed along in Jean's wake until the trio coasted to a stop right in front of Abby. At least they blocked her view of Tripp and the woman he would now escort to the dance. She really didn't want to discuss the situation, but it was a relief to no longer be staring straight at Mr. and Mrs. Tripp Blackston. Heck, even she had to admit they made a handsome couple.

She fought the urge to curse or cry or maybe both. In all the time she'd known him, Tripp had never once even hinted he was married. The deception was upsetting enough on its own, but that darn man had kissed her, and not just once. Granted, it usually happened right after she'd been through some harrowing, life-threatening situation. Regardless of the reason, those kisses had packed one heck of a toe-curling punch. Nothing like what she would've expected from a friend merely expressing relief that she was still alive.

For a man whose sense of honor had defined his entire life, the whole situation seemed out of character for Tripp. Had it just been wishful thinking on her part that his feelings for her were more than a tenant for a favorite landlady?

"Who is that . . . that *woman*?"

From the venom in Jean's voice, Abby wasn't the only one feeling betrayed right now. "I'm not sure."

Okay, that was a lie. But until Tripp offered her a more in-depth explanation about what was going on, she wasn't going to spread rumors about him. Hoping to change the subject, she said, "The veterans group is going to be thrilled with how much money we've taken in tonight. The auction was a huge success."

Glenda sat down next to Abby and gave her a disgusted look. "Seriously, Abby? That stranger is over there hanging on Tripp like she owns him, and you're sitting here talking about money."

What was she supposed to say?

Abby tried to put a positive spin on the situation. "Tripp clearly knows the woman, Glenda. Considering the amount of cash she just donated to support a cause that's important to him, it's no surprise he feels obligated to spend time with her."

The other two women took their chairs and turned them so that they had an unobstructed view of the couple. Jean pursed her lips and glared at the blonde. "The three of us would've enjoyed having a handsome young man escort us to the dance, but we would've been just as happy if he'd been your date for the evening. After all the work you've done to set this whole thing up, you certainly deserve to have a good time at the dance, but now it's too late for you to bid on someone else. I hate that you might have to go alone."

Louise shook her head. "That won't happen. There's plenty of room in Glenda's car for Abby. She can go with us."

Now that was an awful idea. Her and three octogenarians? Abby loved them dearly, but that was so not happening. "I appreciate the offer of a ride, ladies, but I have to be here hours before the dance actually begins. I can drive myself."

Not that she'd ever envisioned she'd end up going solo to the dance. Considering she and Tripp were supposedly the co-chairs of the whole event, she'd mistakenly assumed they'd be attending together even if she'd had to pay for the privilege. Heck, he'd even begged her to make that happen if for no other reason than to keep him from having to escort Jean and company. Clearly he hadn't been expecting his wife to show up and plunk down the big bucks.

She knocked back the last of her glass of wine. "Look, I should go mingle. I want to thank as many of our donors in person as I can."

Before she stood up, Jean laid her age-spotted hand on Abby's arm. "Just know that it will be a long time before I give that boy another of my casseroles. He doesn't deserve them. Not after this."

Maybe it was the wine, but that struck Abby as really funny. It took considerable effort to choke back the urge to laugh, because that would only hurt the elderly woman's feelings. But still, Tripp would be happy to learn Jean would no longer be showing up on his doorstep with her latest tuna-flavored creation. All it had taken was having his wife show up.

She appreciated her friends' support, but it was important to remember that she had no real claim on the man. "Please don't let this one thing ruin this evening for you ladies or change how you feel about Tripp. We're all here to show our support of the people who served our country. We can't change how things turned out, but we can still enjoy ourselves. I'll send someone over with another bottle of wine for you to share and ask one of the waiters to bring you something to snack on."

After making good on her promise to send them more refreshments, she snagged another drink for herself and began making the rounds.

It took her half a glass of wine and a lot of determined effort to shed some of her anger at Tripp and his wife. Hanging out with Zoe, her husband Leif, and their friends helped a lot. Zoe had been an army nurse, and the guys had served multiple deployments together. Right now they were arguing over who would've brought the highest bids if they'd been single and eligible for the auction.

Leif sidled closer to her. "So, Abby, give us your impartial opinion. Which one of us would've given Tripp a run for his money to earn top dollar tonight?"

All three men immediately struck ridiculous poses and flexed their muscles, no doubt thinking they looked sexy as heck. She gave each of them a long look and then fanned herself with her hand. "Guys, please don't make me choose. You're all too totally swoon-worthy."

Rather than being disappointed, they all high-fived one another as their wives shook their heads at their antics. Leif gave Zoe a fast kiss. "What? The woman's clearly got good taste."

Abby moved on from that group to talk to Pastor Haliday. He was standing in the back corner by himself, his gaze trained on someone across the room. Abby followed his line of sight to realize he was watching Connie Pohler as she chatted with the mayor and Gage Logan. If she'd had to describe the look on his face, she would have said he looked . . . hungry. Interesting.

Maybe he finally sensed he wasn't alone, because he blinked and then turned in her direction. "Hi, Abby. Congratulations on turning all of this into such a huge success."

His approval pleased her. "You know I couldn't have done it without the full support of the board and all the volunteers."

He gave her a sly look. "I suppose it's a bit too soon to ask if you'd like to head up the stewardship fund drive at my church this fall."

She really hoped he was teasing. She'd made a personal vow to avoid any other commitments for the foreseeable future, but she would have a hard time turning down the affable pastor. "Yeah, it is, especially considering I'm not even a member of your church."

"That can be fixed easily enough. We can make you an honorary member." Then he winked at her. "Or even a real one if you'd like."

That was a slippery slope, one she was in no hurry to go sliding down. Time to change subjects and address the elephant in the room. "So, I take it you were surprised when Connie outbid everyone else for the pleasure of your company."

He immediately turned beet red. "Yes, I was. She could've picked someone who would make for a more exciting date for the dance."

Clearly the man had no idea how attractive he was. After all, Connie hadn't been the only woman who'd placed a bid in the hope of having Jack for her date at the dance; she'd just been the most determined one. "I think she looked pretty darned happy when Bryce declared her the winner."

"If you say so. I've already warned her that I haven't danced in years. Even then, my ex-wife could never understand how I could march in formation with no problem but stumbled over my own two feet on the dance floor."

Abby didn't know anything about his ex-wife, but she pointed out the obvious. "Maybe you were just dancing with the wrong woman."

"Maybe." His smile turned a bit sad. "My ex remarried years ago and, by all reports, is far happier than she ever was with me. I'm truly glad for that. She was a good woman, Abby, just not cut out to be an army wife. It certainly didn't help that I came back from my deployments a different man from the one she'd married."

Abby gave him a quick hug. "I'll have to take your word for that, but I like the man you are now just fine. I'm guessing Connie does, too. Speaking of whom, she's headed this way."

That hungry look made another fleeting appearance as he watched Connie work her way through the crowd in their direction.

Which meant it was time to move on. For one thing,

she needed to give Bryce Cadigan the check for the second half of his fee for the evening and have him sign off on the contract. It took her a minute to pick him out in the crowd. He was in the back corner talking to another man about his own age, perhaps someone he'd gone to high school with back in the day. Although Bryce was smiling, the other man didn't look nearly as happy about being cornered by the town's golden boy. Maybe she was imagining things, but there seemed to be a lot of tension in the way he stood and kept scanning the room beyond, as if hoping for someone to come rescue him.

"Abby, can we talk?"

Darn it, she'd meant to keep an eye on Tripp's whereabouts. The last thing she wanted right now was to talk to him, but he'd managed to slip up behind her unnoticed. The man had uncanny stealth capabilities for someone his size. Must be a talent left over from his days in the Special Forces.

"Sorry, but now isn't a good time, Tripp. I have things to do, people to see."

Before she could walk away, he caught her arm. She stared down at his hand and then back up to meet his gaze. Normally, she liked his touch. This time, though, the small connection hurt her heart.

"Sorry," he mumbled as he let his hand drop back down to his side. "Please, I need to explain."

"Explain what, exactly?"

Like she didn't know. She wasn't playing dumb; she was just angry and hurt.

"Valerie isn't my wife."

Yeah, right. "You said she was. Were you lying earlier or lying now?"

He ran his fingers through his hair in obvious frustration. "She isn't my wife now, but she used to be. Val was in college when we met, and we got married right after I joined the army. The marriage didn't last all that long. I was gone so much in those days that Val said it was like not having a husband at all. It didn't help that while she was going to school, I was going to war. Realizing we lived in two different worlds, she filed for divorce when I left on my third deployment."

The couple had broken up a long time ago, but she could still hear the hurt in Tripp's voice. Maybe the ex-Mrs. Blackston had good reasons to walk away from their marriage, but it was clear Tripp had clearly felt differently about the situation. Knowing him, he saw it as a major failure on his part. Pastor Haliday's comments about his own divorce had echoed that same sentiment. Heck, she had similar feelings about her own marriage falling apart.

Her anger slowly dissipated. "I'm sorry, Tripp. I know how much it hurts."

"I didn't intentionally keep my marriage secret from you. I just don't like talking about it." He stared across the room to where Valerie stood talking to the mayor. "It all happened so long ago that I barely remember what it felt like to be married. I swear I would've warned you if I'd known she was going to show up here tonight."

"So you didn't know she was coming?"

Tripp looked frustrated. "No, I haven't heard from Val in years. I was as shocked as anybody when she plunked down that much money just to go to a dance with me. It makes no sense, and Val hasn't explained why she's here, not just at the auction, but in the area. She lives in Los Angeles. If she had something to say to me, she could've just called."

It didn't seem likely the woman was interested in getting back together with Tripp after all this time, but that might be wishful thinking on Abby's part. There had to be a pretty powerful reason for her to spend thousands of dollars to force him to spend an evening in her company.

"Maybe she was in town anyway and heard about the auction. She could've wanted to see how you're doing these days. You know, for old time's sake."

"I can't imagine why." He frowned as he considered that idea. "She does travel some for work, though. The last I heard Val is the head buyer for Suits-Herself, Inc. You might have heard of it."

"Yeah, I have."

Seriously, was the man totally clueless? Suits-Herself was a chain of high-end clothing stores that catered to women executives. Back in Abby's previous life, she had shopped there, but only when they had a major sale going on. It didn't help Abby's mood to learn that Valerie was both gorgeous and successful. Was it wrong to hate her just on principle?

It was time to change the subject. She really didn't want to stand around and talk about Tripp's former wife. There was one thing that might cheer Tripp up a little. "Just so you know, Jean is mad that you let yourself get bought by someone other than me or her. She said you won't be getting another of her casseroles anytime soon."

Tripp's laughter rang out across the room, turning heads in their direction. "Seriously? All it took was having Val show up? If I'd known that, I would've begged her to stop by weeks ago."

Then his expression sobered. "I guess I should apologize to Jean, too."

"Yes, you should."

Then Abby waited for him to follow that thought to

its logical conclusion. It didn't take long. "And if I do, she'll probably bring me a casserole to let me know I'm back in her good graces."

Now she was the one who was laughing. "I can pretty much guarantee it."

He chuckled again. "Guess I'll just enjoy the respite while it lasts."

"That's the spirit, Tripp. Look on the bright side."

"What bright side is that?"

They both turned to face Valerie. Maybe she'd picked up a few of Tripp's ninja skills while they'd been married, because he also seemed surprised that the woman had somehow slipped up behind them. If Abby had noticed she was headed their way, she would've made some excuse to Tripp and disappeared into the crowded room.

When he didn't respond, Abby struggled to come up with an answer that made sense. While she and Tripp might find Jean's love for sharing tuna amusing, she wouldn't invite the other woman to enjoy a joke at their friend's expense. "I was just telling him that tonight's success has already resulted in someone else wanting me to run a fund-raiser for them. Rather than feel sorry for me, he's celebrating it's not one he would have to help with."

Valerie clearly didn't get it, but that was okay. Meanwhile, she elbowed him in the ribs. "Where are your manners, Tripp? Aren't you going to introduce us?"

"Oops, sorry. This is my landlady, Abby McCree. Abs, this is Valerie Brunn, my ex-wife."

The poor guy just kept stumbling over his own two feet tonight, because neither she nor Valerie were happy with his introductions. Couldn't he have just said Abby was a friend? Calling her his landlady made her sound decades older than he was when she was several years younger. Rather than point it out, she forced a smile and held out her hand. "Nice to meet you, Ms. Brunn."

The handshake was quick and cool as they assessed each other. Valerie immediately latched on to Tripp's arm again, staking out her territory. "Likewise, Ms. McCree. I'm guessing from a few comments I've overheard tonight, you expected to be the one going to the dance with Tripp."

"Really? That's odd since I didn't actually place any bids this evening."

Only because of Valerie's sniper bid, but that didn't make it any less true. Rather than let the conversation deteriorate any further, she aimed for the high ground. "I do want to thank you for supporting the veterans group. I know Tripp and the other members appreciated everyone turning out tonight for a good cause. Now, if you two will excuse me, I have some business to attend to."

Valerie might have said something else, but Abby just kept walking. As she did, she stared at the clock on the wall and begged it to pick up speed. She really needed this evening to end.

It was tempting to drink another glass of wine, but it wouldn't help. Abby had been trying unsuccessfully to corner Bryce Cadigan for the past half hour. She wasn't on the cleanup crew tonight, and the only thing holding her there was the need to hand him his check.

Right after she'd walked away from Tripp and his ex-barnacle, she spotted Bryce over near the stage. By the time she'd gotten there, he was deep in conversation with the high school football coach and a few other men. Maybe she'd have that glass of wine after all.

In just the couple of minutes it took her to flag down a waiter, Bryce had moved on from talking to the coach to having what looked like a pretty intense discussion with another man. This one was older with graying hair worn pulled back in a short ponytail. Bryce was no longer smiling, his usual charm nowhere to be seen. If anything, he looked uncomfortable as he focused on what the man had to say. He took a couple of steps back as if trying to end the conversation, but his companion followed him step for step. What was that all about? Not that it was any of her business.

Rather than interrupt them, she'd stopped to talk to Gage and the mayor, Rosalyn McKay. She found it interesting that the pair had been inseparable all evening,

Rosalyn glanced around at the crowded room. "Abby, I'm impressed. You did an amazing job organizing all of this. I'm really excited about the dance, too. Going World War II retro was such a clever idea."

Abby thought so, too. "I'm glad to hear it. It's a huge relief the turnout has been so great. I've had a few sleepless nights worrying I'd be the only one who showed up."

She didn't regret the evening's success, but impressing Rosalyn McKay might not have been in Abby's own self-interest. The woman had already drafted her into running one committee here in town. She'd already handed that group off to her successor and didn't want the mayor or her assistant deciding they had another perfect spot to plug Abby into their network of boards and committees.

Meanwhile, Abby kept an eye on Bryce, who had finally escaped the man he'd been with a short time ago. Right now he stood still, his attention riveted on someone across the room. After a few seconds, he smiled and cut across the room at a fast pace, barely acknowledging the various people who called out greetings as he passed by. Given his current trajectory, it appeared that his target was the trio of women standing in the back corner.

As he closed in on them, one of them finally took notice and said something to the other two. Although Abby couldn't hear what was being said, it appeared she was trying to shoo the other two away. After a brief hesitation, they gave Bryce one more questioning look before abandoning their friend to face him alone. Even from where Abby stood, it was easy to tell the smile the woman offered Bryce looked a bit forced.

He hugged her, holding on a little longer than the woman appreciated. He grinned when she tried to shove him back. Whatever he said to the woman had her dropping her hands back down to her sides and glancing around to see if anyone was watching them. As their conversation continued, their body language was definitely interesting. Bryce seemed to be enjoying himself, but his companion was anything but relaxed.

When Bryce leaned in close to whisper something close to the lady's ear, she stiffened, her hands clenched briefly into fists. Either the man didn't pick up on the woman's discomfort at being crowded, or else he didn't care. If anything, he hovered even closer for several seconds before finally taking a short step back.

Gage must have picked up on Abby's interest in Bryce Cadigan's ongoing conversation, because he asked, "Is something wrong?"

The woman looked marginally happier now that Bryce had given her a little breathing room, although her smile remained a little tight. Either way, it wasn't

Abby's problem. "No, I was just trying to thin
lady's name, the one talking to Bryce Cadigan ov
the corner. I noticed she ended up with one of the
baskets, and I'm trying to thank everyone who finan-
cially supported our cause tonight."

Both of her companions looked to see whom she was
talking about. It was Rosalyn who answered, "That's
Robin Alstead. She used to teach English at the high
school, but now she works at that big discount store out
near the highway. I don't know much about her other
than she's a member of that really conservative
church about ten miles north of here. Her late husband was a deacon there, I believe."

What little Abby had heard about that congregation explained the woman's rather old-fashioned at-
tire. She wore no makeup, and her hair was coiled in a
braid at the nape of her neck. Her simple white blouse
was paired with a mid-calf-length navy skirt and plain
black flats.

Bryce said something else and then walked away
laughing. Mrs. Alstead appeared to be relieved that he
was gone. After taking a quick look around, maybe
wondering where her friends had gone, she disappeared down the nearby hallway that led toward the
restrooms. She hesitated right at the entrance to
watch Bryce for a few more seconds before disappearing from sight.

Meanwhile, Bryce continued toward the exit. Realizing he might be leaving, Abby said, "If you two will excuse me, I've got to catch Bryce while I have a chance."

Once again, she didn't move fast enough. Before
Abby had gone half a dozen steps, Valerie Brunn
blocked his way, which brought the man to a screeching halt. Abby froze in her tracks, not wanting to cross
paths with Tripp's ex again. On the other hand, the in-

terchange between Val and Bryce was riveting. It looked as if Valerie was reading him the riot act. At the same time, he kept looking around to see if they were drawing any attention from the surrounding crowd.

The second he realized Abby was watching them, Bryce grabbed Valerie by the arm and dragged her through the door that led outside to the parking lot. It was tempting to follow, but whatever was going on between them was none of her business. Still, apparently Tripp wasn't the only reason Valerie had shown up at the auction.

Not that she was going to tell Tripp what she'd just seen, not when he clearly had mixed feelings about the woman. What she would do was stay close by and wait for Bryce to return so she could finally get rid of the stupid check she'd been carrying around all evening. Afterward, she'd head home and get off her feet for a while.

A few minutes later, Valerie reappeared alone, her face flushed. She glanced around the room, her gaze sliding by Abby as if she were invisible. It was painfully obvious the second she locked on Tripp's position and cut through the crowd, headed right for him. Abby turned her back on the situation and continued to wait for Bryce to come back in. To pass the time, she stopped to chat with Connie Pohler and Jack Haliday.

Growing increasingly frustrated with the situation, she checked the time. He'd been outside for almost twenty minutes. If he didn't show up soon, she'd give up and just mail his check. If he didn't like the delay, tough. She had made a good faith effort to find him. On the other hand, there was always an outside chance he'd stopped to talk to someone else on their way out. If she hurried, she might just catch him.

As soon as she reached the parking lot, she re[...] chasing after him was a stupid idea. She had no idea what kind of car he drove, so there was no way to know whether or not he'd already left. Just in case, she walked the length of the lot to look down all the rows of cars and didn't see him standing anywhere.

It was time to go back inside and check in with Clarence Reed. The owner of the local hardware store was in charge of the cleanup tonight. Once she made sure he didn't need her for anything, she was going home. As she made her way back to the door, she heard a faint beeping noise, the kind a car made when the door was left open. If that was the problem, she'd just close it so the battery didn't die. If there was something else wrong, she would memorize the license plate number and make an announcement once she got back inside.

Naturally, the car was parked all the way at the distant end of the lot. As she drew closer, it was clear that the driver's door was still open even though the beeping noise had finally stopped. Odd that someone would've walked away and left it like that, but there was no one in sight. But as she rounded the end of the car, she realized it wasn't only the battery that was dead.

The owner was, too.

Chapter Three

Bryce Cadigan had slumped over and fallen partway out of the door with only his seat belt holding him in place. His head hung down with his mouth open and his eyes looking a bit bewildered as they stared sightlessly down at the pavement. She forced herself to go closer, to make sure she was right about his condition. His unblinking gaze pretty much answered that question, but she forced herself to rest her fingertips against the side of his throat. His skin was warm to the touch, but she couldn't feel a pulse. The only question now was should she call 911 or Gage's number instead? After all, he was right inside the building. She hated to spoil his evening, but he'd get called to the scene, anyway. Might as well let him take charge from the beginning.

He answered on the second ring. "What's up, Abby?"

"Can you come out to the parking lot? Just you. No one else if you can avoid it. I'm in the far back corner."

It said something about their relationship that he didn't hesitate. "I'll be right there."

Good to his word, he stepped out of the building in

a matter of seconds. She waved her hand until he spotted her. If it wouldn't have attracted more attention, she might have asked him to bring Tripp along for moral support. On the other hand, it was unlikely he could've been able to escape the barnacle's clutches, especially if Valerie figured out it was Abby who needed him right now.

Besides, it wasn't fair to expect him to come running every time she stumbled over another dead body. This was the third time in the short time she'd been living in Snowberry Creek. If people weren't already talking about her unfortunate talent for getting sucked into murder investigations, they would be soon.

"What's wrong, Abby?"

She pointed toward the open car door and let Gage draw his own conclusions. After checking for a pulse, he stepped back, now in full-out cop mode. "Have you called this in?"

Now that he was there, she was having a harder time maintaining her composure. She locked her knees to ensure they'd continue to support her. That didn't hide the quiver in her voice when she answered him. "No, but only because you were already close by."

He stepped closer and draped his arm around her shoulders while he called for reinforcements. Then he punched in another number. "Tripp, sorry to bother you, but there's been an incident out here in the parking lot. For the time being, I want the building on lockdown. Can you and Pastor Jack man the doors and explain to people that they need to stay put for a while? My deputies will relieve you in a few minutes."

She couldn't hear what Tripp said in response, but Gage immediately looked down at her and then back toward the body. "Yeah, Abby is with me. She's fine for now."

How had Tripp known she was outside? No matter. For now, he was stuck inside the building and dealing with people who wouldn't appreciate being told they couldn't leave. All things considered, she would happily trade places with him. Based on past experience, she would be tied up for hours answering questions and making a formal statement.

"Thanks, Tripp. Don't hesitate to call if anyone gives you problems, and I'll deal with them."

After Gage stuck the phone back into his pocket, he turned his attention back to her. "You know the drill. We'll get all the details later, Abby, but give me the short version of what happened out here."

"I've been trying to catch up with Bryce for the past hour or so to give him this." She held up the envelope. "The contract stated we had to give him the second half of his fee at the event. Otherwise, I would've just mailed the final payment."

Not that Gage needed to know all of that. Or heck, maybe he did.

"I saw him go outside with someone earlier." Not that she wanted to rat Valerie out if she didn't have to. "After that person returned alone, I waited for Mr. Cadigan to come back inside, too. When he didn't, I went out to see if I could spot him in the parking lot, which I quickly realized was stupid."

"Why?"

"I didn't know what kind of car Bryce drove, so I had no way of knowing if it was gone or not. I was on my way back in when I heard a faint beeping noise. You know, the kind of sound a car makes when a door is left open. I tracked it to this aisle. I was either going to shut the door or memorize the license plate number and make an announcement inside. I was afraid someone would come out to find their battery was dead or something."

She forced herself to look to where Bryce lay sprawled out of his car. "That's the way I found him. I checked to see if he was breathing and felt for a pulse. Then I called you."

By that point, she could hear the approaching sirens. She really didn't want to be there when the deputies started arriving. "Can I go back inside?"

"I'll have someone escort you to the door, but I'd like you to answer one question for me first."

He might have couched the request in polite terms, but they both knew she didn't really have a choice in the matter. "Ask away."

"Who went outside with Bryce?"

Crossing her fingers that Tripp would forgive her for dragging the barnacle into a murder investigation, she sighed and said, "Valerie Brunn, Tripp's ex-wife."

Gage's muttered response was brief but obscene. She knew just how he felt.

Cruisers from the Snowberry Creek Police Department came pouring into the lot. The aid car from the fire department followed close behind. Learning there was nothing to be done for Bryce, the EMTs focused their attention on Abby. She insisted that she was fine, but they ignored her claims and parked her on the back step of their vehicle, anyway. Even she had to admit the warm blanket they wrapped around her shoulders helped ward off the chill of the evening air.

Or maybe the cold came from another source altogether—the shock of stumbling across another dead body. She didn't think she'd ever get used to it and wouldn't want to. Bryce's death was a tragedy and should be treated as such.

"Drink some more of that water, Abby."

She dutifully followed Angela Grosskopf's soft-spoken order. Their paths had crossed before, so at least the EMT was another familiar face.

She took another sip of her drink. "Thanks, Angie. That helps."

Angie scanned the parking lot before looking back down at Abby. "Sorry you got sucked into this."

"Me too. I think I need to stay home more."

Angie arched her eyebrows and gave Abby a doubtful look, which was understandable. They'd first met when Angie responded to an emergency call the night Tripp had been hurt chasing an intruder away from Abby's back door. Then there'd been the time Abby had been badly shaken after crossing paths with a knife-wielding killer.

That train of thought was derailed when a dark sedan pulled into the parking lot. One look at the man getting out of the car had Abby wanting to dive for cover. Ben Earle was a homicide detective for the county. Their relationship had gotten off to a rocky start the previous fall, but they'd eventually made peace with each other. She liked him well enough, but his presence made it feel as if the auction night had somehow morphed into a reunion for every law enforcement officer and emergency responder she'd ever met.

He headed right for her. "Abby McCree, here we are at another crime scene."

Although he smiled as he said it, she bristled in indignation. "This was not my fault, Ben. All I wanted to do was pay the man."

Her eyes stung with the threat of tears. "I didn't mean to find him dead."

As if that even made sense. She sniffled and tried to explain. "He was the emcee for our bachelor/bachelorette auction tonight. The contract required that we pay him half up front and the rest after the auction was over." Not that Ben needed to know any of that. "Will this be your case?"

He shook his head. "Not as far as I know. From what I've heard, so far they're treating this as a suspicious death, not necessarily a homicide. I happened to be in the area and stopped to see if I could help."

The detective frowned as he studied all the activity in the parking lot. It looked like total chaos to her, but perhaps he could see an order that escaped her inexperienced eye. After a few seconds, he glanced down at her again. "Well, I'd better go check in with Gage. Take care, Abby."

"I'll try, Ben."

It was time for her to get moving, too. She threw off the blanket. "Thanks again, Angie, but I need to go back inside. I'm in charge of the event, and they might need me for something."

The other woman folded the blanket as she studied Abby. "Are you sure you're up to it? You still look a bit shaky."

"Thanks, but I'm fine"—she paused to test that theory—"or at least as fine as I can be under the circumstances. Regardless, I have some friends I need to check on."

"Give a yell if anyone needs us."

"I will."

Abby took a couple of tentative steps and decided her legs were back to working normally now. She caught the attention of one of the deputies. "Tell Gage I've gone back inside if he needs me for anything."

"Yes, ma'am."

As she neared the front of the building, she spotted Tripp standing just inside the glass door. He stepped outside and headed straight toward her. As relieved as she was to see him, she wasn't as happy to see the other person watching them from inside. The last thing she wanted to do was contend with Tripp's ex-wife right now. She wrote it off to a guilty conscience for snitching to Gage that Valerie might have been the last person to see Bryce Cadigan alive.

It also didn't help that the barnacle was glaring at Abby with the green-eyed anger of a jealous woman. Rather than get caught up in a stare-down contest, Abby focused her attention on Tripp.

"What the heck happened this time, Abby?"

His gruff concern washed over her and helped calm the rough seas her emotions were riding right now. "I went out looking for Bryce Cadigan to give him his check. When I found him, he was dead."

Her voice cracked a bit on that last word, and the next thing Abby knew she was wrapped in Tripp's arms. "Darn it, woman, I can't leave you alone for two seconds without you getting into trouble of some kind."

She started to protest but then decided he wasn't wrong. "Sorry."

Although it still wasn't her fault. Not this time.

He looked past her out toward where Gage stood directing his people like a general in charge of a battlefield. "Do they know what happened to him?"

Her face was pressed against Tripp's broad chest, so she felt the deep rumble of his voice as much as she heard it. "They haven't told me anything. Ben Earle stopped to see if they needed any help. He thought they were treating it as a suspicious death case. Maybe that's normal when they don't know what happened."

"I guess that would account for the crime scene tape they're stringing all over the place."

He sounded a bit doubtful about that, especially when he went on to add, "But it doesn't explain why they're not letting anyone leave, though."

"Maybe Gage wants to move the body . . . Bryce, I mean. You know, so it doesn't upset everyone to see him that way."

"Hmmm."

Yeah, she saw his point. It had been close to an hour since she'd made that call to Gage. Surely it shouldn't take all that long to move the body and tow away the car, especially if they hadn't found anything really suspicious. She risked a quick peek back toward the center of all the action. From where she and Tripp stood, it was hard to pick out many details, but everyone seemed to be really busy.

"Do you want me to go see what's going on?"

It was nice of Tripp to offer, but she suspected Gage wouldn't want anyone else to go tromping through his crime—

No, she wouldn't call it that. It was a suspicious death scene. That's all. If that was even a thing.

Tripp stepped back and studied her face. She wasn't sure what he saw there that had him looking so worried, and didn't ask. Finally, he said, "Let's get you inside. Jean and the other ladies are concerned about you and have been fretting up a storm. It will help them settle down to see that you're all right."

Tripp kept his arm around her shoulders as they headed toward the door. She was painfully aware that Valerie was still watching while Tripp seemed oblivious to the situation. Short of shoving his arm away, there wasn't much she could do about it. "I'm sorry you and Jack had to hold down the fort for Gage. That couldn't have been easy."

"Most people have been pretty good about it. I let the deputies deal with the few that had issues with being held captive against their will." He smiled and added, "Their words, not mine."

"What a bunch of drama queens."

Tripp grinned at her assessment of the situation. When they reached the door, Pastor Jack stood waiting to let them in. "Are you all right, Abby? I saw you with the EMTs and was worried."

"I'm fine. Angie insisted on checking me over just as a precaution. It wasn't as if they could do anything for—"

Suddenly, she was aware of how many people were crowded close and listening, and changed what she'd been about to say. "For me. Regardless, Gage has the situation under control. That's all I can say."

The sympathy in Jack's eyes was almost her undoing. "Do you know where Jean, Glenda, and Louise are? Tripp said they were looking for me."

She would've asked Tripp, but the barnacle must have pounced as soon as he stepped through the door. The two of them were over in the corner in the midst of what appeared to be a pretty intense discussion. Tripp didn't look all that happy when he tore his gaze away from Valerie long enough to look at Abby.

At the same time, she noticed Mrs. Alstead seated at a table near the door. The woman's eyes were swollen and her face flushed as if she'd been crying. Right now, she was talking quietly to her friends. Abby and Jack were too far away to hear what she was saying, but her companions immediately turned to glare in Valerie's direction. Maybe Abby hadn't been the only one to notice the heated discussion between the barnacle and Bryce.

Meanwhile, Jack pointed toward the stage. "Your friends are waiting at that table on the far side. I'll walk over there with you."

She let him lead her through the crowd. Bless the man, he ran interference for her, telling anyone who tried to approach Abby that the police would have to answer their questions. She didn't know if that was true, but it wasn't as if she had any useful information to share. Well, other than the fact that Bryce Cadigan had died out in the parking lot, but she figured they already knew that much.

Halfway through the room, the crowd thinned out a little. She knew the instant that Glenda spotted them because she said something to Jean and Louise and then charged across the remaining distance to enfold Abby in a Chantilly-scented hug.

"Come sit down, you poor thing."

Abby didn't want to be known as a "poor thing," but she definitely wasn't at her best right now. Jack walked with her until she was seated at the table. "Would you like me to get you a cup of tea?"

"That would be lovely."

He was off and running while her friends fluttered and fussed around her as they filled a small plate with snacks for her. Jean, in particular, seemed the most upset. "I can't believe the police won't let us leave."

Abby glanced back toward the door on the far side of the room. "They're doing their best, Jean. I know Gage Logan will let everyone go as soon as he can."

The older woman sniffed in disapproval. "I hope so. I don't appreciate being treated like a common criminal."

Okay, that was way over the top, and Abby couldn't resist tweaking her friend's nose a bit. "Jean, two things. First, no one is treating the three of you like criminals. And second, if you were ever to decide to cross over to the dark side, there would be absolutely nothing common about any of you. You're far too classy for that."

Her blunt assessment of their character had all three of the women giggling like schoolgirls. Their laughter brightened her own spirits for the moment.

Jack was back with her tea. "I wasn't sure if you took sugar or not, but I figured it wouldn't hurt."

She wrapped her hands around the plain white mug. The heat felt good. "Thanks, that's fine."

He glanced across the room and frowned. "If you don't need me, I'd better head back over to the door in case the natives start getting restless again."

She couldn't tell what had caught his attention while sitting down, but she was too tired to bother standing up. If someone had a problem they needed her to deal with, they could come find her. For the moment, she would sip her tea and settle in for what promised to be a really late night.

Chapter Four

Abby was on her second cup of tea by the time Gage Logan finally put in an appearance. Evidently Pastor Jack had told him where he could find her, because he cut straight through the crowd right to where she was sitting.

As he made his approach, Glenda sniffed with disapproval. "Well, it's about time."

Her rather snarky comment startled Abby into slopping some of the tea onto her hand. She set her mug down and sopped up the small mess with a napkin.

"I told you he'd be back as soon as he could. The man has to do his job, you know, whatever it takes. I seriously doubt he expected to have to deal with this kind of situation this evening."

Gage had arrived at their table by that point and directed his first comment to her companions. "Ladies, I'm sorry you've had to sit here this long. If you'll give your contact information to the deputy who is setting up shop over by the door, you're free to leave."

Jean stood up with the aid of her walker. "And what

about Abby? Can't she leave, too? This has been hard for her, you know."

"Yes, ma'am, I do know. I promise to get her out of here as soon as possible."

As he spoke, he sat down on the chair next to Abby's and pulled a small spiral notebook out of the inside pocket of his suit jacket. Seriously? Did the man ever go anywhere without it? She'd already lost count of the times the two of them had talked while he jotted down notes. Ben Earle had one just like it, so it was definitely a cop thing.

Her three friends lingered close by despite their stated desires to go home. Maybe they were concerned about her, but she suspected a healthy dose of curiosity was also at play. Gage, wily man that he was, remained silent and simply outwaited them. At least he held off grinning until their backs were turned.

The laugh lines bracketing his eyes deepened just a bit. "You know, it would be nice if you could sleep in tomorrow, Abby. However, I'm betting your phone starts ringing at some ungodly hour in the morning. They'll even mean it when they tell you they're concerned and need to know if you're okay."

She couldn't dispute it. "They will be worried, of course, but it's killing them not to know exactly what's going on."

He leaned forward, pen in hand. "Before we get into the nitty-gritty of what you actually saw out there, I wanted to know if you noticed anyone other than Valerie Brunn talking to Bryce for any length of time this evening, even if the conversation seemed friendly."

"Well, his old football coach stopped Bryce when he first got here, but they didn't actually talk much until after the auction. Right after that, I saw him with a guy who looked older than Bryce. He had graying hair pulled back in a ponytail. I thought there was an odd vibe about their discussion, but I don't know that for sure."

She paused to think back over the evening. "After that, he visited with another man I didn't recognize. The two of them looked to be about the same age. Bryce also talked to Mrs. Alstead, that retired teacher. I saw her as I came back in. I think she's taking his death pretty hard, but that's understandable."

Then her gaze drifted over toward the door to where Tripp and Valerie were standing. "The last person I saw Bryce with was Valerie. He could've talked to other people, but right now those are all I can think of. My mind is feeling pretty fried right now."

"That's okay. This is a good start."

She gave his notebook a pointed look. "What happens next?"

"I'll take a quick statement from you while my men get contact information on everyone who was still here at the time of the . . . death."

That slight hesitation had Abby sitting up straight, a frisson of dread dancing along her nerves. "You almost called it something else, didn't you? Do you know how he died?"

Gage glanced around the immediate area as if making sure that no one was paying any attention to their conversation. A few people were watching from a distance, but there was enough ambient noise that it was doubtful they could make out anything Gage and Abby were saying.

"We can't assume it was natural causes, especially considering his age. Until we know differently, we treat everything as suspicious. The coroner won't have a definitive answer until he finishes the autopsy and any other tests are completed. For now, we will proceed with our investigation, which includes interviewing everyone Bryce talked to while he was here. We'll try to track his movements while everybody's memories are fresh."

She shuddered. "Starting with me, I suppose."

Gage stared at her with those lawman's eyes of his that always seemed to see far more than she wanted them to. "Sorry, but yeah. How well did you know him?"

At least he'd started off with an easy question. "Not well at all. A subcommittee on the veterans group researched possible emcees for tonight's event. Bryce topped the list because of his connection with Snowberry Creek. As the committee chair, I'm the one who offered him the contract. After that, we talked on the phone a couple of times, but mostly we communicated by e-mail and text. If you want copies, I can print them out for you."

She glanced at the stage, where Bryce had stood only hours before. "I never met him in person until he walked through the door tonight. We went backstage to go over the final details before he got started. All told, we spent about ten minutes together."

"And after he was done up onstage? Did you talk to him then?"

"No, we never spoke again. I didn't try to catch up with him right away."

Mainly because she'd been reeling from the shock of learning Tripp had a wife. Well, an ex-wife, but that's not how he'd referred to Valerie until later. That wasn't Gage's concern, though, so she gave him another reason for her delay in tracking down Bryce. "He seemed to be enjoying himself and catching up with old acquaintances. I figured he'd come find me if he was in a big hurry to leave."

"Then you saw him walk outside with Ms. Brunn."

"Yes."

She really hoped Gage would leave it at that, but no such luck. "How were they acting?"

Abby replayed the scene in her head. "I was talking to you and the mayor when I saw Bryce walk away from Mrs. Alstead. Since it looked as if he was heading for the door, I excused myself and went after him."

Gage nodded as he kept writing. "And then?"

"Ms. Brunn stepped in front of him and started talking. She looked upset . . . even angry. Bryce didn't look happy to see her, either. He glanced around as if to see if they were drawing unwanted attention. He looked right at me and then took her by the arm and led her out to the parking lot. He didn't give her much choice in the matter, but she didn't try to get away from him, either."

She paused to let Gage get caught up with his note taking. "I wasn't about to intrude on their discussion, so I stayed near the door and waited for them to come back inside."

"How long did that take?"

"Valerie was outside for maybe ten minutes, but she was alone when she returned to the hall. I think she made a beeline for Tripp at that point, but I can't say for sure. I talked to Connie and Jack for a few minutes while I waited for Bryce to reappear. When he didn't, I went looking for him."

She closed her eyes and drew a slow breath as the image of Bryce hanging out of his car filled her head. "I found him and then called you."

"I'm sorry, Abby. It would've been hard on anyone to stumble across his body like that, but I really hate that it was you."

It was hard to be brave, but she tried. "Better me than Jean or one of the other ladies. A couple of them have heart conditions."

His smile was sympathetic. "Those ladies are tougher than you'd think. Still, you're right. You kept your head and handled it better than most. I appreciated being the first on the scene and being able to control the situation from the get-go."

He stuck the notebook back into his pocket. "Are you going to be all right driving yourself home when we get done here?"

Another question she'd been asked by the police on more than one occasion. "I'll be fine. It's not far."

"If I'm tied up, I can have one of my people follow you home. A few reporters have already been sniffing around outside, so I don't want you going out of here alone. Do you want to leave now?"

Yes, she did, but that wasn't going to happen. She wasn't part of the cleanup crew, but she felt duty bound to remain on-site until everyone else was able to leave.

"I need to stick around for a while yet. You know, in case I'm needed."

Gage looked as if he wanted to argue the point, but he didn't. "If you're sure. Just let me or one of my people know when you're ready to go."

He stood up and looked around at the milling crowd. "People are sure to have questions. You've done enough, so aim them in my direction."

In other words, stay out of his investigation. "I'll do that."

Something across the room caught his attention. After a few seconds, he turned back to face her directly. "I take it you didn't know about Valerie's existence before tonight."

Great, another conversation she didn't want to have. "No, Tripp had never mentioned her."

"What an idiot."

The pure disgust in his voice cheered her up a little, and she dredged up a hint of a smile. "No arguments on that score."

"If it's any comfort, she might be standing right next to him, but he's watching us." Then he grinned. "Somehow I doubt it's me he's really interested in."

Abby appreciated Gage's heavy-handed attempt to offer her comfort. "I'll be fine, Gage. As far as surprises go tonight, finding out about her is a pretty minor one."

Okay, that was a lie. Time to move on. "I'm going to check in with my people. Any idea about when you'll have cleared everyone out of here?"

"We're already sending folks home once we have their contact information. I'll be having a personal chat with a few people back at the station before the night's over."

She could guess who most of them would be. "Will they know I'm the one who ratted them out to you?"

"They might guess, but you're not the only person I've talked to about tonight's events, and I have a few more to go. I've also got more names on my list besides the ones you gave me."

That was reassuring, although it wouldn't be the first time she'd had people mad at her, and it wouldn't likely be the last. "I see Clarence watching us. He's head of the cleanup crew, so I'd better go see what he wants."

She headed in his direction while Gage started making his way back over to where his deputies were hard at work. He'd barely gotten there when Valerie Brunn got right up in his face about something. Tripp stood right next to her but didn't look particularly happy about the situation. Good. She was glad she wasn't the only one having a rough night.

Abby turned her attention back to Clarence. "Hi, sorry you had to wait. What can I do to help?"

She had to give Gage and his men credit for being efficient. Once they started releasing the people they'd cleared, the crowd thinned out in a hurry. To keep herself busy, she kicked off her heels and pitched in to help the cleanup crew, who managed to make quick work of their chores. Once Gage shooed the rest of the guests out the door, the crew would do a last check of the area and head out themselves.

Unfortunately, two of the people still lurking around were Tripp and the barnacle. If anything, Valerie looked even angrier now than she had earlier. Even so, she was still perfectly groomed with every blond hair in place and her makeup intact.

Abby, on the other hand, suspected she looked like she'd been stacking chairs and hauling trash. She was about to make another trip out back to the Dumpster when Gage called her name. Considering Tripp and Valerie were standing right beside him, she had no desire to find out what he wanted now.

Unfortunately, Clarence intervened. "I can take those bags, Abby. Go ahead and see what the man wants."

"Thanks, Clarence. You guys have all done a great job under tough circumstances. I really appreciate it."

She dusted her hands off on the skirt of her dress and slipped on her shoes. It was tempting to make a quick detour to the ladies' room to touch up her lipstick and make sure her hair was tidy, but that wasn't happening. She'd been working hard, and if it showed, too bad. Tripp and Gage had seen her look far worse and still liked her. If the former Mrs. Blackston wasn't impressed, Abby really didn't care.

Much.

For now, she kept her eyes trained directly on Gage. Tripp must have noticed, because he shifted to stand right behind Gage's shoulder, enough so that she couldn't avoid seeing him, too. She managed a small nod in his direction before focusing on the man who'd called her over in the first place.

"Did you need something, Gage?"

"A couple of things. First, Ms. Brunn is missing her purse. Has anyone turned it in?"

"Not that they've told me. We found a red sweater, but that's all." She looked at Valerie. "What does it look like? I'll let the owner of the hall know to be on the lookout for it."

"It's a silver clutch. There's nothing valuable in it, so it's no big deal if it doesn't turn up. I had my credit card and hotel key in my jacket pocket."

Gage moved on to the next subject. "Anyway, Abby, it looks as if your team is about done here, and I want to let my people get back to their normal patrols. Can you be ready to go in five minutes? I still want to make sure you get home okay after everything that's happened."

Her nerves had calmed down considerably, but she didn't argue. Both Gage and Tripp had huge protective streaks. They wouldn't be happy until they knew she made it home safely. "Sure thing. I'll let Clarence know I'm leaving."

As soon as she was back, Gage led the parade outside. "I'll follow you guys to your place. Once I know everything is quiet, I'll head over to the office."

Who did he mean by "you guys"? She really hoped he hadn't meant Valerie was going someplace with her. That question was answered when the other woman split off to wait beside Gage's car while Tripp hung back with Abby. She let out the breath she'd been holding. With everything that had happened, she'd almost forgotten that Tripp had ridden with her to the auction. Even though Abby wasn't particularly happy with the man right now, she could handle a short car ride with him. The only way she could've tolerated having Valerie in her car was if she could lock her in the trunk.

That image, evil as it was, cheered her up considerably. She hustled over to the car, so ready for this night to be over. Tripp slid into the passenger side and fastened his seat belt. Neither of them said anything until she pulled out of the parking lot with Gage right behind them.

They'd barely driven a block when Tripp angled himself to look more directly at her. "I meant what I said earlier. I didn't know Valerie was coming tonight."

"I believe you." Not that it changed anything. She had no idea what to say that would make things go back to the way they usually were between them. "Did she say how long she planned to be in town?"

Tripp turned to look out the passenger door window. "All things considered, it seems her plans may have changed."

There was something he was reluctant to tell her, no doubt something she wasn't going to like. "Look, I'm too tired and too frazzled from finding another dead body to play guessing games tonight. Whatever you're wanting to say, just spit it out."

He sat up straighter and sighed. "Sorry, Abs. It's that Valerie was supposed to fly back home to California tomorrow morning, but Gage asked her to stay longer for some reason."

She risked glancing in his direction. "Asked?"

Tripp flexed his hands into fists. "Not exactly. More like, he told her not to leave town until they knew more about what happened to Bryce Cadigan. She tried telling Gage she didn't know the guy at all, but he didn't believe her. Can't imagine why, though. She hasn't lived in this area since my first deployment, so the chances of their paths crossing would've been pretty remote."

Should she admit she'd been the one to rat out his ex-wife to the cops? Deciding she was in no mood to play games, she just blurted it out. "Tripp, I can't imagine why she would tell Gage that. I don't know how or why, but she definitely knew Bryce."

A heavy silence filled the car, and Tripp was back to staring at her. Finally, he asked, "How in the world would you know that?"

The chill in his voice made her shiver. "Because I saw her get all up in his face about something. For the record, I needed to talk to him myself and wasn't spying on your ex-wife. I was supposed to hand over the second half of his fee after the auction."

Tripp crossed his arms over his chest. "What happened between them?"

Was that jealousy she heard in his voice or just concern? Impossible to tell and not really any of her business.

"Whatever she said to him looked pretty intense. She was clearly upset, and he didn't much appreciate her getting up in his face in public. It looked to me like he was the one who insisted they take the discussion outside. After Ms. Brunn came back inside alone, I hung out near the door to see if he was right behind her. When Bryce didn't reappear after a while, I went out looking for him. You know the rest."

"And that's what you told Gage? That the two of them had words right before he died?"

There was no use in denying it. "Yes, I did. He wanted to know if I'd seen Bryce with anyone in particular at the auction."

Tripp glanced in her direction. "I'm sure Val wasn't the only one who talked to him."

"No, she of course wasn't, and I told him that. However, she was the only one I saw who looked that mad."

They reached her driveway. She drove around the back of the house and parked. Tripp didn't say anything as they got out of the car. If he was waiting for her to apologize for telling the police the truth, he was going to wait a long time. Finally, he crossed his arms on the roof of her car and rested his chin on his wrists.

"I really wish you hadn't told him about Valerie talking to Cadigan, but I know you had no choice." He looked back toward the other car. "Although Gage hasn't said so, I get the feeling they're treating the guy's death like a murder, not natural causes."

She couldn't disagree with his assessment of the situation. "I think they have to do that until the coroner makes an official determination. If Bryce died of something like a heart attack, then they'll close the investigation. But until that happens, they have to make sure they protect any possible evidence."

"That makes sense." Although he still didn't look happy about the situation.

Gage was headed toward them, but at least Valerie stayed behind in his car. "I don't mean to rush you, Abby, but let's get you inside. I need to get back to headquarters. The desk sergeant just called to tell me more reporters have caught wind of Cadigan's death. They're already crawling out of the woodwork around city hall with mics and cameras."

Tripp pushed away from the car and walked around to stand between her and Gage. "Just so you know, I plan on following you to the station. Valerie will need a ride back to her hotel after the two of you are finished talking, which shouldn't take all that long."

That he'd insist on being there for Valerie didn't really surprise anyone, and Gage didn't argue. "Fine, Tripp, but no time limits. The discussion will take as long as it takes. I'd also point out I can save you the trouble and have one of my deputies drop her off, but I'm guessing you don't want to hear that."

"Not particularly."

It was clear that Tripp had gone into full protection mode when it came to Valerie and that Gage didn't appreciate it at all. He pointed at Tripp. "Fine, you can come. However, you will stay out of my way or I'll kick your backside to the curb."

Lord save me from stubborn men. Fed up with the whole situation, Abby left them to glare at each other as long as they wanted to. She had already unlocked the back door and let Zeke out before either man caught up with her. It didn't take them long to prowl through her house to make sure no boogeymen were hiding anywhere. She understood that Gage had a job to do, but Tripp's motivations for hurrying were far more confusing. In the past, the three of them would've gathered around her kitchen table for coffee and cookies. Not tonight, though.

She tried to be a good sport about the way they'd rushed through the place. Even waved as they drove away. She just wished she knew when it came to Tripp if she was saying goodbye for the moment or for a lot longer than that. Would he come back to his place tonight or stay with the barnacle?

Rather than dwell on something she had no control over, she patted Zeke on the head. "Come on, boy, it's bedtime."

But not until she took a shower and did her best to wash away the memory of Bryce Cadigan's dead eyes.

Chapter Five

Gage had been right about the crack-of-dawn phone calls from Jean and company, but the knock at Abby's back door was a definite surprise. Granted, Tripp was a morning person, usually going on his daily run well before the sun came up. However, it had been nearly two in the morning before the sound of his truck had rumbled up the driveway. The noise had dragged Abby out of a sound sleep just long enough to note that he was back home. Her ninety-pound mastiff mix, Zeke, had woofed softly in response to the noise; then both of them had dropped back off to sleep.

Nudging Zeke out of the way, she opened the door to let Tripp come inside. She smiled as he grumbled something that might have been a greeting as he headed straight for the coffeepot. A grumpy Tripp was pretty cute. "Good morning to you, too."

He plunked down at the table and sat with his chin down on his chest as if his head was too heavy to support. Rather than try to force him into a conversation, she broke four more eggs into the skillet and turned the bacon. Five minutes later, she divided the food between two plates and carried them over to the table along with a basket of fresh blueberry muffins.

After topping off Tripp's coffee and her own, she sat down, too. He finally showed a little more life as he reached for his fork. "Bless you, woman."

"Considering how late you got home last night, I'm actually surprised you're up and around already."

"Me too, but I've got stuff to do today." He took a bite of the eggs and moaned is if it were ambrosia. "Thanks for feeding me. I didn't expect that."

"It's no big deal. I was cooking, anyway."

For the moment, both of them concentrated on eating. It wasn't long before their plates were empty and Abby was on her second cup of coffee as Tripp finished his third. He then cleared the table and washed the dishes while she sat back and watched.

It didn't take him long, but still he lingered as he slowly dried the skillet and put it away. She settled in to wait him out. Finally, he returned to the table after raiding Zeke's treat jar. He tossed one of the organic cookies in the air and smiled when the dog missed and had to chase it across the floor. He held out a second one so that Zeke could take it straight from his hand. "Sorry, boy. It was my fault that one got away from you."

The dog was always quick to forgive his buddy almost anything, especially if the apology included a treat or two. It was time to jump-start the conversation. "So what kind of stuff do you have to do today?"

Not that it was really any of her business, but he was lingering for a reason. He leaned back in his chair, looking more like himself.

"I plan to mow the lawn and do a few other chores outside. I also have to hit the books and work on a paper that's due this week."

That all sounded pretty normal, but something was obviously bothering him. Rather than wait for him to come to the point, she tried to hurry things along. "So, how did things go at the police station last night? Did Gage keep you and Ms. Brunn there for long?"

Because if he hadn't, what had kept Tripp out so late? Not that she really wanted to know, especially if he and Valerie had been doing something other than hanging out at the police station to all hours.

"Gage had a lot to wade through last night. Like he said, the press was out in droves. Considering how many of them were parked out in front of city hall, it must have been a slow news night. I'd never heard of Bryce Cadigan before you hired him for the auction, but he must have been well-known in the area."

He seemed puzzled why that might be. "Anyway, Gage and even the mayor had to make statements. Meanwhile, Valerie and the other people he wanted to talk to had to cool their heels until he was done. For whatever reason, he made Val wait the longest."

Abby didn't point out that the woman had been one of the last people to see Bryce alive. Tripp already knew that. "So where did Gage leave things with her?"

"The same as last night. He'd rather she didn't leave town until he knows for sure that they're not dealing with a murder case."

He paused to pour another cup of coffee, clearly not happy about Gage's request. Did Tripp want Valerie to be able to leave because he thought she was innocent, or because he didn't want her around? Even if Valerie did go home, she had obviously planned to come back in two weeks. Why else would she have handed over that much money for the privilege of going to the veterans dance with her ex-husband?

After taking another sip of coffee, Abby asked, "When did Gage expect to hear from the coroner?"

Tripp let out a slow breath, clearly frustrated. "He wasn't sure. Today is Sunday, and I don't know if the coroner and his crew work weekends or not."

Neither did she.

It was probably time to change the subject, but not quite yet. "So did Valerie ever tell you what she and Bryce were talking about?"

Which really wasn't any of her business, and Gage wouldn't even like her asking the question. She'd learned the hard way not to tread on his toes when it came to police business.

Tripp reached for another muffin, but he paused briefly before finally picking it up. He broke off a piece and ate it before answering. "Valerie and I didn't actually have much of a chance to talk last night. Gage parked her in an interrogation room while he made me sit out in the lobby. By the time he cut her loose, she had a headache, and all either of us wanted was to get the heck out of there. I drove her to the hotel and came back here."

He finished off the muffin and stood up. "I didn't mean to impose, but thanks again for breakfast. I actually came over to borrow some milk. It was either that or I would've had to eat dry, cold cereal. Bacon and eggs really hit the spot."

He stretched his arms over his head as if trying to work out a few kinks. "The grocery store is also on my chore list today, so let me know if you need anything. Otherwise, I'll go get started on the yard."

She and Zeke both followed him to the door. "Considering how little sleep you got, the grass can wait. Do your homework and buy your groceries."

He stepped out onto the back porch and looked

around. "Thanks, but it will actually help if I do something active. I'll spend a couple of hours on the yard, do the grocery shopping, and then hole up and work on my paper this afternoon."

It was no surprise that the man wouldn't cut himself any slack. She would've offered to mow the grass herself this one time, but there was no way the stubborn man would let her do that. The agreement he'd made with her late aunt when he first moved in was that he got a reduction in the rent in exchange for doing chores around the place. Abby had inherited him as a tenant along with everything else in her aunt's estate.

"Is it okay if Zeke hangs around outside with you? Zoe is coming over in a little while. We're going to total up the take from last night and get it ready to deposit first thing tomorrow morning."

She leaned down to cover the dog's ears. "You know how much Zeke likes to feel useful. While I don't want to hurt his feelings, he's not very good with numbers."

Tripp grinned as he started down the steps with the dog following right behind him. "Come on, dog. Us guys have lots of manly work to do out in the yard. We'll handle the things that take muscles and brute strength, and let the ladies do all that icky math stuff."

Abby laughed. "If you want an audience while you're out there flexing, I can always call Jean and tell her that you're in dire need of something to eat for dinner tonight. I bet she can whip together one of her tuna specials in no time at all."

The look on Tripp's face was priceless. The poor guy didn't have it in him to hurt Jean's feelings by telling her that he didn't much care for her casseroles. He also couldn't bring himself to just toss them in the trash, so he ate them no matter what her latest special ingredients turned out to be. In the past, the list had included anchovies, jalapeño peppers, and crushed barbecued potato chips as a topping.

Abby took mercy on him. "Better yet, why don't we order pizza for dinner?"

That idea improved his mood. "Sounds good to me. It will even be my treat since you cooked breakfast for both of us."

"Great. Make my half the veggie, and I'll make dessert."

"Sounds good." Tripp watched as Zeke bolted past him headed toward the back corner of the yard. "Let's aim for eating around six if that's okay."

"Sure thing." Abby didn't know about Tripp, but she got real tired of cooking for one. Having dinner delivered was definitely an improvement over the left-over meatloaf she had in the fridge. "I'll see you then."

Meanwhile, the dog came trotting back with one of his grimy tennis balls and dropped it at his buddy's feet. Softy that he was, Tripp picked it up and threw it deep into the backyard. Abby left them to play their games so she could get organized for her upcoming meeting with Zoe. Unfortunately, her elderly friends weren't the only ones who enjoyed watching Tripp hanging out with Zeke in the backyard. She gave in to the temptation to observe the pair from her the kitchen window.

Right now, Zeke was running circles around Tripp with the ball in his mouth. Finally, he charged closer and dropped the slimy thing before dancing back to wait for Tripp to pick it up. Evidently mastiff slobber didn't gross Tripp out like it did Abby, because he didn't hesitate to grab the ball up off the ground and send it flying through the air again. Zeke barked and charged after it.

As soon as he did, Tripp turned to look right at Abby. Darn it, he'd caught her staring again. The man hated being stared at, but he didn't seem particularly upset this time. He just waved and headed for the shed, where the lawn mower was stored. She took advantage of the moment to put Zeke's water bowl out on the porch in case he'd worked up a thirst chasing down his ball.

So what dessert should she make for their dinner tonight? A pie would take too long, but throwing together a blueberry buckle wouldn't take long. Her decision made, she gathered the ingredients and set to work.

Twenty minutes later, she put the pan in the oven to bake, and set the timer. A glance at the clock reminded her that Zoe would be arriving any minute now. She quickly made a fresh pot of coffee and added a few more muffins to the basket before carrying it all down the hall to the dining room. The doorbell rang just as she set the tray on the table. Abby dusted her hands off on her jeans and stepped into the entryway. She was about to open the door when she caught a glimpse of the person through the window and froze until she could make sense of what she was seeing.

First of all, Zoe had dark brown hair and was slightly shorter than Abby. The woman waiting for her to open the door was both far too blond and too tall to be Zoe, which left just one possibility that made any sense. But what would Valerie Brunn be doing on Abby's front porch? She wasn't sure she wanted to find out. However, it wasn't as if she could simply ignore the woman and hope she'd go away of her own accord.

Well, she could, but not with Zoe pulling up in front

of the house. Taking a calming breath, she opened the door. "Ms. Brunn, how can I help you?"

"I need to talk to Tripp. Have you seen him this morning?"

As she spoke, Valerie leaned to the side as if trying to see past her. Did she think Abby was holding the man prisoner or something? Come to think of it, though, she hadn't heard the lawn mower, and she hadn't seen either Tripp or Zeke since she'd started making the coffee cake. Had they decided to go on a run? Not that it mattered right now.

She gave Valerie a cool look. "Yes, I saw him earlier. Did you try calling his cell?"

The woman made an exasperated noise. "Of course I did. When he didn't pick up, I had no choice but to come here looking for him. I knocked on his door first, but there was no answer."

By that point, Zoe was walking up the front steps. Abby offered her a much friendlier smile. "Hi, Zoe, come on in. I set us up in the dining room. I thought it would be easier to work there."

Abby moved out of the way just enough to make room for Zoe to come inside while making sure to block Valerie from doing the same. "Ms. Brunn, as far as I know, Tripp is at home. He did mention at breakfast this morning that he planned to work in the yard for a while and then study. Maybe he doesn't want to be disturbed and turned his phone off."

Maybe it was petty of her to enjoy the way the woman flinched when Abby mentioned having breakfast with Tripp. "I'm sorry I don't have time to chat, but I need to join my guest. If I see Tripp, I'll tell him you stopped by. Have a nice day."

Then she stepped back and calmly shut the door in Valerie's face before the woman could respond.

Zoe was waiting for her just out of sight in the living room. "Was that who I think it was?"

Abby felt her cheeks flush hot. It was bad enough she'd been rude to the woman, but having a witness made it that much worse. "Yeah, that's Valerie Brunn, Tripp's ex-wife."

Zoe moved closer to the window and peeked outside. "What did she want?"

"She's looking for Tripp. She didn't say why."

A conscience could be an awful burden sometimes. Her late aunt would've been ashamed of the way Abby had treated Valerie just now. Zoe wasn't looking all that happy about it, either.

"Zoe, if you'll give me a minute, I need to try to catch Valerie. She's alone here in town, and I probably should've been more hospitable."

Even if she didn't want to be. Rather than give herself time to rethink her decision, she charged back out the front door and looked up and down the street to see where Valerie had gone. When she didn't spot her in either direction, she went down the steps and around the side of the house. Sure enough, Valerie was standing on Tripp's front porch with her face pressed up against the window, trying to see inside.

"Ms. Brunn, I just realized my dog is gone, too. When Tripp takes Zeke for a run, they don't usually stay gone long. If you'd like to wait until they return, I have fresh coffee and blueberry muffins. My friend and I really do need to work, but you'd be welcome to sit with us."

Abby held her breath, hoping against hope that the woman would simply give up and leave. No such luck. Valerie was already headed in her direction. "If you're sure you don't mind. I don't want to be a bother."

There was an underlying edge to the woman's

words that made it clear she knew she already was one, and an unwelcome one at that. That didn't stop her from following Abby back around to the front of the house. When they walked inside, Zoe was already seated at the table with the paperwork from the auction spread out in neat piles.

Ordinarily Abby didn't mind serving as hostess, but right now there was a knot in her stomach that made it hard to play that role. "I'll go grab another coffee cup and plate. Back in a second."

She'd barely gone five steps when she realized she hadn't even introduced the other two women. Stopping to do so now would only make things more awkward, so she kept going. From the murmur of voices following her down the hall, it seemed likely that the other two women were making up for her lack of manners.

After grabbing another plate and cup off the shelf, she headed back into the fray. Valerie had taken a seat at the table next to Zoe, who was explaining why she was involved in last night's auction to help raise funds to assist veterans in the area. Abby stepped into the room just as she said, "Abby is heading up the whole project and is doing a great job of it."

Valerie turned her puzzled gaze in Abby's direction. "So you're a veteran, too."

She sounded surprised by that possibility. What did she think veterans looked like? From what Abby had seen, they came in all shapes and sizes. "No, actually I'm not. I owed someone a favor who is, though, and he asked me to help out."

"From what I saw last night, the auction and the dance was a major undertaking." Valerie picked out a muffin and set it on her plate. "Must have been one heck of a favor."

Abby poured herself a cup of coffee. "It was."

Zoe remained silent, but her gaze ping-ponged between Abby and Valerie, her dark eyes alight with curiosity. Considering it was already common knowledge in Snowberry Creek, Abby figured Zoe knew Tripp had helped Abby deal with the aftermath of finding a dead body buried in her backyard. That made it more likely she was waiting to see if Abby was going to explain the situation to Valerie.

Surrendering to the inevitable, she set her cup aside. "Right after I inherited this house from my aunt, Tripp and I were working out in the yard trying to get rid of some blackberry brambles in the back corner when he spotted a patchwork quilt buried under some old plywood. Well, technically, the goats found the quilt, but Tripp was the one who realized what else they'd uncovered."

By that point, Valerie looked confused, not that Abby blamed her. She'd had trouble making sense of the situation at the time, and she'd been standing right there when Tripp tried to keep a goat from eating the quilt.

Zoe evidently didn't know as much as Abby had thought because she was looking a bit bewildered. "Goats? Why on earth would you have goats in your yard?"

"It sounds strange, but if blackberries are taking over the place, you can rent a bunch of goats to come in and eat them. We were watching them work when Tripp realized one of them was chewing on a piece of cloth. He took it away from the goat and then tried to pull the rest of the quilt out from under the plywood. That's when he realized it was wrapped around a dead body."

Valerie looked a bit ashen. "So last night wasn't the first time you found a . . . well, you know?"

Actually, it was the third time, but Abby was ready to change the subject. She settled for simply saying, "No, it wasn't. But like I said, I owed him."

Pasting a bright, if somewhat brittle, smile on her face, she reached for the stack of papers and the lockbox that contained the checks and other cash they'd taken in the previous night. "Zoe, should we get started?"

Valerie looked as if she wanted to ask another question but seemed to think better of it. She sat quietly while Abby and Zoe started sorting through the pile of checks and credit card payments. After a few seconds, she reached for the bag of cash that had been collected by the people selling chances on the goody baskets. "I can count this for you if it would help."

"That would be great."

While Valerie started sorting the paper bills and coins by denomination, Abby and Zoe worked on matching up payments with the winning bids. They'd been working for maybe fifteen minutes when the lawn mower roared to life right outside the dining room window. Just that quickly, Valerie was up and moving. "Tripp must be back."

In her hurry to leave, she bumped the table hard enough to knock over two of the piles of coins she'd been working on.

Abby did her best to ignore the situation, concentrating on the check she'd been about to record. That would've been easier if her vision hadn't suddenly blurred for some reason. She blinked furiously, trying to refocus both her eyes and her mind. There was no way she wanted to know what was going on outside, although it was impossible to miss noticing the sudden silence as the lawn mower shut off within seconds of Valerie leaving.

Zoe, on the other hand, set down her pen and walked over to look out the window. Then she glanced back at Abby. "They're headed back toward Tripp's place."

Of course they were. It was his home, after all. Where else would he entertain a guest? Not that he'd ever invited Abby inside in all the time she'd known him.

"Zeke's with them, by the way."

Great, another male smitten by the barnacle. "He hangs out with Tripp a lot."

Zoe rejoined her at the table. "Want to talk about it?"

Abby shook her head. After all, what was there to say? "Thanks, but no."

"Okay."

Zoe picked up her pen as if ready to get back to work. Still, she hesitated long enough that Abby looked up to see if something was wrong. Her friend's gaze was sympathetic, her smile a bit edgy. She held up a hand. "One more thing, and then I promise I'll shut up. If Leif had an ex-wife who looked like that, I'd hate her, too. I don't know what that woman's game is, but I'm sure Tripp is smart enough to see through it."

For some reason, that comment brightened Abby's mood considerably. She wasn't sure what that said about her, but she didn't really care. Crossing her fingers Zoe was right about that, she said, "Yeah, he is."

After all, he'd known all along where Valerie lived and worked. If he'd wanted the barnacle back in his life, he'd had plenty of opportunity to make that happen. With that realization, she managed a happier smile.

"Thanks for reminding me of that, Zoe."

"You're welcome. Now, let's get this finished up. I

can't wait to see how much we took in last night. I'm betting we're going to be able to help a lot of our veterans this year."

She was right. Despite everything that had happened last night, a lot of good was going to come from their efforts. For now, she'd concentrate on the job at hand and not worry about why her lawn wasn't getting mowed.

Chapter Six

Zoe left right after twelve thirty, which had left Abby to her own devices all afternoon. Rather than sit around feeling sorry for herself, she'd spent much of the time in her late aunt's quilting room up on the third floor of the house. When Sybil died unexpectedly, she'd left several projects unfinished. It had been several months after her death before Abby got up the courage to try her hand at completing one of them.

Normally, Zeke slept at her feet while she worked, but he'd chosen to stay with Tripp and his guest. While she missed the dog's undemanding company, she wasn't about to call Tripp and ask him to return her pet. It wasn't until late afternoon that the lawn mower had finally started back up again. She was rather proud of herself for continuing to sew quilt squares into long strips rather than dashing over to the window to see if Tripp was alone or if his ex was keeping him company while he worked in the yard.

When the last of the squares were sewn together, she debated whether to start joining the strips together or call it quits for the day. Too restless to sit at the sewing machine any longer, she headed back down-stairs to take care of a few other chores before setting the table for dinner. The only question was if she should set it for two or three. At about five, Zeke finally scratched at the back door. When she let him inside, he made a beeline for his food bowl, reminding her that it was his dinnertime, too.

She filled his dish with kibble and pondered what she should do next. If Tripp had changed his mind about dinner, he would've let her know by now. When her land line rang, she jumped to answer. "Hey there, are we still on for pizza?"

The silence coming from the other end of the line made her wish the old-fashioned phone had caller ID. When it was Gage who finally spoke, she did her best to hide her disappointment.

"I really wish I was calling about pizza, Abby, but this is an official call. I tried your cell, but it went to voice mail. I wanted you to hear the news directly from me. We got the preliminary autopsy report back, and Bryce Cadigan's death is now officially a murder inves-tigation. He was poisoned, but that's all I can tell you right now."

She managed to reach the kitchen table and sit down on her suddenly wobbly legs. "I'm sorry to hear that, Gage. I know these cases are tough to handle."

Especially when it was the third one since she'd moved to Snowberry Creek. "Is there anything you need me to do now that you know?"

He huffed a small laugh. "Other than to let us han-dle it?"

She closed her eyes and bit back the urge to sigh. "Gage, that's so not funny."

Even if he had good cause to feel like she might

need that reminder. In her defense, it was hardly her fault that she'd been the one to discover the body in all three cases. Well, to be fair, she should only have to take partial credit for the first case. Tripp was the one who actually uncovered that victim.

"Sorry, Abby, I shouldn't tease you. It's already been a long day with no end in sight. Can you hold a second?"

She waited patiently until he came back on the line. "Anyway, I just wanted to give you a heads-up. I've had reporters parked outside my door all day. Once they find out it's a homicide case, they might start looking for fresh blood to interview about what happened. For what it's worth, you can never go wrong with a simple 'no comment.' They won't like it, but you're strong enough to stick to your guns."

When someone called his name, Gage said, "Look, I've got to go. Like I said, call me if you have any problems."

"I will."

She sat staring at nothing until the beeping sound signaling the phone was off the hook finally jarred her out of her reverie. After hanging up the receiver, she looked for her cell phone, only to discover the battery had run down. She plugged it back into the charger and waited for it to start. There were two voice messages and a pair of texts from Tripp. She listened to the voice mail first. One was from her mother, who said she was just calling to say hi; the other from Gage telling her he needed to talk to her.

From there, she braced herself before looking at what Tripp had to say. The first one was from earlier to let her know he and Zeke were hiking over to Main Street to get gas for the lawn mower. So that's where they'd disappeared to. The second message was from just a few minutes ago. As soon as she read it, she was sorry she'd bothered to plug in the phone.

Hey, Abby. We're still on for dinner. I'm not sure, but there's a chance Valerie may be joining us. I hope that's okay.

Well, no, but there was no way she could tell him that. For one thing, had anyone told Valerie that Bryce's death was now officially being considered a homicide? If not, Abby sure didn't want to be the one to deliver that particular news to Tripp, much less Valerie herself.

Should she cancel pizza night? She could always make some excuse like she had a headache or that she was allergic to barnacles, but that would mean Tripp would likely end up having dinner alone with Valerie. Abby didn't like that idea either, which left her with no choice but to say it was fine with her.

But it wasn't. It really wasn't.

The past hour had ticked by slowly. Abby had spent part of it taking a shower and blowing her hair dry. It was surprisingly hard to decide whether to wear it up in a ponytail or to leave it down around her shoulders. Finally, she left it down but pulled the sides back with a matched set of combs. After a touch of lipstick and the barest hint of eye shadow, she was good to go.

Well, except for deciding what to wear. When she and Tripp had one of their pizza nights, they usually ended up out on the porch eating off paper plates and drinking beer out of red plastic cups. A dress would be overkill, and even nice slacks might make Tripp wonder what was going on with her. Finally, she settled on her newest pair of jeans and a blue cotton shirt over a white tank top.

As ready as she would ever be, she went downstairs

to the kitchen to wait for her guests to arrive. It was a nice day out, the perfect weather for eating on the porch. However, the threat of reporters lurking in the area meant that might not be a good idea. That left two choices—the kitchen or the dining room.

The kitchen was fine for dinner with Tripp. After all, they'd shared a lot of meals there. Valerie, however, wasn't that kind of casual guest. But again, Tripp would wonder what was going on in Abby's head if she served dinner in the formal dining room. Finally, she decided they'd eat in the kitchen but on her everyday dishes instead of paper plates.

Her decision made, she quickly set the table. The knock came just as she finished. Zeke beat her to the door. It was a huge relief to see Tripp standing there with an extra-large pizza box and no sign of the barnacle anywhere.

"Come on in." She looked past him. "No Valerie?"

He stepped inside and set the pizza on the counter. "No, she decided to head back to her hotel room a while ago. I think she got tired of watching me do homework."

Then he gave both her and the table a puzzled look and then glanced down at his faded T-shirt and jeans with frayed hems and a hole in the knee. "You look nice. Did I miss the memo that said we were dressing up for dinner tonight?"

Okay, so maybe she'd gone overboard by putting a vase of fresh flowers on the table along with Aunt Sybil's linen napkins. Ignoring the flash of heat in her cheeks, she aimed for sounding nonchalant. "No, not at all. I thought it would be nice to eat off something besides our usual paper plates."

His mouth quirked up in just a hint of a smile.

"Right. And none of this is because I said Valerie might be joining us."

He knew her too well. "Maybe a little of it. After all, she would be a first-time guest. I figured using real dishes might make her feel more welcome."

Rather than continue an awkward discussion, Abby pulled two beers and the salad she'd made at the last minute out of the fridge. "Let's eat before the pizza gets cold."

They settled in at the table while Zeke parked himself between them in case someone dropped food on the floor that would require an emergency cleanup. He was good about things like that.

She took a big bite of the pizza and moaned. It was the perfect mix of buttery mozzarella and tomato sauce topped with roasted veggies. "This tastes wonderful."

Tripp shook his head sadly. "I still can't believe you don't eat meat on pizza."

She eyed his half of their dinner, which was piled high with the stuff. "I'm not sure why I don't like pepperoni or sausage on pizza. I would point out that you never have a problem eating any leftover veggie pizza you find in my refrigerator."

"True enough, but it still seems wrong somehow." He pointed at the baking dish on the counter. "What did you make for dessert?"

It was hard not to laugh. The man definitely had a sweet tooth. "Do you care? Or did you suddenly get picky about what I bake for us?"

"Not at all." His smile was mischievous. "I'm just trying to decide whether I want to eat a whole lot of pizza and a small serving of dessert or the other way around."

"It's a blueberry buckle, a kind of coffee cake. If you don't want to gorge yourself on it tonight, you can take some home with you. It will heat up nicely for breakfast in the morning."

He immediately reached for another piece of pizza. "That's great. I never made it to the store today, and I'll be able to avoid dry, cold cereal for another day."

It was obvious why he hadn't finished his to-do list, but Abby didn't say anything. After taking another bite of her pizza, she said, "I have a new quart of milk in the fridge you can take home with you. I have plenty in the open one to last me for another day or so."

"If you're sure."

"Yeah, it's fine."

After they were done with the main course, they made quick work of the dishes before taking their dessert out onto the porch to enjoy the evening air. Once they were settled in the chairs, they sat in silence, content to enjoy a little peace and quiet. Her schedule for the next few days was pretty open, but after that things would pick up again as the night of the dance approached. She suspected Tripp appreciated the chance to kick back for a while. Between school and the events of the night before, he could probably use a little downtime.

He set his empty dessert plate up on the railing out of Zeke's reach. After a bit, he asked, "Have you heard anything from Gage about the investigation? I expected him to let Valerie know if she could book her flight back to L.A."

Just that quick, the coffee cake lost its flavor. Somehow blueberries and cinnamon didn't go well with a discussion about murder. Setting her own plate aside, Abby forced herself to look directly at Tripp. She hated to be the bearer of bad news, but she wouldn't lie to him. "Yeah, Gage called. I'm sorry, but they're definitely handling the case as a homicide."

His grip on his drink cup tightened enough to make the red plastic groan in protest. "Do you know the actual cause of death?"

She shuddered as images of Bryce Cadigan's dead eyes flashed through her mind. "Evidently he was poisoned, but Gage didn't offer any details. He only called to give me a heads-up in case reporters came sniffing around to get a statement."

Tripp muttered a few pungent words under his breath that she suspected she wasn't supposed to hear. He was normally pretty careful with his language around her, but she couldn't blame him for being upset about the situation. Not only was Abby a chief witness in the case, but his ex-wife had to be near the top of Gage's list of potential suspects.

She did her best to reassure him. "Tripp, I know you're worried about Valerie, but you know Gage won't jump to any conclusions or settle for an easy answer. You've told me over and over again in the past to trust him to do his job."

Before he could respond, his cell phone chimed. He jerked it out of his pocket and glanced at the screen as he read a text message. His expression hadn't been particularly happy before, but now it was definitely grim.

He lurched up out of the chair and stalked off into the back corner of the yard to make his call. She couldn't hear what he was saying, but his body language made it clear it wasn't a happy discussion. Zeke had been dozing in the grass near the porch steps, but evidently he also picked up on Tripp's sudden tension. He stood up and gave himself a good shake from head to toe before trotting over to lean against his friend's leg. Tripp reached down to pet the dog's head while he listened to what the person on the other end of the call had to say.

Abby assumed he was talking to Valerie. It made sense she would reach out to Tripp if she'd heard from Gage, too. Whatever her reasons had been to appear out of nowhere to buy an evening with her ex-husband, she hadn't come to Snowberry Creek prepared to get caught up in a murder investigation.

Well, unless she had come to cause one.

Not that Abby should be thinking that way if for no other reason that it would upset Tripp. She didn't particularly care what Valerie Brunn thought of her, but Tripp's opinion of her mattered. Still, he hadn't seen the absolute fury in Valerie's eyes as she'd confronted Bryce Cadigan. The lady had been packing a whole lot of anger around, all of it aimed right at the handsome emcee.

Gage had undoubtedly questioned the woman about it, but it didn't come as a surprise that he hadn't shared any details with Abby. Tripp hadn't mentioned if Valerie had told him what she'd been so upset about, and Abby hadn't wanted to ask her when Zoe had been there with them.

Right now, Tripp was wearing a path in the grass as he paced back and forth, still listening to whatever Valerie had to say. He ended the call and dialed another number. That call didn't appear to go well; for sure, it didn't last long. He stomped halfway across the yard and back again before making a third call. He was facing the wrong direction for Abby to try to read his lips, but the tension in his shoulders was all too clear even from a distance.

Finally, he turned back in Abby's direction, his dark eyes staring straight into hers as he jerked his head in a couple of quick nods. Who was that directed at, especially considering the person on the other end of the call couldn't see him? If he was trying to communicate something to Abby, she had no idea what it was.

He abruptly ended the call and shoved the phone back into his pocket. Then he tilted his head back to stare up at the sky for a few seconds before starting back toward her, his expression unreadable. Well, other than it was obvious that whatever he was dealing with wasn't good.

As he walked, Tripp pulled out his key ring and started flipping it back and forth on his finger. Stopping just short of the steps, he said, "I have to leave. Valerie needs me."

Of course she did. "What's happened now?"

"Those reporters you mentioned have figured out where she's staying. They're camped out in the lobby, so she can't leave her room without being bombarded with questions."

Abby felt a little guilty being relieved that the reporters weren't parked on her doorstep instead. "Can't Gage do something about them?"

Tripp looked frustrated and ticked off in equal measures. "It's not private property, and some of them are staying there, too. No legal way to run them off if they're paying guests."

The last time a reporter bothered Abby, Tripp had claimed to have a few grenades left over from his time in the army and offered to lob one at Reilly Molitor if he continued to pester her. Of course, considering he'd said it right in front of Gage Logan, he'd been kidding. Probably, anyway.

For now, he was looking at her as if wondering how she was going to react to whatever he was about to say.

To prod him into just laying it all out there, she said, "So what does she expect you to do about it?"

"She wants to stay here. Is that okay?"

They both knew he didn't need her permission, and there wasn't anything in his lease that would prevent him from having overnight guests. She managed to stand up despite the swirl of mixed emotions rushing through her veins. The stubborn man continued to stand there as if he'd wait forever for her to respond. What did he want her to say?

"I guess I'd better get you that quart of milk. Sounds like you'll be needing it."

Then she walked into the house and closed the door.

Chapter Seven

Abby made it as far as opening the refrigerator before Tripp caught up with her. His big hand settled over hers and gently shoved the door back closed. She froze, not at all happy that he was crowding her, both physically and emotionally.

"I was just going to get the milk for you." Then she pointed toward the counter. "You'd better take the rest of the blueberry buckle, too. You know, in case Valerie doesn't like cold cereal."

He didn't budge an inch, the stubborn man.

She kept her eyes pinned on one of the magnets stuck on the fridge. "Won't Valerie be wondering what's taking you so long?"

When he still didn't respond, she ventured a quick peek over her shoulder to see why he wasn't springing into action. As soon as she made eye contact, he set his big hand on her shoulder and slowly urged her to turn around and face him.

"That's better. Now, what's really going on, Abby? Do you really think I should leave her in that hotel to be hounded by reporters every time she steps foot out of her room? You usually have more empathy for people than that."

Great. With just that last question he'd managed to make her feel petty and small. It was the second time in one day that her conscience had to kick her in the behind to get her to do the right thing. She knew full well Tripp was a born protector. She'd benefited from that part of his personality on too many occasions to think he wouldn't feel obligated to help Valerie. Heck, he'd even spent time in jail to help a homeless veteran. That was just the kind of man he was.

And if Valerie were anyone else, Abby would've been the first to volunteer to offer the woman a safe haven. She drew a slow breath before once again lifting her gaze to meet Tripp's. "You're right, of course. She needs you right now. Let me know if I can do anything to help."

He only looked marginally happier, so there was clearly still something wrong. "What is it, Tripp?"

He took a step back, finally giving them both a little breathing room. "Here's the thing. My place has only the one bedroom, and the sofa is a love seat. There's no way either of us can sleep on that thing."

Yeah, she knew that. While she thought that was a problem, she hadn't been sure if he would see it that way, too. From the way his ex-wife had been clinging to him, somehow Abby doubted Valerie would mind sharing close quarters with Tripp. Meanwhile, he stood rock-still as if waiting for her to connect some dots and figure out for herself what he was really asking.

It finally hit her. He might have only one bedroom, but he knew she had rooms that weren't being used right now. He'd even slept in the one across the hall from hers one night when he'd been injured. It was too much to hope that Tripp wanted to move back in and turn his place over to the barnacle.

Abby bowed to the inevitable. "You want her to stay with me."

He nodded. "I know it's a lot to ask."

Darn straight it was. He believed Valerie was innocent, but Abby didn't know the woman well enough to have that kind of faith in her. She'd also learned the hard way since moving to Snowberry Creek that murderers came in all shapes and sizes.

"Do you really trust her, Tripp? How well do you really know Valerie after all these years apart?"

At least he gave the matter some serious thought before answering. "The woman I knew wasn't capable of killing someone. I used to laugh when she would capture spiders and set them free outside rather than squashing them. I may not have seen her in years, but I can't believe she's changed that much."

Abby didn't bother to point out that he'd undoubtedly changed quite a bit over that same period of time. He would only say that working as a buyer for a high-end store didn't have the same effect on people that multiple combat deployments did. She still wasn't ready to roll out the red carpet. "Did Valerie tell you why she suddenly reappeared in your life?"

"Yeah, she wanted my help with something."

He clearly didn't want to say anything more on the subject. Abby crossed her arms over her chest and prepared to wait him out. "Spit it out, Tripp. If I'm going to let that woman live under my roof, I need to know what I'm getting myself into."

He frowned, but there was a hint of a humor in his dark eyes. "Anyone ever point out how stubborn you are?"

She gave him a narrowed-eyed look. "Pot, kettle, Tripp."

That made him smile. "Yeah, well, can't argue with you about that."

He started flipping his keys back and forth again. "She had a problem that she was hoping I could help her with. Something to do with her younger sister, who used to live in this area. Although I guess Becca recently moved to L.A. to stay with Valerie. With everything else that's happened, she hasn't told me any more than just that. As far as Bryce Cadigan goes, she swears she'd never met the man in person before last night. I believe her."

Zeke picked that moment to nudge Abby, his way of letting her know that he was wanting a bit of her attention for himself. She used getting him a treat as an excuse to put a little more room between her and Tripp.

"And that's all she said?"

"Pretty much." Tripp took the opportunity to get the milk out of the fridge. "I'll take the open carton since there'll be two of you and only one of me."

Abby put her hands on her hips. "This is not a done deal, Tripp. I still have questions, and you're not doing a very good job of answering them. What else did she tell you?"

He shrugged. "She didn't tell me much of anything. To be honest, I had no idea even what to say to her. I can't even figure out why she would've plunked down that much money at the auction instead of just calling to ask me for help. Did she think I wouldn't have at least listened to what she had to say?"

She had to agree that the barnacle's behavior didn't make much sense unless, as Abby suspected, the woman was also interested in rekindling her relationship with him. If he hadn't picked up on that possibility himself, Abby wasn't about to point it out to him. For now, he was still talking. "When she was here earlier, I was too busy mowing the lawn and doing homework for any heartfelt discussions. What little talking we did do was mostly about small things. You know, about old friends, her job, and stuff."

This line of conversation was going nowhere fast, but she didn't get the impression that Tripp was holding out on her. He really didn't know for sure why his ex-wife had hunted him up after all this time.

Abby couldn't assume that his relationship with Valerie was anything like the one she had with her own former spouse. The few encounters she'd had with Chad since their divorce had felt more like running into someone she used to go to school with than it did like talking to a man she'd once loved. It was as if she'd never really known him at all. It had nearly crushed her to learn that Chad had been happily carrying on an affair for more than a year before she realized what was going on.

With Tripp, what you saw was what you got. The man took things like honor and duty pretty darn seriously, and he would never knowingly put Abby in danger. So it all came down to which would be easier to tolerate—Valerie living with her for a few days, or watching the woman move in with Tripp.

In the end, it was no contest.

"Fine, go get her. While you're gone, I'll put fresh sheets on the bed in the guest bedroom up on the third floor. That one has a bathroom right next to it, so she'll have more privacy that way."

He didn't ask why she would make Valerie trudge up to the third floor when there was a perfectly good room on the second. Maybe he realized that both women would be happier with some distance between them. After all, the only thing they had in common was the fact they both knew Tripp. Well, and that Abby was a witness and Valerie was a suspect in the same murder case.

Happy times all around.

"Okay then. We'll be back shortly. I'll do my best to make sure I don't lead the reporters right back here."

"Good idea."

He started for the door but turned back at the last second as if he'd forgotten something. Before she could ask what it was, he stopped right in front of her. Her pulse skipped a beat as he gathered her in close for a hug. She relaxed into his embrace and wrapped her arms around his waist.

For a second, she thought she felt him press a soft kiss near her temple, but it might have been just his breath brushing across her skin as he said, "Thanks, Abs."

Then he was gone.

Some mornings really sucked. For the second day in a row, Abby's best efforts to sleep late had failed miserably. It wasn't even eight o'clock, and she was already bored and restless. She'd been looking forward to enjoying a few days of relative peace before she had to handle the rush of final preparations for the veterans dance. Instead, she had an unwelcome houseguest and no idea of what to do with her time.

Zeke perked his ears and looked down the hall toward the staircase. Maybe Valerie was about to make an appearance. Abby closed her eyes to listen. Sure enough, she heard the familiar creak of the step right below the second-floor landing. She remained seated, figuring Valerie could follow the scents of coffee and burnt toast to the kitchen if she couldn't remember where it was. Abby had offered to give her a brief tour of the place last night, but the other woman had clearly had a rough day and was more interested in going to bed than learning the floor plan of the house.

She appeared in the doorway a few seconds later and made a beeline right for the coffee. Abby had left a clean mug sitting on the counter for her. She waited until Valerie had poured herself a cup before speaking. "If you're hungry, I have yogurt, cereal, or I can fix you some bacon and eggs."

Valerie sat down at the table. "Yogurt would be fine. It's what I usually have. With my work schedule, I rarely have time for anything elaborate. I also travel a lot for my job. Maybe Tripp told you that I'm a buyer for Suits-Herself, Inc."

"He did. They carry nice clothes. I've shopped there myself."

Valerie gave Abby an assessing look. "He didn't mention what kind of work you do."

"I was the chief financial officer for the company my husband and I started. He bought out my half when we divorced a while back." She paused to sip her coffee and decide how much sharing she wanted to do. "Right after that, my aunt died and left me this house. I'm still working on what comes next."

She set her coffee down. "I'll get the yogurt for you. I have strawberry, raspberry, and there may be a peach left, too."

"I'm not picky."

Abby set a container of strawberry yogurt on the table for each of them. While Valerie peeled the lid off of hers, Abby put a plate full of mini muffins that she'd taken out of the freezer earlier into the microwave to warm. After glancing out of the window, she got another cup down off the shelf and set it by the coffeemaker. Tripp was headed toward the porch with his backpack slung over one shoulder. He probably had classes this morning and wanted to check in before he left.

She opened the door just as the microwave beeped. "Hi, come on in. The coffee is fresh, and I was just heating up some cinnamon walnut muffins if you're hungry."

"I've already eaten, but coffee sounds good. I've got to leave in a few minutes, but I wanted to see if either of you need anything from the store. If I don't restock today, I'm going to have to see if Zeke would mind sharing his kibble."

The dog in question perked up at the mention of food and stationed himself in front of the counter, where Abby stored his treat jar. Tripp took the hint and grabbed a few for his furry friend. "I was only kidding, Zeke. I wouldn't get into the secret stash of food you keep at my place without asking first."

Abby frowned at the two males in the room. "So that's why he's packed on a few extra pounds lately. If you feed him, Tripp, the least you could do is let me know."

The man looked totally unrepentant. "Zeke, you promised to tell her whenever you have dinner at my house."

It was impossible to know how much human speak the dog actually understood, but right now Zeke's tongue was hanging out in a huge doggy grin. Clearly he enjoyed being the center of attention. Abby relented and patted his head. "Don't worry, boy, it's not your fault. You're not supposed to be the adult in the room."

He rewarded her with a slobbery lick on her hand, which she promptly wiped on her jeans. She watched as Tripp proceeded to spoil the dog with even more organic cookies. Valerie slowly ate her yogurt as she shifted her gaze back and forth between Abby and Tripp. Her expression was hard to decipher. If Abby were to hazard a guess, Valerie wasn't all that happy to see the easy camaraderie between her ex-husband and his landlady. Too bad. Abby and Tripp were friends, and she wouldn't pretend otherwise just because Valerie didn't like it.

Finally, the other woman said, "When did you become a dog person, Tripp? As I recall, you were never interested in having a pet when we were together."

Tripp didn't look as if he appreciated the question as he reached over to gently rub Zeke's ears. "Between your classes and my deployments, we didn't have room in our lives for a dog. Besides, Zeke here belongs to Abby. She just lets me borrow him sometimes."

It was time to divert the conversation into safer territory. "You'd better finish your coffee before it gets cold, Tripp. If you want some to go, you know where the travel mugs are."

"Thanks."

He chugged down the rest of his coffee before getting one of the to-go cups down from the cabinet and filling it. Abby hadn't meant the offer to be a reminder to Valerie how familiar Tripp was with her kitchen, but she did notice the woman had tightened her grip on her own coffee mug.

By that point, Tripp was heading for the door. "I've gotta go, but I'll be back around three. Text me if you want anything from the store."

"Will do. Do you want to have dinner with us tonight?"

Before he could answer, Valerie spoke up. "Abby, I'm sure you have better things to do with your time than feed us. I thought I'd take Tripp out to eat someplace nice. You know, to thank him for everything he's done to help me out."

Tripp had a bit of a deer in the headlights look going on as he met first Abby's gaze and then Valerie's. Finally, he said, "I'm sorry, but I can't. I've got an exam to study for."

Then he was out the door, leaving Abby alone with his unhappy ex-wife. Great. Abby was pretty sure Valerie muttered something under her breath that sound liked "he still needs to eat, doesn't he" as she carried her empty yogurt container over to the sink. After rinsing it out, she tossed it in the recycling bin in the corner. With that done, she looked a little at a loss as to what to do next.

Welcome or not, she was still a guest, so Abby pointed out the few amenities she had to offer. "Help yourself to any of the books in the den if you need something to read. You can also watch a movie if you'd like. I'm going to take Zeke for his walk, and we'll be back in about an hour."

"Actually, I need to work. Can I use your Wi-Fi?"

"Sure thing. I'll get the password for you."

Fifteen minutes later, Valerie was ensconced at the dining room table working while Abby and Zeke headed out for a long, leisurely stroll. It bothered her to leave an almost total stranger alone in her house, but right now she needed some room to breathe.

The whole situation was really frustrating. Clearly Valerie was no more anxious to have dinner with her than Abby was to cook it for her. On the other hand, it would be beyond rude to fix a meal for herself and not offer to share. Maybe Valerie would go out by herself, but it wasn't clear to Abby how the woman had been getting around town. Uber, maybe.

Regardless, once she and Zeke got back home, she'd ask Valerie what her plans were and go from there. For now, she was going to enjoy the sunshine and Zeke's undemanding company.

However, there was one thing she knew for sure. She really hoped Gage Logan made quick work of solving Bryce Cadigan's murder, because if she and Valerie spent much more time together, things might get really ugly.

Chapter Eight

Forty-five minutes later, Abby and Zeke were just finishing up their walk. She'd driven them over to the park to stroll along the river. It was one of Zeke's favorite places to go, and she found the soft murmur of the river soothing. They left the trees along the trail to cut across the grassy slope back toward the parking lot.

To her surprise, a police cruiser was stopped right behind her car, blocking her in. Gage Logan stood leaning against the front fender of his car, clearly waiting for her. What did he need now? She tugged on Zeke's leash and started walking faster. Gage straightened up as soon as she got close.

"Hey, Gage, what's up?"

"Sorry to bother you and your buddy here, Abby, but I happened to spot your car as I was driving by." He bent down to pet Zeke. "I'm actually looking for Tripp. Have you seen him? He's not answering his phone."

She pulled out her water bottle and took a long drink. "He had classes this morning. I can give him a message if I see him, but I'm not really expecting to. He said he had an exam to study for when he gets home."

Gage sounded pretty frustrated when he spoke again. "I need to talk to Ms. Brunn, but she's not answering her phone, either. Evidently she checked out of the hotel yesterday evening, and the clerk on duty at the time remembers her walking out with a guy that fits Tripp's description. I'm not going to be at all happy with either of them if she headed back to California without telling me."

Abby wanted to bash both Tripp and the barnacle. "Let me get this straight. Are you telling me that neither Tripp nor Valerie bothered to tell you where she was going?"

Gage jerked his head in a quick nod. "Yes, that's exactly what I'm telling you. Why? Do you know where she is?"

She and her tenant would definitely be having words later. Tripp knew Gage hated being left out of the loop when it came to police business. She shouldn't be the one dealing with a ticked-off police chief when none of this was her fault. Heck, she wasn't any happier about the situation than he was.

"Yeah, I do. Or at least I know where she was as of an hour ago. I have no idea why she's not answering her phone, but she's staying at my house."

The stark lines bracketing Gage's mouth deepened. "Dare I ask why you'd invite her to move in?"

"I didn't, or at least it wasn't my idea. She called Tripp yesterday to tell him that the reporters were pestering her at the hotel. Tripp said there wasn't any way to stop them. Something about it being a public place, not to mention some of them had booked rooms there."

She'd also thought maybe Tripp had talked to Gage about the situation, but obviously she'd been wrong about that.

Clearly frustrated, Gage asked, "So why didn't she just check in somewhere else? There's a couple of places out closer to I-5 that aren't that far from here."

Another good question, one she had no good answer for. "All I know is that Tripp asked if she could use one of my guest rooms. His place only has one bedroom, and the only sofa he has is too short to use as a bed."

Gage didn't say anything for a few seconds. "Are you headed back home from here?"

She decided to be honest with him. "Yeah, I actually hated to leave Valerie alone in my house at all, but I needed to take Zeke for his walk. And frankly, I needed to clear my head. I don't know the woman at all, and I'm not all that happy about the situation."

"I don't blame you." Gage hesitated a second before adding, "But for what it's worth, she seems to have a clean record. Not even a parking ticket."

It was time to go home. After unlocking the car, she opened the back door so Zeke could climb in. "Do you have a message for Valerie?"

He opened the driver's door for her. "No, I'll follow you home and talk to her myself."

Great. Somehow she doubted Valerie would believe that Gage had sought out Abby and not the other way around. Well, too bad. If the woman wasn't happy, she could just move to one of the hotels that Gage had mentioned.

"I'll see you there, but I'll make myself scarce so you can talk to her in private."

"Sounds good."

As she started to get into the car, he stopped her. "I

said this before, but I'm really sorry you got caught up in this mess, Abby. I'll do my best to make sure that my investigation doesn't impact you any more than it absolutely has to."

"I appreciate that, Gage. Besides, it's not your fault that Valerie is staying at my place. That's on Tripp."

Gage sighed. "What was he thinking? Even if she's innocent—and that's still a big if at this point—a possible suspect shouldn't be living with one of the primary witnesses in the case. I'll be having a talk with Tripp later. It won't be a pleasant one."

There wasn't much she could say to that. She hated that this mess with Valerie was causing problems for the two men. They'd served together at some point in the past and so had known each other for longer than Tripp had been living in Snowberry Creek. She hoped their friendship would survive long term.

"I'll see you at the house."

Tripp's truck was the last thing Abby wanted to see when she got home. The darn man was supposed to be gone. Gage was already unhappy that Valerie moved out of the hotel without notice. Having Tripp underfoot while she was once again being interrogated wasn't likely to help matters.

He stepped out on his front porch as soon as she parked the car. She let Zeke out, who immediately trotted over to join him. "Why aren't you at school?"

Okay, that came out more accusatory than she'd intended. He gave her a puzzled look. "My teacher had a family emergency and had to cancel class. Is there some reason I shouldn't be here?"

Before she could answer, the sound of another car in the driveway caught his attention. As soon as he recognized Gage's cruiser, Tripp's expression went from curious to concerned.

"What's he doing here?" Then he gave Abby a suspicious look. "Did you call him to complain about Valerie staying with you?"

Really? That was his first thought? Even if she had admitted to Gage that she wasn't happy about the arrangement, she hadn't sought him out. "Gage spotted us heading back to the car at the park and stopped to talk. Seems he'd been trying to call you, but it kept going to voice mail."

By that point Gage was out of his car and close enough to join the conversation. He gave Tripp a hard look. "Don't blame Abby for me being here. I was looking for you. Since neither you nor your ex-wife were answering your phones, I asked Abby if she'd seen you."

There was a heavy thread of anger woven through his words. Tripp growled back, "I didn't answer because I was in class up until thirty minutes ago. Your message didn't say it was anything urgent. I was about to call you back when I heard Abby's car in the driveway."

Tripp stepped down off the porch with Zeke trailing right behind him. "I'm here now. What did you want?"

"I told Valerie that I'd need to talk to her again today. Imagine my surprise when I called the hotel to set up a time to get together only to find she'd checked out with no notice. The only reason I knew to call you is because the evening clerk gave me a good description of the man she left with."

Tripp gave Abby another hard look before turning back to Gage. "You told Val she needed to stay in the area, not that she had to stay at that particular hotel."

"I also told her to keep me in the loop if that changed."

Okay, from his look of confusion, that last bit of information was news to Tripp. "I'm sure she planned to let you know that Abby invited her to stay here."

Maybe he really believed that, but Gage clearly didn't. Regardless, Abby really hated that Tripp's first instinct was to defend the barnacle. Maybe he was right, and Valerie had planned to let Gage know about the change in her location. That didn't explain why she hadn't told Tripp that she was supposed to keep the police apprised of her living arrangements in Snowberry Creek. This conversation was accomplishing nothing.

"Gage, if you need me for anything, I'll be in the sewing room on the third floor. Just walk on in the house whenever you and Tripp finish your . . . discussion."

Argument was more like it, but that was their problem, not hers.

"Come here, Zeke." The dog was obviously reluctant to leave the two men, but he finally padded over to stand beside her. "Good boy, let's go."

The two of them had gone only about half the distance to the back steps before Gage caught up with her, and Tripp loomed up on her other side. Neither man said a word, which probably meant they were only moving their disagreement inside. She didn't bother to speak to either of them until they were in her kitchen.

Rather than risk getting embroiled in what could be another angry conversation, she kept moving. "Like I said, I'm going upstairs to work on Aunt Sybil's quilt. Help yourself to anything you want out of the fridge."

She hung up Zeke's leash and headed down the

hall to the staircase. As she passed by the door to the dining room, she was relieved to see Valerie was still sitting at the table. Whatever she was studying on her laptop had her full attention, making it unclear if she was even aware she was no longer alone in the house.

Abby hurried on by and hustled up the stairs. She'd only reached the first landing when she heard Gage's deep voice calling Valerie's name. Although she was curious what Gage was in such a hurry to talk to the barnacle about, right now it was probably smarter to disappear for a while.

She'd barely had time to sit down at the sewing machine when she heard the stairs creak. Zeke was already curled up on the rug in the corner, so it wasn't him coming up the steps. Rather than stare at the door in anticipation, she chose two strips of quilt squares and began pinning them together.

When Tripp appeared in the doorway a few seconds later, she didn't bother to look up from what she was doing. "Did you need something?"

He remained on the far side of the room. "Look, I'm sorry."

Okay, his visit might warrant her full attention after all. She set the quilt squares back down. "For what, exactly? I can think of a few things I'm not happy about right now, and I want to make sure I know exactly which one you're apologizing for."

The fact that he grinned at her assessment of the situation didn't help her mood one bit. At least he had the good sense to wipe the smile off his face the second he realized it was only fanning the flames of her temper.

"I thought you might want a snack." He ventured a little closer to offer her a bottle of water and a couple of the mini muffins wrapped in a napkin. "And I should've known you wouldn't call Gage to complain even if you aren't happy about Valerie staying here."

"That's a good start." She pointed toward the chair near the quilting frame on the other side of the room. "Have a seat if you want, but close the door before you do. I promised Gage he'd have privacy while he talks to Valerie."

"Yeah, he made it clear that my presence wasn't wanted or appreciated." He sat down and leaned forward, resting his elbows on his knees and staring down at the floor. "I hate this for her, but I do know he's only doing his job."

To give herself something to do, Abby opened the bottle of water and took a small drink. "He also knows this is hard for you, Tripp, what with your ex-wife appearing out of nowhere only to get caught up in this murder investigation."

"I'm also sorry I strong-armed you into letting her stay here, but she didn't want to be alone."

While that last bit might be true, Abby was willing to bet she wasn't the person Valerie had been hoping would keep her company. Tripp might still be blissfully unaware of the barnacle's interest in him, but it seemed all too clear to Abby. Valerie had told Tripp she needed his help with a problem, but she also looked at him like a woman looked at a man she wanted.

When Abby remained silent, Tripp finally looked up. "I should've found a different hotel for her."

It was too late now. "Probably. Gage wasn't happy to find out one of his suspects was currently living with a witness. It might complicate his investigation a little."

Or a whole lot if it turned out that Valerie was indeed the one who killed Bryce Cadigan.

From the big-time frown that just settled on Tripp's

face, some of what she'd been thinking must have shown in her own expression. Fine. Neither of them was happy right now. She picked up her quilt squares and went back to work pinning them together. Tripp watched every move she made as if it were the most riveting thing he'd ever seen.

"Did Gage tell you who his other suspects might be?"

Abby paused to consider how much she should share before responding. "Not exactly. He wanted to know everyone I'd seen Bryce talking to both before and after the auction. There weren't that many, and I didn't know everyone's name. I have no idea if Gage was able to identify any of them based on my description alone. Since he was asking some other people the same question, he might have figured out who they were that way."

Another long silence.

"We need to figure out who they are. You and me, I mean."

Tripp's bald statement startled Abby into almost knocking her bottle of water over on her quilting. She managed to catch it and quickly screwed the lid back on.

"Gage is already unhappy with you, Tripp. If you go sticking your nose in his investigation, it's only going to make him madder."

To her surprise, Tripp laughed. "Seriously, Abby? Since when have you let that stop you? Besides, I didn't say we would actually talk to these people, but I want to help get his focus off Valerie. If we can figure out who they are, you can give that information to Gage and let him run with it."

He made it all sound so easy, but she knew from personal experience that even brushing up against a murder investigation could go horribly wrong. "How do you suggest we go about figuring out who they are?

Neither of us have lived here long enough to know all that many people in town."

"Good point." He went back to staring at the floor. "What can you tell me about the people you mentioned to Gage?"

She picked up a pin and started working again. "I saw Bryce talking to his old football coach, but I'm guessing Gage already knows who that is. Bryce also talked to one of his former high school teachers, so I'm sure Gage will be talking to her if he hasn't already. She seemed to take Bryce's death hard."

"Tell me about the ones you didn't have names for. What did they look like?"

Rather than argue, she let her thoughts drift back to the auction and tried to dredge up a clear picture of the other two men she'd seen with Bryce.

"One was about Bryce's age. I have no way of knowing this for sure, but I suspect they might have gone to high school together. At least they looked to be about the same age. There was only one other man I saw Bryce talk to for any length of time, but he was older. Probably in his late forties. There was definitely some tension between them, but I wasn't close enough to hear what they were talking about."

"We'll start with the younger guy. There must be some way to track him down."

Abby really didn't want to get sucked into Tripp's personal crusade to clear the barnacle's name, but there didn't seem to be any way to avoid it. "I'll go to the library either later this afternoon or first thing tomorrow. I could be wrong, but I'm betting they have a set of the high school yearbooks in their collection. If I can find the one with Bryce's class in it, I might be able to pick out the other guy's picture. It's worth a try."

She finished pinning the two strips she been working on and set them aside. "It's a long shot, though. His looks could've changed over the years. Heck, I could be completely wrong thinking he and Bryce went to school together, so no promises."

"I just appreciate that you're willing to try."

He stood up and stretched. "I'd better get back over to my place and hit the books. Let me know if there's anything I can do to help."

"The dinner offer still stands. It won't be anything fancy. Just sandwiches and some of that *pasta e fagioli* soup you like so much."

"If you're sure it's not too much trouble."

She had to smother a laugh. Heating up a bowl of soup for a friend was a no-brainer. Sharing a meal with that friend's ex-wife, who may or may not be a murderer? Now, that fit her definition of trouble with a capital T. Guessing Tripp wouldn't appreciate her take on the subject, she settled for simply saying, "We'll eat at six."

Chapter Nine

Looking at old yearbooks turned out to be incredibly boring. Abby flipped through the last few pages of the third one she'd taken off the shelf and closed the cover. It would help if she actually knew the year Bryce had graduated from the high school in Snowberry Creek. His exact age would make things easier, but she couldn't risk asking any of her friends if they happened to know.

After all, what plausible excuse could she come up with for needing that information? She was feeling twitchy enough just knowing the police department was right next door to the library. After asking the librarian about the yearbooks, she'd grabbed three off the shelf and found an empty table in the back corner of the library that was out of sight of the door.

She returned them to the shelf and picked up the next four. If she didn't spot Bryce in any of those, it was time to give up. Tripp wouldn't be happy, but at least she could tell him she'd tried. However, luck was with her this time. Rather than going through the rows and rows of individual pictures, she concentrated on the group photos. The one thing she knew for sure about Bryce was that he'd been on the football team.

Yep, that was him in the middle row. Better yet, standing right next to him was the mystery man he'd been talking to at the auction. According to the list of names under the picture, his name was Denny Moller, and they were both listed as juniors. While she was at it, she turned to the staff pictures. It was easy to recognize the football coach, Roy Tull. He'd put on some pounds and lost some of his hair, but the face was still the same.

Picking out Mrs. Alstead proved to be much more of a challenge. For one thing, she'd been Miss DeWitt back then. Abby angled the book to catch the light better. Wow, she'd changed a lot over the years, and not for the better. Back then, the clothes she had on were stylish, and she'd worn just enough makeup to highlight her fresh beauty. In fact, she could've easily passed for one of her students. Regardless, she wasn't the target of Abby's search, and it was time to get back on task.

She opened the next yearbook to the football team picture. Bryce was there, but Denny was missing. His senior picture was there, though, so he hadn't moved away. That might not mean anything, but her spidey senses were tingling. For now, she needed to leave if she wanted to get dinner on the table on time.

Even if she couldn't do any further digging right now, at least she now had a name to give Gage. Before she did, though, she'd have to come up with an explanation about how she'd learned it. While he might find the information useful, he wouldn't necessarily appreciate her poking around even on the edges of his investigation.

She'd worry about that later. Right now, she had to get home and play hostess to her unwanted house-guest.

The kitchen was normally one of Abby's favorite rooms in the house. It was large and had enough counter space for two people to work without crowding each other. Certainly, she and Aunt Sybil had done a lot of baking together whenever Abby had come for a visit. She and Tripp had also managed to throw together some quick meals without stepping all over each other's toes. The same couldn't be said for her and the barnacle. The past hour had shown her that there was a great deal of wisdom in the old saying about too many cooks spoiling the broth.

Valerie stirred the pot on the stove. "I tasted the soup a little while ago and thought it needed more oregano."

Abby didn't appreciate the uninvited critique of her cooking. "I put in what the recipe called for."

Valerie dipped a spoon into the pot and held the steaming hot soup up to Abby's lips. "Here, taste it. See if that isn't better."

What was she supposed to say? It wasn't as if she could take the additional spice back out of the pot. "It's fine."

Of course, it had been all right in the first place. Telling herself Valerie was only trying to help, she forced a smile. "I'll slice the tomatoes for the sandwiches. Would you open those two packages of cheese and put the slices on that plate over there?"

They immediately bumped hips when she reached for the same knife that Valerie wanted. When Abby jerked her hand back, she accidentally knocked over the salt shaker, which promptly rolled off the counter to land on the floor. It didn't break, but the lid popped off and spilled the contents all over the place.

She almost stomped her foot in frustration. "I'll get the vacuum cleaner."

Valerie didn't say a word, although Abby thought the woman was fighting the urge to laugh. Let her. Right now Abby had more important things to do. She'd barely started vacuuming up the mess when Tripp knocked on the back door. Valerie darn near vaulted over the kitchen table to be the one to let him in.

He stepped inside and looked around the kitchen. "Hi, I hope I'm not late."

Valerie gave him a high-wattage smile. "No, you're right on time."

Tripp gave Abby a puzzled look as she jerked one of the chairs out of the way to sweep underneath that side of the table. After making quick work of the floor, she used the brush attachment to clean along the edges of the tile. She should probably greet Tripp, too, but right now she didn't trust herself to be civil. None of this was his fault. Well, that wasn't exactly true. Valerie wouldn't be there to irritate her so much if he hadn't taken pity on the woman.

She shut off the machine and tried to yank the cord out of the wall from where she stood several feet away. When it didn't come loose, Tripp walked over and unplugged the vacuum for her. Instead of dropping the cord onto the floor, he carried the end over and handed it to her personally. "Kind of late in the day to be cleaning house, isn't it?"

His half smile was a strong clue that he was only teasing, but Abby still didn't appreciate it. Rather than responding, she concentrated on winding up the cord.

Valerie, ever the helpful one, didn't miss the

chance to poke her perfect nose into their conversation. She moved closer to Tripp before speaking, drawing his attention back in her direction. "Abby somehow managed to knock the salt shaker off the counter. It made quite the mess."

Did she really have to make Abby sound like the biggest klutz ever? Evidently. "Yes, Valerie, I spilled the salt. I also cleaned it up. I assume that's all right with you."

Even if she was overreacting, she couldn't seem to help herself. "I'm going to put the vacuum away now. Dinner is ready. The soup is on the stove. The sandwich makings are all on the table. Feel free to help yourselves."

After shoving the vacuum back where it belonged, she forced herself to close the closet without slamming it. There was no way she wanted to go back to the kitchen right now. Instead, she headed toward the front door and out onto the porch. Eventually she'd have to go back and deal with her guests, but not until she let the fresh evening air cool her temper a bit.

A few seconds later, the door opened behind her. She knew without looking that it was Tripp who had followed her. She gave it two minutes tops before Valerie came trailing after him.

He moved up beside Abby, standing close but without actually crowding her. It was too much to be hoped that he would leave her alone for a few seconds.

The clueless male asked, "Abs, what's really going on?"

She closed her eyes and drew a slow breath. "Sorry, it's been a long day, and I have a headache."

Both of those things were true. She couldn't very

well tell him that the real pain was standing back in her kitchen.

Tripp edged a little closer. "Want me to get you something for the headache?"

"That would—"

Before she could finish, Valerie appeared right on schedule. "Tripp, your soup's getting cold."

He glanced back over his shoulder. "I would guess that means Abby's soup is, too."

Valerie gave him a wide-eyed look. "I didn't dish hers up. She said for us to help ourselves. I assumed that meant she'd serve herself whenever she was ready."

His expression went totally blank. At least he wasn't buying Valerie's innocent act at all. "Come on, Abby. Let's get you some ibuprofen."

Tripp brushed by his ex as if she were the doorman whose job was to greet people entering the house. Abby followed close on his heels, leaving Valerie to bring up the rear. When they got to the kitchen, the table was no longer set for three. One plate and bowl were now sitting on the counter, leaving the two remaining place settings in front of adjoining chairs. How cozy.

Tripp pulled a chair out and motioned for Abby to sit down. Then he looked at Valerie and pointed toward an empty seat on the far end of the table. She wasn't happy, but she surrendered to the inevitable and followed his directions.

He pushed the other bowl of soup over in front of her, along with the necessary flatware and plate. That done, he got the ibuprofen out of the cabinet and set the bottle in front of Abby and then brought her a glass of water.

Finally, he dished up another bowl of soup and picked up the plate Valerie had put back on the counter. Before sitting down, he asked, "Can I get anybody anything else?"

"I'm good, Tripp." In fact, Abby was already feeling a lot better. On the other hand, Valerie looked like she might have her own headache brewing.

No one seemed inclined to talk as they passed the sandwich makings back and forth. While the silence wasn't exactly uncomfortable, Abby had certainly had more pleasant meals. She managed to finish her soup and half of her sandwich. Valerie ate most of her sandwich but only toyed with the soup. Maybe it had too much oregano for her taste.

Tripp, on the other hand, devoured two bowls of soup and the enormous sandwich he'd made for himself. "Thanks, that hit the spot, Abs."

Valerie immediately set her spoon down with more force than was necessary. "Tripp, now that you're finished with dinner, let's go for a walk."

He'd been about to take a drink of the beer Abby had put out for him when she set the table. "Sorry, but I can't."

That clearly wasn't the answer Valerie was hoping for. She shoved her chair back from the table and stood up. "Can't or won't?"

Tripp either didn't hear the note of temper in Valerie's voice or chose to ignore it. Either way, he responded in a reasonable tone. "Since Abby was nice enough to fix dinner for us, I'm going to do the dishes. That's the deal when I eat over here. After that, I need to study for an exam and do a final polish on the paper I've been working on."

Making good on his stated intentions, he picked up

his dishes, carried them over to the counter, and came back for the rest.

The barnacle tried again. "Please come with me, Tripp. We won't be gone for more than an hour. I've been shut up in this house all day, and I really could use a breath of fresh air."

She sidled around the table to stand next to him at the sink and put her hand on his shoulder. "Back when we were married, we always enjoyed a long walk after dinner. It will be like old times."

Abby wanted to hurl. Instead, she fed Zeke and started putting the condiments and leftover meat and cheese back in the refrigerator. Meanwhile, Tripp held firm on his refusal. "Sorry, Val, but I really need to head back over to my place and get to work. If you're interested, though, I usually go for a five-mile run at six in the morning. You're welcome to join me."

Valerie looked genuinely horrified. "Why on earth would you get up at the crack of dawn to go running?"

He shrugged. "After twenty years in the army, it's become a habit."

The woman turned her attention in Abby's direction. "And do you like to run in the mornings, too?"

When Tripp cracked up laughing, Valerie gave him a puzzled look. "Did I say something funny?"

Abby answered before Tripp could. "He knows the only way I'd run at that hour of the morning would be if the house was on fire, if then."

She looked around the kitchen to see if there was anything else she needed to do, but Tripp had made his usual quick work of cleaning up. "Now, if you two will excuse me, I think a good soak in the tub will be just the ticket to finish getting rid of my headache. Thanks for doing the dishes, Tripp."

As much as she hated leaving Valerie alone with him, she walked away without a backward look. It wasn't as if she had any real claim on the man. That didn't keep her from peeking out of her bedroom window to see if he did go back to his place. He was just stepping up on his front porch with no sign of Valerie anywhere. Funny how that helped ease the last bit of her headache.

Tripp opened his front door but stopped before going inside. He walked back to the front edge of his porch, looked straight up at her bedroom window, and waved. Clearly busted, she waved back and slunk off to her en suite bathroom to take that long soak in the tub she'd mentioned.

She left the overhead light off, instead lighting the row of her favorite pear-scented candles on the shelf above the tub, and turned on some soft music. She left the door ajar in case Zeke decided to come visit. After putting her cell phone within easy reach on the small table next to the tub, she pinned her hair up on top of her head, stripped off her clothes, and tossed them in the hamper.

Slipping into the steaming hot water, she rested her head against her bath pillow. It felt like heaven, soothing both her headache and her mood. A few minutes later, her cell phone chimed, signaling a new text. It was tempting to ignore the summons, but curiosity got the better of her.

Just as she suspected, the message was from Tripp. *Feeling better?*

Yes. How is the homework going?

I hate writing papers. I also need to study for an exam. Shouldn't take too long.

What class?

Biology.

You've never told me what your major is.

No, I haven't.

Secretive jerk.

I prefer to think of myself as a man of mystery.

Yeah, right. BTW, I know who the guy was that Bryce was talking to at the auction. I found a picture of him standing next to Bryce in one of the yearbooks. Now I just need to find a way to tell Gage without making him mad.

Since you did it as a favor for me, I promise not to let him beat up on you . . . too much, anyway.

Thanks a lot, mystery man.

One more thing, Abby. I'm sorry Val is being such a problem. I owe you.

Yeah, he did, but she also knew he was caught between her and a woman he still felt some obligation to protect.

I'll survive. Maybe I'll see you tomorrow.

You can always go running with me.

No pigs have flown by my window lately, so I'm pretty sure that's not happening.

LOL. Good night.

She set her phone back on the table and then added some more hot water to the tub. What else could she do to identify the older man Bryce had spoken to? If the archives of *The Clarion* were online, she could do some poking around to see if anything about Bryce popped up. She was still pondering that idea when Zeke wandered in. He sat down and gave her a reproachful look. He wasn't all that fond of baths and never understood why she was.

Still, he'd come close enough to let her scratch his head for him. "Hi, boy. I promise I won't stay in here much longer. Then the two of us will curl up on the bed and watch a movie. Maybe I'll even sneak back downstairs and fix us both a snack."

That last word perked him right up. His tongue lolled out of his mouth in a hopeful doggy grin. It would've taken a much harder heart than hers to deny those big brown eyes. She pulled the plug on the tub. "Okay, Zeke. Give me a minute and we'll go forage."

And while she was downstairs, she'd grab her laptop, too. It was time to go hunting.

Chapter Ten

Abby had learned one really important fact soon after moving to Snowberry Creek: the ladies on the quilting guild were her best source of information about anything and everyone in town. After a frustrating evening delving into the rather limited online archives of the local newspaper, she called her friends and invited them over for an early afternoon tea party.

She didn't bother to warn them about her houseguest. Valerie had disappeared right after a late breakfast, saying she'd be back in time for dinner. She offered no explanation about where she was going, and Abby hadn't asked.

The front doorbell rang right on time, and she opened the door to let Glenda, Louise, and Jean file inside. "Welcome, ladies. I'm so glad you could come."

Glenda, the chief spokesperson for the trio, gave Abby a quick hug. "We're so relieved you called. We've been worried about you but didn't want to intrude."

Louise sighed dramatically. "It was bad enough that *woman* interfered with your plan to bid on Mr. Blackston yourself. Then she had to go and murder Bryce

Cadigan. I just don't know what the world is coming to. Rumor has it that Gage Logan ordered her to stay in town until he has enough evidence to toss her in jail."

Naturally Jean had to add her two cents' worth to the conversation. "I'm still not happy with that young man, but we can hardly hold Tripp responsible for his ex-wife's murderous tendencies. Just knowing she's out wandering around our town unsupervised gives me the shivers."

It was hard not to laugh at their rather melodramatic take on the situation. While Abby was certainly no fan of Valerie Brunn, she felt some obligation to correct her friends' understanding of the situation.

"Gage hasn't told me much about the investigation, but I do know Ms. Brunn isn't the only person Gage and his people were talking to regarding the case."

That last tidbit definitely piqued their interest. She could almost see the wheels turning in their minds as she guided them down the hall toward the kitchen. Glenda was the first to realize they weren't headed into the dining room, where they usually gathered. Abby had been reluctant to pack up Valerie's laptop, as well as all of the paperwork she'd left scattered on the dining room table.

Jean stopped to look out the kitchen window before picking a seat at the table, no doubt hoping to catch a glimpse of Tripp working in the backyard. "Why are we meeting in the kitchen? Not that it's a bad thing. It's always bright and sunny in here."

Abby brought the teapot over to the table and filled everyone's cup. As the ladies passed around the sugar bowl and creamer, she set out two plates of cookies. "I thought it was a bit cozier. Besides, there's a mess of paperwork on the table in the other room."

Louise usually let Glenda take the lead on any conversation, so it came as a bit of a surprise when she was the one to ask, "So, Abby, what's the problem this time?"

Then she frowned. "I'm sorry, that came out wrong. I just want to know if there is anything we can do to help. I know it has to be hard for you to be involved in another such tragic situation."

"Yes, Abby, we hope you know that we're always here for you, and not just because you're Sybil's niece. Your aunt was our dear friend, of course, but we've all become quite fond of you in your own right."

Jean's heartfelt comment almost brought tears to Abby's eyes. While she missed her late aunt, these three women had gone a long way toward filling the hole in her heart left by Sybil's death.

"That means a lot to me, Jean. And, Louise, you're right. I do need your help again." She paused to sip her tea to collect her thoughts. "Gage asked me if I'd seen Bryce Cadigan talking to anyone in particular the night of the auction. I've figured out the name of one of the two men I didn't recognize, but I was hoping you could help me identify the other one."

All three ladies immediately went on point, their faded eyes glittering with intense interest. Glenda set down her teacup and leaned back in her chair. "What can you tell us about him?"

Before launching into her description, Abby needed to caution them. "Promise me you won't talk about this with anyone else. You know how Gage gets if he thinks I act too curious about his business."

She waited until all three women nodded, not that they were happy about it. No doubt they were thinking there was no use in knowing something their friends didn't if they couldn't lord it over them.

Abby cautioned them again. "Mind you, there was

nothing inherently suspicious about Bryce talking to anyone at the auction. No doubt he ran into quite a few people he knew from when he still lived here. Don't you agree that it would be only natural for him to want to catch up with old friends and acquaintances?"

She waited for them to acknowledge the truth of that statement before continuing. Finally, Louise responded. "I'm sure that's true. After all, he lived here his entire life until he left for college. His father died while Bryce was in high school, and his mother passed away a few years after that, so there was no particular reason that he would come back to town except for a special occasion like the auction."

Not to be outdone, Glenda added her own bit of information. "His family lived on the other side of town near the hardware store. I didn't know Mr. Cadigan at all really, but Mrs. Cadigan belonged to the same circle at church as Louise and I do. She was a nice lady, but she had her hands full with Bryce. He was quite the scamp when he was in junior high and high school. You know, the usual hijinks common in boys that age."

That information was interesting, but not particularly helpful. It was time to redirect the conversation back to the mystery man she was trying to identify.

"The guy I saw Bryce talking to looked to be in his late forties and was about five foot nine. His hair was going gray, and he wore it pulled back in a ponytail."

While her friends pondered that information, she replenished both their tea and the cookie supply. The ladies rivaled Tripp when it came to having a sweet tooth.

After tossing around a few possibilities, they quickly whittled the list down to a few final names. Abby waited patiently as Glenda gave the matter a little more thought. Finally, she nodded. "We think the man you saw might have been one of the Pratt brothers. They would be about the right age, and both of them were still wearing those ridiculous scraggly ponytails the last time I saw them."

She reached for another cookie. "I have no idea if either one of them was at the auction, though. At least I didn't see them. How about you, Louise?"

The other woman shook her head. "Neither did I, but that doesn't mean much. We pretty much spent the evening in that one area. Unless Gil or Gary happened to pass right by our table, we wouldn't have seen them. The hall was awfully crowded."

Jean rejoined the conversation. "That's true, which is a sign of how successful the auction was, Abby. You should be proud of that."

She was, but it wasn't a solo effort. "I had a great team of volunteers. I couldn't have done it without them."

Once again, Abby steered her friends back to the topic at hand. "So, why do you think it was more likely one of the Pratt brothers instead of the other names you were considering?"

Louise held out her cup for a refill. "For one thing, the Pratts lived next door to the Cadigans. As far as I know, the two brothers still live in that same house."

Now they were on a roll. Abby should be able to find their exact address easily enough. If she drove past the house, she might be able to determine for sure that one of the two brothers was the man she'd seen with Bryce.

She gave her friends a bright smile. "I knew I could depend on you ladies to help me out. And for the record, remember that there's no reason to think whichever of the Pratt brothers I saw at the auction had anything to do with Bryce's death. I'm just trying to provide Gage with the most complete information I can about what I saw that night."

Before the ladies could respond, the back door opened with no warning. Even Zeke failed to announce that Valerie had returned hours and hours before Abby had expected her. Glenda sat facing the door, so she was the first to realize who had just strolled into the house as if she owned it. Her horrified gasp had both Louise and Jean twisting around in their chairs to see what had caught Glenda's attention. She pointed at Valerie and announced in dark tones, "It's that woman!"

For her part, Jean's eyes widened in shock and then narrowed just as quickly into anger. She glared up at Valerie. "Abby, call the police. Tell them to hurry before she murders us right here in your kitchen."

Louise nodded like a bobbleheaded doll. "Even if Gage can't throw her in jail for murdering that poor man, he can arrest her for unlawful entry."

Abby wanted to bang her head on the table. Again, could they be more melodramatic?

Valerie stayed by the door as if considering making a quick exit, but Abby couldn't be that lucky. Instead, her unwanted guest locked her sights on her. "Don't you want to tell them I'm staying here before somebody has a stroke?"

No, actually, she didn't, but Abby caved in to the demands of the four sets of angry eyes staring at her. "I'm letting Ms. Brunn stay here as a favor to Tripp."

Evidently that was enough to put him firmly back on Jean's bad list. She gave Valerie a scathing look and then turned back to Abby. "Seriously? He actually asked you to do that? Did they run out of rooms at the hotel, or did they just run her out, period?"

Louise wasn't any happier. "How can you sleep nights knowing a potential murderess is living under your roof?"

It was far past time to put a halt to this discussion. "Ladies, I appreciate your concern, but she is a guest. Please treat her as such."

Valerie finally stepped farther into the room. She helped herself to a couple of cookies and got a soft drink out of the fridge. "If you charming people will excuse me, I'm going to work in the dining room."

Then she nonchalantly sailed out of the room, shoulders back and head held high. Abby had to give the woman kudos for having such style. She wasn't sure she would've had the strength to carry off an exit like that after being accused of murder. Abby hated envying anything about Valerie, but right now she'd love to be the one working at the dining room table instead of sitting here with three women waiting for her to offer up an explanation that they'd understand.

"The reporters were bothering her at the hotel. When she called Tripp to help her, he asked if she could use one of my guest rooms. It was that or he would have to let her move in with him." She held up her hands to forestall any interruptions and lowered her voice to a quiet whisper. "His house has one bed-room. What would you have done?"

Her blunt statement took the wind out of their out-raged sails. While they pondered the situation, she poured herself a cup of lukewarm tea. It tasted bitter, but that could've just been her mood.

"For what it's worth, Tripp doesn't believe she's ca-pable of killing someone."

Glenda rolled her eyes. "From what my late hus-band shared with me from those awful true crime books he read, I would point out that anyone is capable of murder if the circumstances are right. People can be living a normal life and then something goes wrong. All it takes is for someone to threaten their family or their livelihood, or maybe to reveal some dread secret that they can't afford to have come to light."

She was right about that, and Abby should know. After all, she'd met two murderers up close and personal since moving to town.

Glenda wasn't done. "Having his ex-wife reappear in his life after all these years had to come as a shock to Tripp. There's a good chance he isn't thinking straight when it comes to her. What do your own instincts tell you?"

Abby didn't answer right away, preferring to give the matter some serious thought. Finally, reluctantly, she gave them the best answer she could. "I might not trust Valerie, but I do trust Tripp."

Her three friends exchanged glances and then nodded. Glenda gave her a sympathetic smile. "He's never betrayed you yet, so we'll give him and his judgment the benefit of the doubt. We'll assume she's innocent until proven otherwise."

Then she shook her finger at Abby. "That doesn't mean we're happy about her staying here and taking advantage of you and your hospitality."

Neither was Abby, which meant she needed to figure out which Pratt brother had been at the auction and then find a way to let Gage know the man's identity along with Denny Moller's. The sooner he had all the information he needed, the sooner he and his men could solve the case and Valerie could go back to California—preferably alone.

* * *

After that, none of them were in the mood for any more tea and cookies. Glenda left, taking Jean with her and leaving Abby to drive Louise home. The plan was that the older woman would point out where the Pratt brothers lived on the way to her house. Once they were settled in the car, Abby backed out of the driveway and then asked, "Okay, which way do we go?"

"Drive over to Main Street and head toward the center of town. You're going to want to turn left about two blocks past city hall."

Ten minutes later, they turned into the area where the Pratt brothers lived. Louise pointed toward the intersection ahead. "Turn right at the corner and then slow down. As I recall, their house is at the end of the second cul-de-sac on your left."

That was disappointing. If they didn't spot either of the Pratt brothers on this trip, Abby would have to come back again. It was one thing to drive past a house on a through street. But a cul-de-sac made it more likely someone would notice her if she had to make multiple trips before she got to check out the two men.

Crossing her fingers that luck would be with them, she turned onto their street and slowed down. "Which one is it?"

Louise studied the nearly identical houses for several seconds before pointing toward the one at the top of the circle. "That was where Bryce's family lived. The rambler to the left with the blue trim belongs to the Pratts. Both boys left town when they joined the navy. But when their mother became ill, Gil moved back to take care of her, and Gary returned not long after that. I would guess they inherited equal shares of the place when she passed away."

By that point, Abby had slowed the car to a crawl as she made the turn at the top of the circle. She looked in vain for any sign of life at the Pratt house. Short of walking up to the front door and knocking, she had no choice but to leave and try again later.

"I'd better get you on home, Louise. Thanks for showing me where they live. Maybe they'll be outside the next time I drive by."

As they headed back toward Main Street, Louise appeared to be thinking pretty hard. Abby finally asked, "Is something wrong?"

"I'm still worried about that woman staying with you, not that I think she's any real danger to you. I just find it very odd that she would try to rekindle some kind of relationship with her ex-husband with no warning at all. Tripp is certainly attractive enough, and he's polite and hardworking. But why now? What happened to bring her here to our town? It's not as if she's ever lived here."

Abby couldn't agree more. "I don't understand why she would use the auction as a way to approach him in the first place. She lives in Los Angeles. How did she even hear about it?"

Those were all good questions. Too bad neither of them could come up with any reasonable answers. A few minutes later, Abby pulled up in front of Louise's place but left the engine running. "Thanks for coming over today. Even under such weird circumstances, you guys are always good company."

Judging by Louise's smile, Abby's comment pleased her a great deal. "Well, as Jean said earlier, you've become quite dear to all of us. Keep us posted on how things are progressing, and let me know if I can answer any more questions for you."

Then she let herself out of the car and started up the sidewalk. Abby always waited for her friends to get safely inside before leaving. Louise was almost halfway to her front door when she abruptly turned around and marched right back toward the car. Abby pushed the button to lower the passenger door window. "Did you forget something?"

Louise leaned down to look in the window. "Yes, I did. We were so focused on where Gil and Gary live that I didn't think to tell you that they have their own business. I'm not sure where their garage is located these days, but they build and repair motorcycles. That's what their father used to do, too, but the business closed when he passed away. The boys started it up again right after they came back to town."

"Thanks, Louise. That's really helpful."

Having delivered her message, Louise headed back toward her house. She stopped to wave one last time before disappearing inside. Abby's mood had improved considerably. It should be easy enough to find the Pratts' workshop. With luck, it would be on a busy enough street and Abby could make several passes if necessary without being spotted.

Once she verified that one of the brothers was the man she was looking for, she'd bite the bullet and simply tell Gage what she'd been up to. At least she could also assure him that she hadn't tried to do any sleuthing on her own this time other than to track down a couple of names. That should make him happy, shouldn't it?

Deciding she really didn't want to know the answer to that particular question, she put her car in gear and drove away.

Chapter Eleven

Rather than going directly home to her unwanted company, Abby decided it was the perfect time to make a quick stop at Something's Brewing. With luck, Bridey Kyser, who owned the coffee shop, would have a little time to visit. When she walked in, she was glad to see her friend behind the counter rather than her assistant.

Bridey shot her a friendly smile. "Hey, Abby, I'm glad you stopped by. I've been thinking about you. Seth and I both wanted to congratulate you on the huge success the other night even if the evening didn't exactly turn out as expected. Are you doing okay?"

"I'm fine." Honesty had her adding, "Mostly, anyway. Finding another body was pretty unnerving."

Her friend shuddered. "I can't imagine how awful it was for you. I don't know what this town is coming to for something like this to happen again."

She set down the cloth she'd been using to polish the glass countertop. "What do you say we forget about gloomy stuff for now and take a break?"

"Sounds good to me." Abby eyed the goodies in the display case. "I'll have a piece of that peaches-and-cream coffee cake with a tall latte."

After asking her assistant to take over the counter, Bridey made quick work of Abby's order and then fixed a drink for herself. The two of them sat at their usual table in the back corner. "Whew, it feels good to get off my feet for a while. It's been extra busy today for some reason, and this is just the lull before the high school mob descends upon the place this afternoon."

"Sounds like I picked the right time to stop by." Abby took a bite of her pastry and moaned as the taste of fresh peaches with a hint of cinnamon and nutmeg hit her tongue. "This is absolutely delicious, Bridey."

Her friend looked pleased as she studied Abby over the rim of her coffee cup. "So the big dance is almost here. Seth and I are looking forward to it so much. He's already rented his costume, and I found a vintage dress that is just perfect for the occasion."

She set her cup down on the table. "I can't wait to see Seth in his uniform. How about you? With everything you've got going on, have you found something gorgeous to wear?"

That was one item on her to-do list Abby had already taken care of weeks ago. "Actually, I have. I've been sorting out decades' worth of junk in Aunt Sybil's attic. I was going through an old steamer trunk last month and came across a dark green dress from the right era. The seamstress at the cleaners is making a couple of minor alterations for me."

"It sounds perfect. My dress is pale blue with a swirly skirt. It's so pretty and fits like a dream."

"Ooh, that sounds nice. I bet Seth will love it."

Of course, from what Abby had seen, Seth loved his wife, period. The truth was that Abby envied the couple and their happiness. She'd had that once and missed it even if she didn't exactly miss her ex-husband.

Meanwhile, Bridey was talking again. "Seriously, Abby, the dance is going to be so much fun. I can't tell you how many people have come in here talking about it. In fact, I saw Zoe Brevik just yesterday. Her husband and his two buddies were complaining because they couldn't simply wear the dress uniforms they already have from their time in the army. But when Leif came home from the costume place, he claimed he pulled off the vintage look better than the other two guys. From what she said, they're hoping you're having some kind of 'best in show' contest at the dance."

Abby laughed. Having met the three former soldiers on several occasions, she could just picture them all vying for top honors. "I'll mention that idea to my committee. Regardless, I'm glad they're having fun with the idea of a USO-style dance. I was really worried no one would want to come, but ticket sales have been great. The last I heard, we've almost sold out."

Bridey seemed delighted by that news. "From what Zoe told me, the auction also did incredibly well. I still haven't gotten over the mayor placing the high bid for Gage Logan, not to mention Connie Pohler forking over the big bucks for a night out with Pastor Haliday."

That had been a definite highlight in the evening's events. Abby was pretty sure neither man had known what hit him. "Gage seemed to be okay with going to the dance with the mayor, but I think Pastor Jack was stunned Connie would want him as her date for the evening. I know she looked really pleased with how things turned out."

When Bridey looked around the shop as if to confirm where her assistant was, Abby was pretty sure that she wasn't going to like what her friend was about to say next. She was right. "I know this is probably a sore subject, but I would guess having that woman unexpectedly slap down five thousand dollars for Tripp didn't hurt the group's bottom line."

Abby said the only thing she could. "Her donation to the cause was very generous."

It was too much to be hoped her flat statement would head off any further discussion on the subject. Bridey immediately asked, "Is it true she's Tripp's wife? Because if it is, I'm not very happy with that man right now."

Fiddling with her napkin gave Abby something to look at besides the sympathy in her friend's eyes. "Actually, she's his ex-wife. They've been divorced for a long time, and he swears he had no idea that she was going to show up at the auction and bid on him. I believe him."

"Well, I'm glad to hear that. I didn't want to think he let you be blindsided like that." Then she frowned. "So if he's going to have to take his ex to the dance, who will you be going with?"

Another sore subject. "I have to be there extra early to make sure everything is ready to go. Going by myself will simplify that. If I had an escort, either he'd have to meet me there or else stand around for hours with nothing to do."

Bridey no doubt recognized that explanation for the rationalization it was. "I'm sure Seth's brother would be glad to fill in for you. Even if you have to be at the hall early, he can come later with the two of us. He's a really nice guy, and I promise I'm not playing matchmaker. I just wanted you to know that you don't have to go alone if you don't want to."

The idea was mildly tempting, but Abby finally shook her head. "Thanks for the offer, but it's probably better that I go alone. Since I'm in charge, I'll probably have to spend much of the evening working behind the scenes."

"Well, let me know if you change your mind. On a different subject . . . well, sort of, anyway. Have you heard if Gage has made any progress on the murder investigation?"

Before Abby could respond, the bell over the shop door jingled. Both women turned to see who had come in. Great, it was as if just mentioning Gage's name had conjured up the man himself. He looked around the shop as he took off his sunglasses and stuck them in his shirt pocket. As soon as he spotted the two of them, he headed their way, pausing only long enough to tell Bridey's assistant that he'd have his usual drink and a piece of the coffee cake.

"Mind if I join you? I won't be staying long. I'm meeting with the mayor in an hour."

Abby couldn't resist the urge to tease him a bit. "To coordinate what you're going to wear to the dance?"

It was fun to see the big man's face flush a bit red. "Very funny, Abby. Rosalyn was just showing her support for a good cause, so don't read anything into it."

Bridey wasn't having it. "She could've simply made a cash donation, Gage, or maybe put together a basket so the group could sell chances on it. That's what Seth and I did."

He glowered at both of them. "Maybe I should get my order to go."

"No, please stay." Bridey held up her hands in surrender and then caught her barista's eye. "Gage's order is on the house today, and please bring Abby another latte."

Turning her attention back to Gage, she added, "We promise we'll behave."

When he settled back in his chair, Abby couldn't resist stirring the pot a little. "Speak for yourself, woman. For one thing, I want to know why Gage blushed when we brought up the subject of his hot date with the mayor. I think there's an interesting story behind it."

Gage rolled his eyes. "There's no story, and I did not blush."

When they both snickered, he drew a deep breath and let it out. "Seriously, have you two regressed back to a middle school mentality?"

Abby didn't bother to deny the allegation. "Probably. After we get done with you, we might just hunt down Pastor Jack and tease him a little, too."

Gage finally chuckled. "Go easy on him. Don't spread it around, but right before he went out onstage, he admitted to me he was afraid no one would bid on him at all."

That had Abby grinning as she remembered the look on Jack's face when they'd talked after the auction ended. "Connie sure proved him wrong, not to mention those other very determined ladies she managed to outbid."

Her smile faded when she noticed the calculating look on Gage's face. He sat up straighter to look at her more directly. "I've been wondering about something, Abby. Bridey here is married, so I get why she couldn't volunteer to be up there on the stage."

Okay, she really didn't like where this was headed. "None of the auctionees were married."

He nodded. "That's true, but you're not married. So why weren't you up there strutting your stuff like the rest of us suckers?"

Abby choked on the bite of coffee cake she'd just eaten. Ever helpful, Gage reached over to pound her on the back several times. As soon as he stopped, she reached for her drink and took several small sips. When she could talk, she gave him the only answer she could. "It never even occurred to me."

That wasn't exactly true. The idea had crossed her mind, but only very briefly. She still didn't know all that many people in Snowberry Creek, and she couldn't imagine any of them paying cash to spend an evening with her. She'd assuaged her conscience with the knowledge that she needed to keep herself available to handle any problems that arose that evening. That was her story, and she was sticking to it.

But now that Gage had brought it up, what if she'd volunteered to be the one up onstage instead of forcing Tripp to be her sacrificial lamb? Would he have bid for her company? And would Valerie have still shown up at the auction?

The bell over the door jingled again as several customers walked in together. Bridey picked up her cup. "If you two will excuse me, I'd better get back to work. Abby, let me know if I can do anything to help with the last-minute stuff for the dance."

"I will. Thanks, Bridey."

When she was out of hearing distance, Gage lowered his voice and said, "I was going to check in with you this afternoon to see how things are going with Valerie staying at your place. Any problems I should know about?"

Rather than gloss things over, she gave him a partial

truth. "Things haven't exactly been smooth sailing, but nothing I can't handle."

He definitely had his cop face on now. "Like what, for instance?"

Telling him that Valerie had removed Abby's setting from the table seemed petty and a little too much like snitching. "We're not particularly comfortable around each other, but that's understandable. We're complete strangers sharing the same house. The only thing we have in common is Tripp, and I suspect he feels like he's caught in the middle."

Gage looked disgusted. "That's his own stupid fault."

"True enough. It also didn't help that Glenda, Louise, and Jean were over earlier today. Valerie left before they got there and said she wouldn't be back until after dinner, so I didn't warn them she was staying there. When she waltzed back in hours too early, they wanted me to call nine-one-one and have her arrested for unlawful entry. After she left the room, they asked how I could sleep nights knowing a murderess was living under my roof."

By that point, Gage was pinching the bridge of his nose as if the conversation was giving him a headache. "Seriously, are you really all right with her being there, or are you just being polite? I can have another talk with her as well as Tripp about the subject if you want."

"No, I told Tripp she could stay there. Unless she causes me any real problems, I won't renege on the deal. Hopefully, she won't be there all that long."

She gave Gage a questioning look, hoping he'd update her on the status of his investigation. He didn't speak for several seconds, but then he finally nodded just a little. "Things are moving along, but that's all I can tell you. We're still following some leads and interviewing everyone who was at the auction. We hoped to be finished with that last part in the next day or so."

Maybe this was a good time to let him know what she'd learned since the last time they'd spoken. "I was going to call you later. I figured out that one of the two men I saw Bryce talking to was Denny Moller."

Gage had been about to take a drink of his coffee, but he froze midmotion. "Abby, what have I told you about messing in police matters?"

She held up her hands in surrender. "I know, I know. You want me to stay out of your business."

"And yet you clearly don't seem to understand what that means." He set his coffee cup back down on the table with unnecessary force. "Do I really need to toss you in Tripp's old cell to get the idea across?"

He wouldn't do that, would he? "On what charges?"

"Protective custody because of chronic stupidity."

Whoa, he really was mad. "Before you go to that extreme, can you at least let me explain?"

She held her breath until he finally jerked his head in a quick nod. "I'm listening."

"I was afraid you might not be able to figure out who the guy was based on the vague description I gave you. He looked to be about the same age as Bryce, so I thought maybe they went to high school together. I went to the library and looked through the yearbooks until I found their pictures. They were on the football team together their junior year, but Denny Moller wasn't in the team picture when they were seniors."

Gage relaxed back in his chair. "Guess I need to talk to Denny myself."

Maybe she wasn't going to end up behind bars after all. That was a relief even though she was pretty sure he'd been kidding about that. Probably, anyway. On the other hand, she hadn't told him about the Pratt brothers.

"Come on, Abby. You're already in trouble. You might as well confess. It's good for the soul even if it's bad for my blood pressure."

Darn it, she was really going to have to work on her poker face. "How did you know there was something else?"

"I didn't." Gage was looking pretty smug about then. "Not for sure, anyway. I've learned never to under-estimate your total inability to stay out of trouble, but also every guilty thought you have flashes across your face like it's a billboard."

She was mildly offended by that assertion. "That's not true."

"If you don't believe me, ask Tripp the next time you see him. Now tell me what else you've been up to, or I can call over to the jail to make sure your room is ready when we get there."

"Well, at least if I'm staying in your fine accommodations I won't have to be rooming with Valerie."

He laughed at that. "Come on, Abby, tell me."

It was tempting to make a break for the door, but she'd never outdistance Gage. "Fine."

Oddly enough, confessing to Gage was thirsty work. She took a long drink of her latte before launching into the second part of her tale. "I asked some, um, friends if they had any idea who the other guy I saw Bryce talking to might be."

"Translation, that's why Glenda, Louise, and Jean were at your house earlier. You invited them to a gos-sip session."

The man was a mind reader. No wonder he had such a good reputation as a cop. "Please don't be angry with them, Gage. They didn't know what I wanted until they came over."

"Don't worry about them, Abby. It's not their fault that you suck them into your misadventures."

"You're right, of course. Regardless, I told them that I wanted to give you the most accurate information I could, but I haven't lived in Snowberry Creek long enough to know as many people as they do. I also said there was no reason to believe that the man I'd seen had done anything other than talk to Bryce, so they couldn't tell anyone I was trying to identify him. Basically, I swore them to secrecy before I gave them any kind of description of the man. They won't say anything to anyone else."

Gage looked pretty skeptical. "Go on."

"They think the man might be one of the Pratt brothers, but I can't say if it was Gary or Gil without actually seeing them first."

"And how were you going to do that?"

Now she was treading on pretty thin ice. "One of the ladies pointed out their house for me, which is right next door to where Bryce Cadigan's family used to live. She also mentioned the Pratts own a motorcycle shop somewhere in the area."

"So you did a drive-by."

"I did, but just the house. I don't know where the shop is."

"And what did you learn?"

"Nothing, because no one was outside. I still have no idea which brother I saw at the auction. Heck, I don't even know for sure it was either of them."

Gage was back to pinching the bridge of his nose. "Let's agree that you've done your due diligence, Abby. I'll check in with the Pratt brothers myself. Hear me when I say I don't want you anywhere near that pair or their shop. Gary and Gil don't often cause me any serious problems themselves, but some pretty rough characters hang out at their garage sometimes. Believe me when I say you do not want to end up in their crosshairs."

She shivered even though the coffee shop wasn't actually chilly. "Fine. I won't go near them."

"Good." He finished his drink and stood up. "It's time for my meeting. Where are you off to next?"

"That depends." She decided to tease him a little. "Do I need to go home and pack a bag for an extended stay at your fine establishment?"

He glowered at her. "I'll put your reservation on hold for now. But one hint that you're up to your old tricks again, all bets are off. And for the record, if I do toss you in jail, I won't be letting Tripp sneak you cookies or burgers from Gary's Drive-In."

"Now that's just mean."

"Consider it tough love."

He waved at Bridey on his way out. After he was gone, Abby headed back over to the counter to buy a piece of the coffee cake for Tripp. She considered buying one for Valerie, too, but didn't. There was only so far she was willing to go to make the woman feel welcome.

As she waited for Bridey's assistant to pack up the coffee cake, she considered her options for the rest of the day. When she got home, she'd take Zeke for an extra-long walk. By the time they got back, it would be time to start dinner. When she dropped off Tripp's treat, she'd invite him over to join her and Valerie again. If he hesitated, she'd remind him the woman was really his guest, not hers. It was his duty to referee.

Once they all got through what could be another stressful meal, she'd catch up on e-mail and a few other things. And maybe, just maybe, she'd do a little more poking around online, this time to see what she could learn about Valerie Brunn. Despite the woman's protests to the contrary, there was a connection between her and Bryce Cadigan. There'd been too much anger, too much emotion in their confrontation at the auction.

The only question at this point was whether that connection was worth killing over.

Chapter Twelve

A short time later, Abby let herself back into her house. She stood just inside the kitchen door and listened. The place was eerily silent except for the normal creaks and groans of a grand old dame of a house. Even if Valerie had disappeared again, where was Zeke? She immediately glanced at the row of coat hooks on the wall next to the door and noted his leash was missing. Interesting.

Abby checked her phone to see if she'd missed any messages. Sure enough there was a recent text from Tripp saying Zeke was keeping him company while he did his homework. That didn't explain the missing leash. It wasn't as if Tripp would've needed it to coax the dog to come over to his place. Zeke loved hanging out over there.

Maybe Valerie had needed to go somewhere and dropped Zeke off with Tripp rather than leaving the dog all alone in the house. It could've been her way to check up on her ex-husband, especially if she was hoping he'd blow off his classwork to spend time with her.

Abby gave herself a stern reminder that it was not

really any of her business what Valerie was up to even if it involved both Abby's dog and her tenant. Besides, she had no room to talk. Even if Valerie had used Zeke as an excuse to approach Tripp, Abby had bought peach coffee cake for that exact same purpose.

Only one way to find out what was going on. She even had a legitimate excuse to reclaim her pet. She really did want to fit in their daily walk before it was time to get back and start cooking. She stuck two bottles of water and Zeke's collapsible bowl into her pack, grabbed her keys, and headed out the back door and across the yard.

Tripp opened his door before she even had a chance to knock. Zeke stuck his head out through the opening, his tail wagging happily. She held up the bag containing the coffee cake with one hand and gave the dog a good scratching with the other.

"I've come to get Zeke. It's time for our walk."

Usually any mention of an outing was enough to have the dog ready to charge off on an adventure with her. Right now, though, his entire attention was riveted on the bag she was still holding. So was Tripp's, for that matter.

She handed it to him. "I stopped by Bridey's shop earlier and thought you might like to try her new peach coffee cake."

He peeked inside the bag and drew a deep breath. "That smells delicious. I'd say you shouldn't have, but I'm not a fool. Thanks."

"You're welcome. I was wondering if you happened to have Zeke's leash. It's not on the hook where I usually keep it."

"Yeah, I do. Valerie brought Zeke over this afternoon before she left." He opened the door wider. "I'll get it for you."

He wasn't gone long. "By the way, she said not to hold dinner for her. She called Uber for a ride to the closest car rental agency. She figured she might as well rent one to use as long as she's going to be here for a few days. She planned to head up to Seattle from there. If I understood her right, she needed to check in with the local Suits-Herself store about some shipment. Val is friends with the manager there, so they planned to have dinner together."

That bit of news improved Abby's mood considerably. "So what are your plans for dinner? I thawed a chicken to cook, but it's too much for just one person."

Tripp frowned and glanced back at the papers he had spread out on the table he used for a desk. "I really need to work tonight, but a man's still got to eat. What do you say we hit Gary's Drive-In? That way neither one of us has to cook or clean up, and Zeke can come, too."

"Perfect. I'll text you when Zeke and I get back from our walk."

"Sounds like a plan."

And if she crossed her fingers that Valerie wouldn't make another earlier-than-expected return, she kept that to herself.

The drive-in was located a couple of miles outside of town along the river. Since the weather was nice, Abby and Tripp decided to stop and eat at one of the picnic tables by the water. After the past few days, she could use the momentary escape from reality.

While they waited at the drive-up for their order, Tripp glanced in her direction. "You doing okay over there?"

She leaned back against the headrest and closed her eyes. "Yeah, I am. It's just been a really long day."

"Sounds like it. Valerie told me about the ladies wanting to have her arrested. I'm not sure if it was because of the murder or because she is staying at your house."

Abby smiled a little. "Actually, for both reasons. I convinced them to give her the benefit of the doubt for your sake."

"Thank you for that."

She angled herself in the seat to look more directly at Tripp to better gauge his reaction to her next piece of news. "On the other hand, Gage threatened to throw me in your old cell and lock the door. He even said he wouldn't allow you to bring me cookies or one of Gary's burgers while I was a guest in the Snowberry Creek jail."

Tripp's eyebrows were riding low over his eyes when he looked at her again. If she had to guess, it meant he wasn't sure whether or not she was joking. "Was he serious?"

"I'm still not sure. I ran into him at Something's Brewing this afternoon. I decided to tell him that I'd found out the names of the men I'd seen Bryce talking to at the auction. To say he wasn't happy is putting it mildly."

Tripp tightened his grip on the steering wheel. "I'll have a talk with him."

Abby could just imagine how that would go, so she did her best to head off the confrontation. "No need. He calmed down when I explained that I'd figured out the one name by looking at old yearbooks. He was a little crabbier about me asking Glenda, Louise, and Jean for help with identifying the other one. I don't think he was impressed by the fact that I swore them to secrecy before I told them anything."

"Really? I can't imagine why." He slanted her another look. "If there's a Gossip Central in this town, those three would be on the executive board."

She couldn't really fault his logic, but there was no way she would admit that. "They promised not to say anything to anyone else, and I believed them. Evidently Gage did, too, because he said he would put my reservation at the jail on hold for the time being."

"So, tell me about these two guys."

Would he feel obligated to share the information with the barnacle? Deciding that it wouldn't be fair to put him in that position, she shook her head. "I'm not sure that's a good idea."

"Come on, Abby. You know I won't go after them. I just want to know how likely it is that Gage would view them as credible suspects."

"Will you promise not to share their names with Valerie?"

His silence was telling. Even Zeke picked up on the sudden surge in tension because he whined and nudged her shoulder. She patted his wrinkly face. "It's okay, boy. We're not fighting."

Not exactly, anyway.

"Fine, I promise I won't say anything to her unless I think it's necessary."

"Not good enough, Tripp. I told Gage I wouldn't do anything to interfere with his investigation. He won't be happy if he thinks I'm feeding insider information to one of his suspects."

Tripp immediately started to protest, but she cut him off. "No, I mean it. I know you trust Valerie, and I said I'd give her the benefit of the doubt. That's as far as I'm willing to go."

While waiting for Tripp to launch another attempt to convince her to share everything she knew, a loud rumble caught her attention. She looked around until she spotted several large motorcycles headed their way. They drove past and veered off onto a secondary road, one she wasn't familiar with. At first she thought they were headed for a cinder block building with a single neon light flashing in the front window that simply read BEER. Instead, they kept going even though a road sign said it was a dead end.

"Do you know where that side road over there leads to?"

"I've heard there's a motorcycle repair shop at the far end. Spence, one of the guys at the veterans group, mentioned getting parts for his bike there."

It almost had to be the Pratt brothers' garage. After all, how many motorcycle shops could there be in a town the size of Snowberry Creek?

Tripp looked a bit puzzled by her interest. "Why are you asking?"

She considered lying, but what if Gage was right about every thought she had playing out in real time on her face? He'd suggested asking Tripp to verify his claim, and there was no time like the present. "Answer me this. Can you sometimes tell when I'm trying to avoid telling you something?"

His answer was short and to the point. "No."

Relieved to find out she wasn't that transparent, she tried to come up with a believable yet fictional excuse for her interest in where the bikers had been going. Before she could, Tripp's next words reined her back in.

"Not just usually, Abby. I can *always* tell. You get this guilty look in your eyes if you're just holding back pertinent information. But if you're about to tell a whopper, you bite your lower lip right before you start talking."

He grinned and pointed at her face. "Just like that, in fact."

Well, rats, so much for that plan. She settled on telling a half-truth. "Someone mentioned a pretty rough crowd hangs out at a local motorcycle shop. I was curious where it was."

"Why? Are you thinking about transforming yourself into some guy's biker babe? 'Cause I've gotta say, somehow I don't see that happening. You don't exactly fit the profile."

She arched an eyebrow and gave him a cool look. "I'm not sure if I should be insulted or complimented by your opinion of my assets."

The jerk actually laughed. "I like your assets just fine, Abby, but you lack the hard edge that a lot of those ladies have."

Feeling slightly mollified, she finally gave him the answer he'd been waiting for. "The other man I saw Bryce talking to at the auction might be one of the two brothers who own that shop. Gage plans on talking to them. He also warned me to stay away from their place. He didn't think either of them would present any kind of threat to me, but I guess he's had problems with some of their clientele."

By that point, their order was ready. After paying for it, Tripp said, "Thanks for telling me, Abby. Since Gage is already on it, I don't see any need to talk to them myself or to tell Valerie about them."

He parked the truck and turned off the engine before adding, "For now, anyway. But if Gage comes after her, all bets are off."

"Fine, but don't bother asking me who the other guy is."

Before he could protest, she held up her hand. "Listen, I was really hoping for a relaxing meal. Do you think we can forget about anything and everyone connected to Bryce Cadigan long enough to do justice to one of Gary's meals?"

Tripp stared at her for several long seconds before nodding. "It's a deal. Now, let's give Zeke his burgers."

By agreement, they limited their dinner conversation to non-murder-related topics. Abby didn't know about Tripp, but it felt good to concentrate on happier subjects. Although he'd made it clear that he really did need to get back to his homework, he decided there was time to squeeze in a long walk along the river after they finished eating.

Finally, they headed back to the house. Abby really hated the moments of awkwardness between the two of them since the auction and wished their outing wasn't coming to an end. It would've been nice if their mellow mood could have lasted a little longer, but that wasn't to be. When they pulled into the driveway, there was a strange sedan sitting where Tripp normally parked. As soon as he turned off the engine, Valerie got out of the car and headed straight for them. The expression on the barnacle's face made it clear that the good times were definitely over.

Valerie ignored both Abby and Zeke but tore into Tripp but good. "Where have you been all this time? You never gave me a house key, so I had to sit out here cooling my heels while you two were out doing whatever you were doing."

Before Tripp could respond, she crossed her arms over her chest and glared at Abby and then back at him. "You keep saying you don't have time to do any-

hing other than study, but you seem to find plenty of
ime to spend with your landlady."

Tripp mirrored the barnacle's angry stance. "That's
:nough, Valerie. Not that it's any of your business, we
ust went out for burgers and shakes at the local drive-
n. Besides, you said you were spending the evening in
jeattle."

He glanced at his watch. "Considering it's only six
hirty, there was no reason for us to expect you back
his soon."

"My evening got cut short. Seems I've been put on
idministrative leave until this mess is over, and my
upposed friend wasn't into spending time with a mur-
ler suspect."

"I'm sorry to hear that, Val, but I don't see how
hat's our fault."

Rather than immediately answer him, Valerie paused
o glance in Abby's direction. "Do you mind? This is a
)rivate conversation."

Tripp went on point, clearly getting ready to leap to
Abby's defense, but she wasn't going to let Valerie
harpen her claws on him when he'd done nothing
vrong. "I'm sorry if we kept you waiting." Then she
hook her head. "No, actually, I'm not sorry at all, Ms.
3runn. As far as I'm concerned, neither of us are at
our beck and call. If you had asked me for a key ear-
ier, I might have given you one. However, considering
ou left before I got home, there was no way I could've
lone that even if I wanted to. This is my house, not
[ripp's, so you shouldn't expect him to provide you
vith a key, either."

It was probably beyond rude to be venting like this,
)ut she'd had it with the woman's attitude. "For the
ecord, I will remind you that it was not my idea that
ou stay at my house. If you're unhappy here, you're

more than welcome to go find a hotel room some-where. It wouldn't hurt my feelings one bit. If you want to stay, fine. However, I'd recommend you go straight up to your room and stay there for the rest of the evening. I find I'm not really in the mood for com-pany. Especially yours."

Abby directed her next remarks to Tripp. "Zeke and I are going inside now. Thank you for dinner. I had a really good time."

While she hated to abandon Tripp, by that point even Zeke was growling. She walked away without a backward glance, her only regret that Valerie wasn't immediately leaping back into her car and driving away.

Chapter Thirteen

Back in the house, Abby paced the length of her living room and back again as she considered her options. It would be cowardly to retreat to her own room rather than face her unwelcome guest. On the other hand, the confrontation outside had left her more shaken than she was willing to admit. She was tired of that woman's presence in her home . . . in her life . . . in fact, even in her town.

The only way to get rid of her resident barnacle once and for all was to find out who had killed Bryce Cadigan. She would hate it if the culprit turned out to be Valerie, mainly because of how it would affect Tripp. There wasn't much she could do tonight but work on her list of other possible suspects. After writing down everything she already knew about them, she'd spend some time online to see what else she could learn.

The sound of the back door opening spurred her into action. She wasn't going to lurk around downstairs and have to deal with Valerie. For one thing, her pesky conscience was starting to act up again. She wasn't going to apologize for anything she'd said out in the backyard but she also didn't want to pick up the discussion where she'd left off.

"Zeke, I'm going upstairs."

Evidently he wasn't ready to call it a night yet because he remained sprawled on the living room floor. Rather than insist that he come, she gave him a quick pat on the head and then hurried upstairs to the sanctuary of her bedroom. After closing the door, she leaned her ear against it to listen for any sign that Valerie was on her way upstairs as well. Nothing but silence. Despite Abby's suggestion that the woman retire to her room for the night, she really didn't care where Valerie was right now as long as it wasn't anywhere close to her.

Or Tripp. She really hoped he was back at his own place and getting a chance to study in peace. Even if she didn't want to offer Valerie any kind of apology, she did feel like he might be entitled to one. Not right now, though. She'd already taken up enough of his time for one night.

No sooner had the thought crossed her mind than her phone pinged. That didn't stop her from looking though. Sure enough, it was her tenant checking in.

You okay?

Yes. Mostly, anyway. How about you?

I'm fine. Sorry Valerie took her temper out on you. should've thought to give her a key.

Abby closed her eyes and counted to ten before trusting herself to answer. *Again, it's my house, not yours. I didn't think to give her a key, but she could've also asked for one. Either way, it's not your problem. It's hers.*

As she waited for him to respond, she could almost hear him praying for patience. At least his next comment made her laugh. *Let me know if I need to come referee. Better yet, can I sell tickets and popcorn for the big smackdown? Maybe even take bets.*

For the record, I can take her fair and square.

Not that she had any intention of fighting fair if she could help it. Tripp responded with an entire row of laughing emoticons ending with a single sentence. *I'd never be stupid enough to bet against you.*

Thanks . . . I think.

My homework is calling. Talk to you later.

Her mood was considerably improved by the brief exchange. She kicked off her shoes, grabbed her laptop, and climbed on the bed, sitting with her back against the headboard. After opening a new document file, she began typing in all the information she knew about the people Bryce Cadigan had talked to at the auction. It was likely her list was incomplete since she hadn't tracked his every movement. There was also no guarantee that the murderer had even been at the auction.

If that were the case, how had the person known where to find Bryce in the first place? She brought up his website and studied it. Sure enough, there was a tab that read "Upcoming Events." When she clicked on it, a calendar popped up that listed all of his scheduled appearances including dates, times, and locations. Anyone who was interested in tracking Bryce's movements could've easily figured out he would be at the auction that night and been waiting for him out in the parking lot. Someone who wasn't even on anyone's radar.

That complicated things considerably. Had Gage figured that out as well? She'd have to assume he had. After all, from what she'd heard, Gage had had a successful career as a homicide detective with one of the big-city police forces before returning to his hometown to take over as the local chief of police.

But back to the problem at hand. There wasn't anything she could do to track anyone who might have accessed Bryce's calendar, so it was time to move on to other options. She reviewed everything she'd learned so far and found it to be a pitifully short list of information.

To begin with, she didn't know how Bryce had actually died. According to Gage, he'd been poisoned. But how? Had he ingested it, or had it been injected somehow? What kind of drug had been used? Clearly the whole process could've taken only minutes at best. The sudden realization of how close she'd come to stumbling into the middle of an actual murder didn't bear thinking about. Shoving that scary thought to the back of her mind, she kept going. What threads could she tug on without putting herself in the crosshairs of the killer or even the police?

She'd already promised to stay away from the Pratt brothers, so she put them at the bottom of her list. Her gut feeling was that the football coach wasn't actually a suspect. Both he and Bryce had seemed genuinely happy to see each other. That left Denny Moller and Robin Alstead, the former teacher. The few notes next to their names were pretty sparse. Denny graduated with Bryce. The retired teacher was a widow who now worked at the discount store at the edge of town. She also belonged to a local church. Too bad it wasn't Pastor Jack's. Abby might have been able to find out something about the woman from him.

Now that she'd exhausted the information she'd already garnered on everyone on the list, it was time to turn to the Internet to see what more she could learn

there. She'd barely started working when she heard
Zeke whine and softly scratch at her door. Setting the
laptop on the bedside table, she hurried to let him in.
He stayed out in the hall, making it clear that wasn't
what he was wanting.

"Okay, boy, I'll come let you out."

He woofed and trotted back down the steps. She followed him to the kitchen and opened the door. Zeke
bolted out onto the porch and then down the steps to
the yard. Knowing his nightly patrol could take several
minutes, she stepped out to enjoy the evening air. The
sun had gone down in the time she'd been upstairs
working, so it took her a few seconds to realize that she
wasn't alone.

Valerie was sitting in one of the chairs with a glass of
wine in one hand and a small tablet in the other. From
where Abby stood, it appeared as if Valerie was reading
an e-book. While it was tempting to ignore her as much
as she was pointedly ignoring Abby in return, that
seemed foolish considering they were living under the
same roof for the time being. Eventually they would
have to speak to each other again. The longer the silence continued, the more awkward things would become.

Someone had to make the first move, so Abby
asked, "Are you reading something interesting?"

At first it didn't seem as if Valerie would respond,
but she finally turned off her tablet and set it aside.
"Not particularly, but it's probably not the book's
fault. For obvious reasons, I'm not in the right mood
for a murder mystery."

Abby couldn't help but laugh just a little. "Gee, I
can't imagine why."

Valerie stood up and walked to the far corner of the
porch, the one spot that offered an unobstructed view

of Tripp's house. "I know you won't believe me, and I'm not even sure why I care what you think. Even so, I didn't kill Bryce Cadigan."

Abby didn't know, either. "From what I saw at the auction, it was obvious you knew him. Why lie about that?"

The heavy silence was back again. Finally, Valerie turned her back on Tripp's place to look directly at Abby. "It's not really a lie. Before that night, I'd never been in the same room with him. That's all I'm going to say on the matter."

Fine, but that didn't make any sense. Valerie's anger had been too real, too personal. For his part, if Bryce had had no idea who she was, why hadn't he simply brushed her aside and gone about his business? Instead, he'd forced her to take the discussion outside. That only made sense if one or even both of them had something to hide.

Abby leaned against the porch railing as she pondered the situation. It would be so much easier if Valerie would simply tell her what was going on, but the woman stared at her as if waiting to see if Abby was smart enough to figure it out on her own. There was only one thing that made any sense—if Valerie hadn't had problems with Bryce herself, then maybe she was protecting someone else.

Abby studied the other woman for a few more seconds and then offered up her thinking on the matter. "You're not the type of person who would suddenly go off on a total stranger for no reason. If Bryce wasn't a problem for you, he must have been one for someone you care about."

She paused briefly to see if Valerie would deny or confirm Abby's conclusion. When she didn't say anything, Abby played the only other card she could. "I'm guessing that someone would be your sister. Tripp said she recently left this area to move to Los Angeles, where you live. Was Bryce Cadigan the reason for that move?"

Valerie didn't confirm or deny the allegation. Instead, she picked up her tablet and the wineglass and headed for the door. "I believe you were told to stay out of the investigation. That sounds like a good idea to me. You don't want to get caught in the middle of a situation that has already turned deadly once."

Well, okay then. Abby supposed Valerie had just offered her a bit of good advice. Even though she hated the thought of having Valerie underfoot for an unknown amount of time, she should probably even follow it. The trouble was, she wanted the woman gone and for things between her and Tripp to go back to the way they were before the auction. That wasn't going to happen as long as the barnacle remained stuck in Snowberry Creek. Abby watched the clouds drifting slowly across the sky and pondered her predicament. How could she help move the investigation along without getting sucked in too deep? Sadly, neither her mind nor the clouds offered up any viable suggestions.

Maybe tomorrow would be more productive than today had been. She looked around the backyard to locate Zeke. She patted her leg and called out, "Hey, boy, it's time to come in."

He briefly looked up from whatever he had been sniffing on the ground but made no move to come running, so Abby pulled out the big guns. "Okay, stay out here if you want. Maybe some other dog will enjoy the pumpkin blueberry cookie I was going to give you."

That did it. He bolted across the yard and up onto the porch. She hurried to get the door open when it

appeared he wasn't going slow down anytime soon. Inside the kitchen, she bent down to give Zeke a stern
look as she offered him the promised goody. "Next time
you ignore me, young man, there will be no treats."

He scarfed down the cookie and then snorted right
in her face, splattering her skin with a sticky layer of
cookie crumbs and mastiff love. As she wiped her face
with a paper towel, Abby tried to imagine how Valerie
would've responded if he'd done the same to her, and
couldn't quite bring the image into focus. What did it
say about her that all she could do was laugh and pat
him on the head?

"I don't know about you, big guy, but I'm ready to
call it a day."

As the two of them made their way up to her bedroom on the second floor, it dawned on her that she'd
never gotten around to personally thanking Mrs. Alstead for supporting the veterans group by buying
chances on one of the baskets. Maybe tomorrow
would be a good day to do a little shopping at the discount store. If she happened to cross paths with the
woman, well, wouldn't that be interesting?

Since Abby had no idea what hours or even what
days Robin Alstead worked, it was a crapshoot if her
quarry would even be at the store. Mayor McKay also
hadn't mentioned what the woman did there. If she
worked in back or in one of the offices, Abby might
not even be able to get near her. At least the trip
would get her out of the house for a while.

After their unsatisfactory discussion last night, she
was in no hurry to cross paths with Valerie again. As
far as Abby could tell, the woman was still asleep when
she left the house at nine thirty. Zeke was clearly dis-

appointed to be left behind, but she didn't want to leave him shut up in the car while she did her errands.

Over a quick breakfast, she'd considered what she actually wanted to ask the former teacher if she did manage to find her. The goal was to garner some information without setting off any alarms. Right now, she'd settle for just getting a better feel for what kind of man Bryce Cadigan had been. Even if the teacher hadn't seen him in years, she might be able to offer up some insight into what he'd been like when he still lived in Snowberry Creek.

As usual, the store was really busy. After parking, she grabbed a cart and headed for the entrance, falling into line with the other customers on their way inside.

While it would've been handy if Mrs. Alstead was one of the greeters, that would've made it awkward to carry on any kind of conversation without clogging up the busy entrance. She also didn't want to get the woman in trouble for discussing private matters on company time. Her frustration grew as she started walking up and down the aisles. Obviously this wasn't going according to plan. She tossed a box of crackers in her cart and then tried to get a box of her favorite cereal from the top shelf. It slid back just out of her reach even when she stood on her tiptoes.

She was about to give up when someone walked up behind her. "Here, let me get that for you. I've got my stepladder with me."

Miracle of miracles, her would-be helper turned out to be Mrs. Alstead. Clearly the gods were smiling down on her today. Abby stepped back out of the way while the woman set her three-step ladder in place. She handed down the box of cereal and then used the opportunity to straighten the other boxes on the shelf before stepping back down.

As she folded the ladder, she offered Abby a practiced smile. "Was there something else I could help you with?"

It was now or never. Abby smiled back. "You're Mrs. Alstead, aren't you? I'm so glad to have run into you. I headed up the committee that organized the veterans auction the other night. I believe you were one of the lucky folks who actually took one of the baskets home."

Then she held out her hand. "I'm Abby McCree, by the way."

Mrs. Alstead looked a bit hesitant, but she finally gave Abby's hand a halfhearted shake. "The basket was lovely."

Still trying to establish some sense of rapport, Abby asked her another question even though she already knew the answer. "Which one was it?"

"The one for knitters."

"Oh, that's right. The yarn shop did a lovely job on that basket. Personally, I put all of my tickets in the bag for the one from the bookstore. My to-be-read pile just got a whole lot taller, so I'm all set when those rainy days start again next fall."

To delay moving on, Abby made a show of picking another box of cereal and adding it to the cart while she kept talking. "The committee is so pleased with how much money we raised for the veterans in the area."

"I'm glad to hear it. My late husband was a veteran, so I wanted to show my support."

"Well, just know it was much appreciated." Then Abby sighed. "It's just a shame that the success was overshadowed by the tragedy at the end."

Mrs. Alstead's expression hardened. "I still can't believe Bryce is dead. That awful woman was clearly furious with him for some reason, but that doesn't excuse her killing him."

Maybe Abby wasn't the only one who'd seen Valerie arguing with Bryce. "Do you have any idea what she was so upset about?"

Mrs. Alstead's mouth was a straight slash of anger. "No, but I think she was determined to embarrass him in public."

If that was true, why would Valerie have waited until she could catch him alone near the door? And why would she have let him take their discussion outside? Since that line of questioning was going nowhere, Abby shifted gears. "I only met Mr. Cadigan on the evening of the event, but I'm guessing you knew him much better. I understand you were his teacher in high school."

The woman looked a bit puzzled and took a step back. "Yes, I was, but how would you know that?"

Abby hurried to explain before Mrs. Alstead went into full retreat. "I was trying to make sure I thanked everyone I could the night of the auction including those who bought chances on the baskets. I was going to approach you, but I saw you were standing with friends and didn't want to interrupt. Meanwhile, I was talking to Mayor McKay and asked if she knew your name. She told me you used to teach at the high school. I guess I just assumed that you would've had Bryce in your class."

Looking only slightly mollified by the explanation, Mrs. Alstead said, "Oh, of course. That makes sense. Despite the tragic ending to that evening, I was so glad he found time to talk to me. Bryce was such a nice young man and a good student back in the day. I've followed his career for years and was pleased to see the amazing career he built for himself."

How had Abby so totally misread the body language when Bryce had cornered his former teacher at the auction? "So you two were still close?"

That garnered Abby a firm denial from the woman. "Not at all. It's just that particular graduating class was extra special to me since it was my first year of teaching. I had those kids both as juniors and seniors. Regardless, I think all teachers take personal pride when one of their students achieves greatness. Everyone who knew Bryce took pride in his success."

Okay, that wasn't true. Abby could name several people who didn't fit that description, but the woman was entitled to her opinion. Maybe it was time to change subjects. "I also saw Denny Moller at the auction, too. Was he another of your students?"

At the mention of his name, Mrs. Alstead relaxed and smiled. "Yes, he was. Denny was one of my best students. I had great expectations for him, but unfortunately he lost his chance for a football scholarship during his junior year. That accident involving his knee was a real tragedy. I tutored him at home to help him keep up with his studies while he recuperated from one of his surgeries. I know he was disappointed to not be able to go away to college like Bryce did, but he's built a nice life for himself as a plumbing contractor."

Before Abby could figure out a way to press her for details on the nature of the accident, the radio clipped to Mrs. Alstead's apron pocket crackled. She snatched it up as if she were drowning and someone had just thrown her a lifesaver.

"Mrs. Alstead here."

The disembodied voice was staticky and difficult to understand, but it evidently presented no problem for Mrs. Alstead. The person on the other end said something about needing her to check in the stockroom for another case of the macaroni and cheese that was on special.

"I'll take a quick look and let you know."

Then she turned her attention back to Abby. "It was nice meeting you, Ms. McCree. Now, if you'll excuse me, I should get back to work."

"No problem. Thank you again for supporting the auction the other night and your help getting the cereal for me."

She watched as Mrs. Alstead hurried away. The brief conversation had created more questions than answers, but there was no way she could hang around the store and hope to be able to ask them. For now, she'd finish her shopping and then return home to see if she could learn more about how Denny Moller had lost his scholarship. She might be completely off base, but right now she'd bet anything that Bryce Cadigan was involved.

It could be nothing more than that they played on the same team. But maybe, just maybe, what had happened in the past might be worth killing for in the present.

Chapter Fourteen

Abby's eyes felt like sandpaper. She'd spent hour
on the computer reading up on the football season
when both Bryce Cadigan and Denny Moller had
been on the Snowberry Creek team. She'd started
with their freshman year and worked her way through
all four years of Bryce's high school career. It told a
fascinating story. She just wished she knew if she wa
reading too much into what was actually being said.

It was clear that Denny was the upcoming star, scor-
ing the most points and garnering the biggest head
lines. The reporter who had covered the games for
The Clarion at the time clearly thought Denny had a
shot at a successful college career and even hinted
that he might even get to go pro after that. He'd been
the total package with size, speed, and great hands.

The few mentions of Bryce Cadigan weren't nearly a
glowing. She had to wonder how well that went with
him. Granted, she hadn't spent much time in his com
pany, but it was clear to see that he took great pleasure in
being the center of attention. Hardly an expert on the
game of football, Abby had watched enough games with

her ex-husband to understand the difference between Denny being the starting receiver while Bryce had been his backup.

That had changed after Denny got hurt. There were remarkably few details about the exact nature of the injury, but it was clear that it had taken multiple surgeries to repair the damage. There had been an investigation afterward, but apparently the final report had been sealed. In the end, the reporter had described it as an "unfortunate accident" that had ended not just the season for Denny, but his entire career. The article had gone on to say that a scout from a prestigious university thought it was a real shame because the boy had shown such promise.

During their senior year, Bryce Cadigan's name had replaced Denny's as the headliner in the paper's coverage. The team ended up with a winning season but didn't make it past the first round of the postseason tournament.

In the end, Denny had become a plumber while Bryce had gone on to a successful career in broadcasting. Abby printed the last article, stuck it in a file folder with the others, and set it aside. That done, she didn't want to think about anything more complicated than which flavor of doggy treats she should bake next for Zeke. Better yet, she'd stock up on some of Gage Logan's favorite cookies in case she needed to have a bribe handy.

There was no sign of Valerie when she went back downstairs, which was fine with her. Zeke was dozing in his own personal sunbeam in the living room. He lifted his head long enough to blink at her sleepily. Evidently deciding she wasn't doing anything exciting, he dropped his head back down on his paws and resumed snoring.

She headed for the kitchen, turned her aunt's old radio to a classic rock station, and then began pulling out all the ingredients she needed to make Zeke's favorite treats. Twenty minutes later, she finished cutting the dough with a paw print–shaped cookie cutter and slid two trays of cookies into the oven. It didn't take long for Zeke to appear in the kitchen doorway as he sniffed the air with great interest. She laughed and wagged a finger in his direction.

"Sorry, but your share of the booty is still baking. Then they'll need to cool before you can have any."

He gave her a reproachful look about the delay and then plunked down on the floor in the far corner, clearly moving his nap into the kitchen to monitor the progress on his cookies. She didn't blame him. Although she'd never actually tasted the batter herself, the combined scents of blueberries and peanut butter made it tempting.

She turned on the mixer to cream the butter and sugar for a double batch of chocolate chip cookies. While that processed, she gave in to the urge to sing along to the music as she chopped the walnuts.

"Something smells good."

Tripp's deep voice startled Abby into nicking her finger with the knife. She whirled around and pointed the sharp blade right at him. "Darn it, Tripp, what have I told you about sneaking up on me like that?"

He reached around her to snag a paper towel off the roll while somehow managing to look both apologetic and amused at the same time. He put pressure on the small cut on her finger. "Sorry, but I did knock before I came in. I guess you were singing too loudly to hear me. At least I assume that's what that noise was."

"Very funny."

When she tried to tug her finger free of his grasp, he tightened his hold on her hand. After checking her cut again, he rewrapped it with a clean part of the paper towel. "Give it a minute. It's still oozing. I don't know about you, but I don't particularly like the taste of blood mixed with whatever you've got going on in that bowl. Assuming, that is, that you're willing to share when it's finished."

"I'm making chocolate chip cookies, and right now me sharing them is doubtful."

Her threat didn't seem to impress him at all. "Do you keep bandages in here someplace, or do I need to get one from the hall bathroom?"

What did it say about their relationship that Tripp knew right where she kept the first-aid supplies? At least this wasn't as bad as the time someone had thrown a rock through her living room window while she'd been sitting right in front of it. She'd stepped on broken glass in her efforts to get both herself and Zeke away from the threat.

She nodded in the direction of the other end of the counter. "There are some in that drawer, but I can take care of it myself."

Tripp didn't argue, but he didn't release his hold on her until he checked one last time to see if the bleeding had stopped. As soon as he did, she dug a small bandage out of the drawer and tore off the wrapper. She was still working on it when the timer on the oven started dinging.

Tripp reached past her to get the hot pads. After removing the trays from the oven, he set them on the cooling racks she'd already set out on the table. He drew a deep breath and then let it out slowly. "Gosh, those smell good."

Then he grinned at Zeke, who had lumbered to his

feet and joined him by the table. "Don't worry, boy. I know Abby only makes paw print cookies for you."

He helped himself to a cold drink out of the refrigerator and then sat down in his usual seat at the table. Zeke immediately laid his head in Tripp's lap, who took the hint and started petting him. When they were both settled, Abby asked, "So what brings you over here today?"

"Nothing special." Then he shook his head. "Okay, that's not true. I was wondering how your investigation was going."

That was unexpected. Well, on the other hand, maybe not. Normally he would fight with Gage to be the first in line to warn her off getting involved at all. Clearly he was willing to make an exception this time since his ex-wife topped the suspect list. He probably wanted her name cleared before their big night at the veterans dance next week. It would be hard to enjoy himself if his date was behind bars.

"To be honest, I've got a bunch of information and no idea what any of it means."

She stopped talking long enough to sift the flour and other dry ingredients into a bowl before adding it to the creamed butter and sugar. Once she had the mixer chugging along again, she tried to organize what she knew into some semblance of order.

"I talked to that Mrs. Alstead at the store where she works. She was taken aback a bit that I knew she'd been Bryce's teacher, until I told her I'd learned it from the mayor. I also told her I was trying to thank everyone personally who had supported the auction, which again is true. By that point, she was more relaxed."

She opened the bags of chocolate chips and dumped them into the batter along with the walnuts, holding back a few of the chips to share with Tripp. "Anyway, that lasted right up until I brought up Bryce Cadigan's death. She also saw him with Valerie, by the way. She thought Valerie was trying to embarrass Bryce in public, which didn't exactly jive with what I saw. I mentioned I'd only just met him but assumed she'd known him far better since he'd been one of her students."

Abby shut off the mixer to scrape the bowl. "She claimed his entire class was special only because that was her first year of teaching. Well, and that all teachers are pleased when a student achieves success. She claimed to have been happy that he'd found time to talk to her."

Tripp popped a couple of the chips into his mouth. "I take it you didn't believe her."

"Maybe I misread the body language when they were talking, but I swear he enjoyed crowding her like he did. When I brought up Denny Moller, she sounded more sincere when she said he was one of her best students. She said it was a real shame he'd lost his chance at a football scholarship because of an injury his junior year. Before I could press her for more details, she had to respond to a customer service request. I think she was only too glad to have an excuse to get away from me by that point."

Rather than working at the counter, she carried the bowl over to the table and started scooping the dough onto another pair of cookie sheets. As she worked, she continued talking. "I did some poking around online to learn what I could about the years where both Bryce and Denny played football here in town. I'd like your take on what happened if you wouldn't mind reading through the stack of articles I printed out."

Her sneaky tenant used his lightning-fast reflexes to grab one of the balls of dough off the cookie sheet.

She tried to smack his hand, but it was already too late.
"No more of that or you won't get any of the cookies
after they're baked."

Tripp didn't look the least bit worried as he staged
another attack. "I like the dough as much as I like the
cookies. At least I know I'll get my fair share this way."

Like she hadn't been keeping him supplied with
cookies and other treats on a regular basis. "I might
need them as a bribe for Gage if things go south."

Because they usually did.

She managed to fill the trays despite Tripp's continuing efforts to eat more of the dough. When the first
batch was in the oven, she fetched the folder of articles and handed it to him. "I'm going to clean up the
dishes while you read."

It didn't take long to pack up the treats she'd made
for Zeke and stick them in the freezer. Well, except for
the couple she gave him to eat. Then she quickly washed
the newly empty trays and refilled them with the chocolate chip dough. When the oven timer buzzed, she removed the finished cookies and replaced them with the
new trays.

By the time she'd finished cleaning up, Tripp was
almost to the bottom of the stack of articles. Judging
by his frown, something about what he'd read bothered him a great deal. She waited until he finished the
last one before speaking.

"What's wrong? What did you see?"

Tripp's eyes looked troubled when he stuck the
stack of papers back in the folder and finally met her
gaze. "It's actually what I didn't see. This all happened
long before people worried so much about protecting
a patient's right to privacy. The only thing they mention is that Denny was hurt. No details about what
kind of injury it was or even how it actually happened.

Later on, it does say he had multiple surgeries to fix it, and he wouldn't be playing football again."

Then he yanked the papers out again and shuffled through them until he found the one he was looking for. He scanned down the page, following the words with his forefinger. "It also mentions an investigation of some kind. Why would they need to investigate an injury if it was just an unfortunate accident?"

"Both of those things bothered me, too, but I thought maybe I was reading too much into the situation. You know, wanting there to be someone who had a good reason to kill Bryce. Well, besides Valerie, of course."

Tripp's temper immediately flared hot. "Considering she'd never met the man, she didn't have a reason to kill Bryce."

The stubborn man continued to believe every word Valerie said. Rather than respond to that, she asked him, "Did she ever tell you what the problem was that she wanted your help with?"

"I did ask her, but she said it didn't matter now."

"And why is that? Could it be because the problem died with Bryce?"

Tripp's hand came down on the table hard enough to rattle the cooling cookie trays. "Abby, for the last time, she doesn't have it in her to kill someone any more than you do."

Responding to his temper with her own would accomplish nothing. "But what if she was trying to protect someone else? Could Bryce have presented a threat to someone she cared about, like maybe her younger sister?"

That stopped him cold. "I don't know. Maybe. The two of them were always really close. Even more so after their parents died. Back then, Becca was still in high school. She lived with a family friend so she could stay and graduate. Val and I had just gotten married and were living in base housing. The two of them were on the phone for hours every week. It nearly killed Val to be so far from her sister, but she couldn't afford to walk away from her classes at the college, either."

He stared into the distance or maybe into his past. Whatever he was looking at didn't make him happy. "She would've done anything to protect Becca. There's no reason to think that's ever changed."

Abby hated seeing Tripp hurt that much. "That doesn't mean she did this. It just means we have to work harder to figure out who did."

He slowly nodded. "Where do we go from here?"

"We still don't have a good feel for what kind of man Bryce Cadigan was. You know more of the guys around town. Do you think any of them might have gone to school with him?"

After a minute's thought, he nodded. "I know Spence Lang grew up here in Snowberry Creek."

"I've met him a couple of times. He served with Leif and Nick."

"Yeah, that's the guy. I'm not sure how close in age he would be to Bryce, though. It could be their paths never crossed at all."

"Well, at least it's a starting point. When do you think we can talk to him?"

"I might have to do this on my own, but I'll let you know. Maybe I can get him and the other two to meet me at that bar we passed the other night. If their wives decide to come, you can tag along, too."

"Sounds like a plan."

"I'll go make some calls and get back to you."

She quickly transferred a few cookies to a plastic

bag and handed it to him. "Take these with you. It sounds like hungry work."

"I thought you needed these as a bribe."

"I can always make more."

He headed for the door, but stopped to look back at her. "For the first time I can see how you got sucked into investigating on your own, Abs. I still think it's dangerous, but at least now I understand."

Then he was gone.

Chapter Fifteen

Tripp pulled into the parking lot in front of the cinder block building they'd driven past the other night on their way to Gary's Drive-In. The only indication that the place was actually a bar was the blinking neon light by the front door that simply said BEER. She was pretty sure she'd never before set foot in a place like this one and wasn't sure she'd have the courage to now if Tripp wasn't right there beside her.

She glanced in his direction. "Do you come here often? And does this place even have a name?"

He smiled as he parked the truck and turned off the engine. "I don't know what the owner calls it, but we always just refer to it as Beer because of the sign. I occasionally meet Gage and a couple of the guys from the veterans group here to play pool and knock back a few of our favorite microbrews. You might not believe it by the looks of the place, but the burgers here rival those Gary sells at his drive-in, and the onion rings are even better."

If that was true, then the evening was already looking up. Abby slid down to the ground from the truck cab and landed with a bit of a jolt. Sometimes she forgot how much higher his truck rode than her sedan did. Tripp waited for her by the tailgate. "Anything I should know about proper etiquette before we go in?"

His laughter rang out across the parking lot. "You know, I'm not sure the word *etiquette* and Beer have ever been used in the same sentence before. As long as you don't get too rowdy or cheat at pool, you should be fine. I know it's sometimes hard for you to stay out of trouble, but at least try. Gage gets testy when he gets called out here to break up fights."

She punched him on the arm. "I do not cause trouble or cheat."

Tripp smirked as they started toward the door. "If you say so."

Even if he was teasing, she felt obligated to defend herself. "Seriously, I don't go looking for trouble, Mr. Blackston."

"Maybe not, but it does seem to find you, anyway." He frowned a little as they walked past a row of motorcycles. "If something does happen, stick to me like a tick, and we'll head for the nearest exit. Got that?"

Okay, maybe insisting on coming with Tripp wasn't the smartest idea she'd ever had. "Would you feel better if I waited in the truck?"

He wrapped his arm around her shoulders and shepherded her toward the entrance. "No, it'll be fine. Besides, nothing like an occasional bar fight to add spice to life."

She was pretty sure he was teasing her again, but there was an odd gleam in his dark eyes that made her think he was mentally reliving some past moments of bar-brawling glory. Before she could decide if she wanted to ask for details, they'd reached the door and stepped inside. The combination of loud music and people doing their best to talk over it resulted in a blast of noise that almost sent her into full retreat.

Tripp either didn't notice or didn't care. He hesitated long enough to look around and then dove straight into the crowd, dragging her along in his wake. She held on to his hand like a lifeline until he came to an abrupt halt. When he tugged her out from behind him, she was relieved to spot at least one familiar face. He leaned down close to make himself heard over the surrounding noise. "I'm going to get a beer. What would you like?"

"Whatever you're having will be fine."

After he walked away, she turned her attention to Zoe, who waited nearby. "I'm so glad to see you. It's nice that you guys could come tonight on such short notice."

The other woman smiled. "Leif and I were only too happy to come. We could both use a night out. Follow me over to the back corner. Leif, Nick, and Spence have staked out a couple of the pool tables for the night. Nick's wife, Callie, is protecting the stools we dragged over there so we'd have a place to sit as the guys practice the manly art of billiards. Spence's wife is running late, but she should be here any minute now."

A few seconds later, the two of them were ensconced on their stools watching Nick and Leif duke it out while Spence offered unwanted and definitely unappreciated advice from the sidelines. Nick finally threatened to skewer him with a cue if he didn't shut up and leave them alone. Luckily, Tripp was back with the beers. He and Spence picked up cues and launched into their own game at the next table.

Zoe and Callie took turns rooting for their husbands, applauding great shots and booing when the opposing team scored. It was hard not to be a bit jealous of the two couples. Not only were the pairs both happily married, but their friendships were obviously set in stone. Rather than dwell on not really being part of a couple, Abby swiveled on her stool to face the other table more directly as Tripp and Spence started their second game.

Tripp had just sunk his third ball when she spotted Spence's wife wending her way through the crowd. Abby waved to get Melanie's attention and then pointed at the empty stool beside her. Spence stepped away from the table to kiss his wife before once again putting on his game face.

Then Spence smiled at Abby. "I don't know whose idea it was to do this, but God bless them. We've been doing inventory at the factory, and I'm ready to take a breather."

She grinned back at him. "Glad you could make it. From the sound of things, it's been one of those weeks for most of us."

When he returned to his game, Melanie asked, "Are you doing okay, Abby? The night of the auction had to have been a tough one for you. From what Spence told me, it was definitely a night of surprises for both you and Tripp."

It was hard not to sigh. She'd give anything to move past that evening and everything that had happened since. "Yeah, it was rough. I just hate that the success of the evening was overshadowed by the tragedy at the end. The fact that the police haven't yet made an arrest just keeps my nerves all stirred up."

"I bet it does. I'd say not to worry, but that's easier said than done. Still, I'm sure Gage Logan will get it all sorted out eventually." Melanie paused to clap her hands when Spence made his shot. "We've heard Tripp's ex-wife made Gage's short list of possible suspects. Do you know if the police are looking at other possibilities?"

Abby sipped her beer. "Not for sure, but I hope so. That's one of the reasons Tripp wanted to meet with all of you tonight. We were wondering if any of you went to the local high school at the same time as Bryce Cadigan and Denny Moller."

Melanie had been watching her husband try to make a tough bank shot, but she immediately turned to face Abby more directly. "Actually, Spence, Callie, and I all did. Nick and Leif moved here from out of state, so it's doubtful they would know anything helpful. Zoe was a few years ahead of us, so she wouldn't have had classes with either of them. What did you want to know?"

How much should Abby share? Deciding it wasn't worth dancing around the issue, she settled for the blunt truth. "Tripp's ex-wife is stuck here in Snowberry Creek until things get settled, so we wonder who else might have had it in for Bryce. When I saw him talking to Denny at the auction, things looked a bit tense between them. It probably didn't mean anything, but it's hard to know if that's true. I know they were on the football team together until their junior year."

"Spence might remember if anything happened, since he was on the team, too." Melanie wrinkled her nose. "I didn't exactly run with their crowd. I was the typical shy and geeky good student, so I never hung out with the popular kids."

It was hard to picture Melanie as being anything other than the confident woman she seemed to be, but high school had been a long time ago for all of them. Abby had changed a lot since that time, too.

"What about Spence? Was he one of the popular kids?"

Melanie laughed and shook her head. "He was the bad boy your mother warned you about, so good looking and wild. Gosh, I had such a crush on him back then."

And still did from what Abby could see. For now, there was one other person she was curious about.

"Did either of you have Mrs. Alstead for English? She would've been known as Miss DeWitt back then."

Melanie was already nodding. "I did. As I recall, a lot of the guys had kind of a crush on her. It was her first year of teaching, so she wasn't much older than the seniors."

Wow, Abby would've guessed the woman was a decade or even more older than that. "Really? She looks a lot older to me."

"She does now, but not back then. In fact, I seem to remember that she'd graduated from both high school and college early, so she was barely twenty when she got the job. She took a year off right after our senior year, maybe to finish her graduate work or something."

Okay, that was interesting. Mrs. Alstead hadn't mentioned that fact. Of course, why would she? It had all happened a long time ago.

Meanwhile, Melanie waved at her husband to get his attention when he stepped away from the pool table to let Tripp take his turn. He held up a hand to acknowledge her but stayed where he was until Tripp took the shot. When the last ball on the table dropped into the pocket, Spence muttered something under his breath and reached for his wallet. Tripp grinned as he accepted the twenty Spence slapped down on his hand, and headed straight for the bar.

Spence joined his wife but gave Abby a dark look. "Did you know that man cheats?"

She snickered but felt obligated to defend Tripp's honor. "I know he can be sneaky, but just how does one cheat at pool? You were watching him like a hawk, so he couldn't have tilted the table or manually dropped a ball in the pocket without you seeing him do it."

The former soldier remained unconvinced. "I don't know. It's probably some scary ninja mind game skill he learned while he was in the Special Forces. There's no telling what all those guys could do."

Spence glanced back over his shoulder to where Tripp stood near the bar as he waited for their second round of drinks. "The sneak probably mesmerized all of us long enough to clear the balls off the table."

Melanie wasn't buying it. "So it's not just because he's better at pool than you are?"

Spence gave his wife a disapproving look for doubting his skills, but then grinned at Abby. "Well, I suppose that's another possible explanation, but I like mine better."

While they waited for Tripp's return, Melanie asked, "Spence, Abby and Tripp were wondering if you remember anything from high school that might have caused bad blood between Bryce Cadigan and Denny Moller."

He finished his beer and set it aside. After glancing around, maybe to see if anyone else was listening, he nodded. "Yeah, as a matter of fact. It would've been their junior year when Denny got hurt during football practice. I never saw how it actually happened, but it really messed up Denny's leg bad. They carted him off the field on a stretcher. He had surgery and missed a bunch of school that year. I graduated that spring, so I don't know what happened after that."

Tripp was back bringing four more beers with him. "I just caught the end of that. Are you talking about Bryce and that other guy?"

Spence nodded. "Yeah, there were some whispers that Bryce might have been involved somehow, but it was all kept hush-hush. After they took Denny to the hospital, the coach made it clear that if any of us were caught spreading rumors about the incident, he'd suspend us from the team. He was a real hard-ass when it came to breaking any rules he put in place."

He took a long drink from his beer. "I know the cops got involved and interviewed some of the other players. They never talked to me since I was doing drills at the other end of the field when it happened. I do remember that Bryce wasn't at school or at practice for a few days after it happened. The investigation was closed a week or so later. They ruled it was an accident, and Bryce came back acting like nothing ever happened."

Maybe Tripp was better at reading between the lines than she was because he was already shaking his head. "Sounds like a cover-up of some kind to me. How did Denny's family take it?"

"Not well. I forgot something in my gym locker and went back after school to get it. I overheard Mr. Moller hollering at the coach big-time. When the coach spotted me, he motioned for me to get lost, so I did. Considering how many college scouts were keeping an eye on Denny and everything, the injury had to come as a devastating blow to his entire family."

"How about Bryce's parents? Did they get involved?"

Spence frowned again. "Sorry, I don't really know.

For what it's worth, Mr. Cadigan was the kind of man who would try to throw his weight around if the situation called for it. Not sure if he would've had the clout to protect his son if Bryce actually had done something really bad. To be honest, I was going through my own rough spot about then, so I wasn't paying much attention to what was going on in anyone else's lives."

Melanie reached out to take Spence's hand in hers. He immediately swooped in for another quick kiss before reaching for his pool cue. "Come on, Blackston. You've gotta give me a chance to even up the score. Best two out of three, and then it'll be time to grab some burgers."

Tripp picked up the chalk and used it on the tip of his cue. "Sounds good. Winner buys the onion rings."

"It's a deal."

Abby waited until their attention was back on their game before saying, "Sorry if talking about that stuff brought back some bad memories for Spence."

Melanie shook her head. "Don't worry about it. Spence put all of that behind him a long time ago. Anyway, did any of that help?"

"Yeah, I think it did. Even without a lot of details, at least we do know that whatever happened back then was pretty bad. We won't know unless we find a way to talk to Denny directly if he was still holding a grudge."

"Good luck with that." Melanie set down her drink. "I'm going to head over to the ladies' room. Let Spence know I'll be back in a minute if he wonders where I've gone."

Right after Melanie disappeared into the crowd, Zoe tapped Abby on the shoulder. "Two tables just opened up that we can scoot together so we can all sit in one place. We should grab them while we can."

"I'll let Tripp know and be right there."

She waited until he took his shot before laying her hand on his arm. "We're going to claim those tables over in the corner. Join us when your game is over."

"You doing okay in this rowdy place?"

"Actually, I am. It's been a long time since I spent a night out on the town with friends."

He leaned in close. "Never let it be said that I don't know how to show you a classy time. Nothing like cheap beer and free peanuts to impress the ladies."

For a second, she thought he was going to kiss her, but then he backed off when Spence called his name. "Are you going to play or flirt?"

Abby wasn't sure if the interruption left her feeling disappointed or relieved. She also suspected Tripp was feeling some of the same confusion. Finally, he smiled just a little. "Spence and I will be over in a couple of minutes."

"See you there."

The food was every bit as good as Tripp had promised, and the company was even better. She hadn't been lying when she'd told Tripp that it had been a long time since she'd been out with a crowd to share laughs over burgers and beer. It had been even longer since she'd gone dancing. It wasn't something Chad had ever particularly enjoyed, so they'd only done so when a social occasion made it necessary.

But as everyone finished up their meals, Callie announced to her husband that he owed her a dance. Even though Nick put up a bit of a fight, it was easy to tell that he really didn't mind. Spence and Melanie immediately followed them out onto the small dance floor on the far side of the room, but Zoe told Leif they could wait until something slower came on the jukebox. He glanced at Abby and patted his leg. "My ankle is a bit cranky. A little present from my last deployment."

Tripp trailed his last French fry through a puddle of ketchup as he quietly asked, "Where were you stationed?"

Leif named some town Abby had never heard of, but Tripp knew right where it was. The two men and even Zoe launched into a brief discussion about the various places where the three of them had seen duty while serving in the military. Although it left her very little to contribute to the conversation, she found it fascinating to learn more about Tripp's life in the army. It wasn't something he often talked about.

Then the quick-paced song ended. After a brief silence, an old classic by The Righteous Brothers started. Zoe's face lit up as she grabbed Leif's hand and dragged him out onto the dance floor. That left just her and Tripp sitting alone at the table. She tried desperately to come up with a topic of conversation to fill the time while the others were gone. But then to her surprise, Tripp took her hand in his and tugged her up off her chair.

"Come on, Abby, let's show them how it's done."

Before she could think of any reason they shouldn't, she was wrapped in Tripp's arms in the middle of the other dancers. It took them a few seconds to fall into an easy rhythm together, but maybe that was just her overthinking the situation. Neither of them spoke as they swayed to the familiar ballad about heartbreak and loss. She'd always loved this song, but now it made her think of Chad and all that they'd lost somehow along the way. Was Tripp thinking along the same lines about his own past experience with Valerie?

She wasn't sure she wanted to know. It also didn't help knowing the big veterans dance, which she'd hoped to attend with Tripp, was just over a week away. Well, that wasn't going to happen, not even if they managed to clear Valerie's name once and for all. So for now, she'd shove everything else out of her head and just enjoy the moment.

Tripp eased away from her just far enough to be able to look down at her. "You doing okay?"

"I'm fine. Why?"

"You tensed up there for a second." He tugged her back in closer, but he was frowning. "I didn't give you a chance to refuse. Would you rather sit this out?"

That was absolutely the last thing she wanted to do. "Not at all. I'm really fine. I was just thinking about what Spence told us about Bryce and Denny."

He drew a deep breath and let it out slowly. "There's definitely something there, but we can't do anything about it tonight. What do you say we just relax and enjoy ourselves?"

He accompanied the proposition by spinning her out and then back into his arms. She loved the slick move and was about to tell him so when she spotted someone standing against the wall near the door. It was the Pratt brother she'd seen talking to Bryce at the auction. This time he wore jeans, a white T-shirt, and a leather biker vest instead of a suit, but there was no mistaking him.

She still had no idea if he was Gil or Gary, but that didn't matter. Right now, he was slowly scanning the crowd as if looking for someone in particular. For a brief second, his eyes locked onto hers. There was no glimmer of recognition, no real threat, but nonetheless a cold sensation washed over her that was almost reptilian in nature. Now she understood why Gage had warned her to stay away from the man.

He might not have been the one who killed Bryce, but there was no doubt in her mind that he could have and not even blinked.

Chapter Sixteen

When she stumbled a little, Tripp tightened his hold and glared down at her. "Now I know something's wrong, Abby. What's going on?"

By that point, Pratt had pushed away from the wall and was working his way through the crowded dance floor on his way to who knew where. His route brought him all too close, so she ducked her head, resting her face against Tripp's chest to avoid any chance of once again drawing the biker's hard gaze in her direction. She waited until he'd put some distance between them before finally responding to Tripp's question.

"That biker who just walked by is the other man who had issues with Bryce at the auction. Unless I'm mistaken, he's one of the Pratt brothers who own that motorcycle shop down the road." She shivered a little. "You know Gage warned me to stay away from him. Now I know why. He's big-time scary."

Tripp tightened his grip on her as his eyes flared wide and hot. "Did he threaten you in some way?"

"No, not really. We happened to make eye contact as he was looking around the room. I have to say he has the coldest eyes I've ever seen. This might sound stupid based on just one close look at that guy, but I wouldn't doubt for a minute that he's capable of killing a man. I'd be scared to get anywhere near anyone who could do something like that."

Tripp winced as if her words hurt him somehow. He spun her out and then did it again, as if trying to put a little distance between them for some reason. Then it hit her. He'd never said it in so many words, but Tripp had to have seen a lot of combat over the two decades he served in the army. That was true of most, if not all, of the people she'd met while working with the veterans group. She honored the sacrifices they'd made and regretted the emotional price that many of them had paid for their service to the country.

"That came out wrong, Tripp. I'm sorry. I was talking about that scary biker, no one else." He looked dubious, so she tried again. "I trust you, Tripp—period, full stop. Never doubt that."

Then to add a little humor to the moment, hoping it would help, she added, "Besides, Zeke adores you, and we both know what an excellent judge of character he is."

The corner of Tripp's mouth finally quirked up in a small grin. "Come on, Abby. We both know that furry beast's loyalty can be bought for two dog cookies and a pat on the head."

She couldn't argue with the truth of that statement, but at least the knot of tension in her chest eased knowing he had accepted her apology. When the song ended, another immediately started up, this one much faster. She waited to see what Tripp wanted to do.

He stepped back just a little. "I'm up for it if you are. I've never considered myself a great dancer, but I think I can do better than that."

When she looked to see what he was talking about, she spotted Spence over in the far corner busting out some pretty bizarre dance moves. Judging from Melanie's calm reaction to the display, it had to be his usual style.

Abby tried her best to smother a laugh when she met Tripp's grin with one of her own. "You know, suddenly I feel a whole lot better about my own dance skills."

Satisfied that Tripp's good mood had been restored, Abby settled in to enjoy the rest of the evening. As they returned to the table to take a break from dancing, she spotted the Pratt brother over by the bar. She waved to get Spence's attention. "Do you know that guy standing over by the bar in the biker vest? The one with a ponytail."

Spence twisted around in his seat to check the guy out. "That's Gil Pratt. He owns the bike repair shop right down the street. Do you want me to introduce you?"

"No, I was just curious. He looked familiar for some reason."

Spence looked as if he wasn't quite buying her explanation, but he didn't press the issue. Instead, he and Tripp launched into a good-natured rehash of their earlier billiard game. Abby laughed as she listened to them while still keeping a wary eye on Gil Pratt. She wasn't exactly sure what about him worried her so much, but there was definitely something off about the way he was acting.

As she watched, several other guys wearing biker jackets crowded closer to Gil on his right. It was easy to tell the logos worn by the new arrivals were different from the one on Gil Pratt's back. When he tried to put some space between himself and the newcomers, several more moved up on his left.

Maybe it was time to talk to Tripp about leaving. Before she could say more than his name, the fists started flying. Within seconds, Tripp and the guys had upended their tables to provide a barricade between them and the pig pile of angry bikers near the bar. Abby couldn't resist peeking over the top edge of the table but quickly ducked back down out of the line of fire.

Tripp wedged himself down beside her and slipped his arm around her shoulders while keeping an eye on the action. "You okay?"

She nodded. "What do we do now?"

"If there's ever a straight shot to one of the doors, we could try to get out of here." He stuck his head up for a brief look around. "Trouble with that idea is that we don't know what's going on out in the parking lot. Right now, we're better off hunkering down and waiting for the cops to get here. I promise we'll do whatever it takes to keep you ladies safe."

The sound of wood splintering had him wincing as he glanced back over his shoulder. "Boy, that had to hurt!"

Abby ducked down lower as Zoe scooted in closer on her other side. Meanwhile, Leif and Nick also took turns scoping out the situation. When someone was knocked into their makeshift barricade, they surged to their feet long enough to send the guy stumbling back into the fray. Abby didn't know what it said about Tripp and the three former soldiers that they all had huge grins on their faces the whole time.

A voice rang out over the crowd. "Cops are here!"

That was enough to start a general rush toward the door. Rather than join the stampede, the eight of them remained right where they were as the shouting and shoving continued for what seemed like forever.

Finally, a calm voice called out, "Everyone, stay right where you are until we get this mess sorted out."

Tripp's tension level immediately ratcheted down several levels, as did everyone else's in their small group. Leif kissed his wife. "Don't ever say we don't take our ladies to the best places."

Zoe reached up to pat his cheek. "I'm proud of you. At least this time you're not going to end the night sporting a pair of handcuffs."

Abby couldn't help but laugh. There was definitely a story behind that comment, but now wasn't the time to ask. This was hardly how she expected the evening to turn out even if Tripp had warned her that it was a possibility. Another couple of minutes passed before someone approached their neck of the woods. At least it was a familiar face.

If Deputy Chapin was surprised to see her, he didn't mention it. "Ms. McCree, are you and your friends all right?"

She let Tripp tug her back up to her feet as she smiled at one of Snowberry Creek's finest. He'd been the officer who had manned the desk when Tripp had been a guest at the town jail a while back. "Deputy Chapin, we're awfully glad to see you."

He nodded as he eyed their makeshift fort. "Glad you didn't get caught in the middle of that mess. It will take a while before it will be safe to step outside, so make yourselves comfortable. The EMTs are dealing with a few injuries, and we're getting ready to transport a few prisoners to the county lockup. I'll let you know when you can head out."

"Thanks, Deputy."

While they waited, she helped the others right the

tables and set the chairs back in place. It was another twenty minutes before the deputy gave the all clear. As the eight of them filed out into the parking lot, Abby drew in a deep breath of the fresh night air, a vast improvement over the stench of spilled beer and booze that had permeated the bar.

The crowd outside was a mix of police officers from at least two different jurisdictions, emergency medical personnel, and bar patrons. It wasn't hard to tell which ones had been involved in the brawl. There were plenty of black eyes, bloody knuckles, and split lips to go around.

As they made their way around the edge of the milling crowd toward Tripp's truck, she spotted Gil Pratt standing next to one of the squad cars, his wrists secured behind his back with one of those plastic zip ties. His right eye was nearly swollen shut, and he looked to be favoring his right side when he moved.

"Tripp, do they usually arrest the guy who was attacked?"

He followed her line of sight. "Why do you ask?"

"I happened to be looking at Gil Pratt when the fight broke out. A bunch of guys wearing a different logo on their jackets surrounded him while he was standing at the bar. One of them swung the first punch, and Gil just defended himself. We need to tell someone."

Tripp tightened his grip on her hand. "I really wish you hadn't seen that. The last thing we need is for you to get caught in the middle of two rival gangs."

She couldn't help but agree with him, but she also couldn't simply walk away without telling the investigating officers what she'd seen. Tripp knew it, too.

He handed her his keys. "Get in the truck and lock the doors. I'll go talk to our friendly deputy."

He was back a few minutes later. "They're going to take Gil to the hospital rather than to the lockup with everyone else. Deputy Chapin will talk to Gage and let him decide how to handle the situation. They'll do what they can to keep your name out of the report.

"Thanks, Tripp."

As they pulled out of the parking lot, she glanced back over her shoulder. "Despite how it ended, I had a great time tonight."

"Me too, although I shudder to think what would've happened if we'd still been out on the dance floor when the fight broke out." Tripp reached over and gave her hand a quick squeeze. "I swear you've turned into a real magnet for chaos."

As they headed homeward, she pondered that last statement and how she felt about it. Maybe she should've been a bit insulted by his assessment of her, but in fact she was kind of flattered by it. That didn't mean she was going admit that much to Tripp, because he clearly had different feelings on the subject. She was still smiling when they pulled into the driveway.

Abby's good mood lasted right up until she walked into her own kitchen to find that her houseguest had evidently decided to wait up for her. How thoughtful.

Valerie looked up from her tablet to shoot a dark look at the clock on the wall. It wasn't all that late, really. Just a little after midnight. Okay, it was closer to one o'clock, but still. For a brief second, Abby felt the same kick of guilty fear when she'd come sneaking in a couple of hours after her curfew back in high school. There was one big difference in the current situation, though.

No, come to think of it, there were actually several. First, she was an adult, not a teenager. Second, this was her house, and she could come and go as she pleased. And finally, it was none of Valerie's business how Abby had spent her evening or whom she'd been with.

Abby hung her keys on the hook just inside the door as Zeke finally put in an appearance and demanded to be let out. She didn't have to look outside to know he'd made a beeline for the small house in back, because she could hear Tripp's deep voice talking to him. No doubt both man and dog were dutifully making their nightly patrol around the perimeter of the yard.

Mostly just to have something to do, she fixed herself a glass of ice water, wishing the whole time she could simply head upstairs without waiting for Zeke to return. It was probably rude to ignore her guest, but she was pretty sure the last bit of her good mood would disappear the second the two of them started talking. She desperately wanted to keep that from happening, mainly because it would be nice to go to bed not tied up in knots over yet another confrontation.

Valerie evidently had no such qualms. "You know, considering your claim to just be Tripp's landlady, you two spend a lot of time together. He mentioned that his rent is discounted in return for services rendered. A more suspicious person might actually wonder what those services actually entail."

Had the barnacle really gone there? Abby tightened her grip on the glass in her hand in an effort to stop herself from heaving its contents right in Valerie's face. She was really proud of herself when she set the glass down in the sink and stepped away from the temptation.

"Believe it or not, Valerie, I don't really care what you think of me or my relationship with your *ex*-husband." She hoped the woman picked up on her slight emphasis on the "ex" part of that statement as she slowly turned to face her directly. "Having said that, despite all the years since your divorce, you should know Tripp better than that."

When Valerie started to speak again, Abby cut her off. "No, you've said enough for one night, so let me finish. For the record, we met with friends who grew up here in Snowberry Creek to see if they knew of anything in Bryce's past that might have resulted in him getting killed."

At least that little bombshell managed to silence Valerie for a few seconds. She sounded a little less confrontational when she asked, "Did you learn anything useful?"

The back door opened and Zeke bolted into the kitchen. At first Tripp remained outside, but it was too much to be hoped that he wouldn't pick up on the tension between Abby and Valerie. He gave his ex-wife a disgusted look and invited himself to the party.

"Okay, Val, what did you do to upset Abby this time?"

The other woman went on the defensive. "How do you know she didn't say something to upset me?"

He leaned against the counter and crossed his arms over his chest. "Because that's not Abby's normal style."

By that point Valerie was on her feet and moving around the table to stand closer to him. "And you think it's mine? Because I'm telling you that all I did was make a simple statement, and she went off on me."

Abby had planned to stay out of the discussion, but enough was enough. "Actually, she was wondering what exactly it is you do for me to earn that reduction in rent you get."

Tripp looked at his ex-wife as if she were a total stranger. "Valerie, if you don't want to have to pack your bags and get the heck out of here right now, you will apologize to Abby. All she's done is offer you a safe place to stay and done her best to help clear your name."

Valerie wasn't having it. "Don't forget that she's the one who sicced that cop on me in the first place. If she hadn't totally misread the situation between me and Bryce Cadigan, I would've been back home by now." She paused to shoot Abby a hateful look. "I'm sure her interference was purely innocent and had nothing to do with the fact that I outbid her in the auction."

That again. "For the last time, Valerie, I didn't bid on anybody at the auction."

Meanwhile, Tripp's hands remained tucked in close to his chest, but now they were clenched in tight fists. "You need to leave, Valerie. Go pack. I'll follow you to one of the hotels out by the interstate to make sure you get checked in safely."

Maybe it finally got through to the woman that she'd gone too far. Her shoulders slumped as she reached out to lay her hand on Tripp's arm. He merely glared at her until she jerked it back down to her side.

"Come on, Tripp. I'm upset because that police chief friend of yours came by again while you two were out having fun to ask me a bunch more questions."

Tripp didn't fall for her play for sympathy. "So how does that translate into you being rude to both me and Abby?"

Valerie looked exasperated. "All right, fine. I over-reacted, and I apologize to both of you. I was pretty shaken by the fact he doesn't seem to be backing off on the idea that I killed Bryce. It seems someone else has been talking to Chief Logan about the discussion I had with Bryce in the parking lot. In that person's opinion, it was on the verge of becoming violent. That's ridiculous, of course, but it's my word against theirs. When I went looking for you, hoping that you could intercede on my behalf, you were nowhere to be found. It didn't take me long to realize you were out with Abby. I guess I was a little jealous."

Abby rolled her eyes but used the excuse of giving Zeke a fresh bowl of water to hide her reaction from both Tripp and Valerie. This discussion was going nowhere. It was time to make herself scarce.

"Look, it's late, and I'm tired. If neither of you need me for anything, it's way past my bedtime. Good night."

Then she walked away without waiting to see if Tripp made good on his threat to force Valerie to find somewhere else to stay for the duration. Her phone was chiming before she even made it to her room.

Should I make her move?

She so wanted to say yes, but she knew herself well enough to know she'd regret the rash decision in the morning. The woman was rude and hateful, but she was also in a tough situation. Besides, the barnacle wasn't the only one who'd said something to Tripp tonight that had hurt him. Abby had been grateful when he'd forgiven her. Maybe Valerie deserved another chance, too. After a brief hesitation, she gave Tripp her answer.

No, but if she ever says anything like that to me again, I will kick her to the curb in a heartbeat.

You're a nice person, Abby McCree.

Not really, but I'm glad you think so. Get some sleep. That's what I'm going to do. We'll figure out what to do with all we learned tonight in the morning. But not too early. I plan to be lazy and sleep late.

It's a deal.

She brushed her teeth and put on her favorite sleepshirt before crawling into bed. She'd just pulled up the covers when she heard the creak of the stairs as Valerie made her way up to her room. Instead of continuing on up to her bedroom on the third floor, she stopped outside of Abby's door.

"I apologize again. Thanks for letting me stay."

If Abby had thought there was even a hint of sincerity in the apology, she would've responded. But she didn't and remained silent. There was a slight hesitation as if Valerie was waiting for their kumbaya moment to begin. When it didn't come, she quietly continued on her way.

The whole sleeping late thing didn't happen. Too restless to stay in bed any longer, Abby gave up and got dressed far earlier than she'd meant to. Tripp must have been watching for her to turn on the kitchen light, because thirty seconds later he was at the door holding up a grease-stained bag and cardboard tray with four cups of coffee that sported the logo from Something's Brewing. Abby immediately unlocked the door.

"I come bringing Bridey's best fresh-out-of-the-oven blueberry muffins and coffee."

She hurried to set out plates, napkins, and forks. "Wow, you must need an extra shot of caffeine to have bought four cups of coffee. You could've just had some of mine when it gets done brewing."

"Actually, this isn't all just for the two of us," he admitted, looking a bit chagrined. "I ran into Gage on my way to the coffee shop and asked him to stop by. He accused me of trying to bribe a police officer by tempting him with coffee and muffins, but that didn't stop him from accepting the invitation."

Abby winced. "Are you sure this is a good idea?"

Not that her doubts about the situation kept her from setting out another plate. She also asked, "Are you going to invite Valerie to this discussion?"

He shrugged. "It concerns her, too, so I sent her a text. Of course, she might not see it in time if she's still sleeping."

Right. If Abby was reading the subtext correctly, he didn't really want to include his ex-wife. At the same time, he didn't want her to think they were sneaking around behind her back again, not that that wasn't really what they'd been doing. After poking and prodding that idea a little, Abby decided she was okay with his thinking.

"So we're going to admit to Gage that we've been doing a little investigating on our own?"

Tripp looked a little worried. "I think we should even though he won't like it. I'd rather he not learn it from someone else, especially if he decides to talk to any of the others and finds out we were asking questions about Bryce and Denny."

Zeke woofed softly to warn her that more company was on the horizon. A few seconds later, Gage appeared on the back porch and walked on in without knocking. He took off his hat and tossed it on the counter near the door.

"Morning, Abby. I hope Tripp warned you he'd invited me over."

"Yeah, he did." Well, sort of, anyway. "Would you two like something besides muffins for breakfast? I've got bacon, eggs, yogurt, and oatmeal."

Gage shook his head as he and Tripp took their usual seats at the table. "Thanks, but I've already had breakfast. That was a few hours ago, though, so a muffin will really hit the spot."

She checked the time. It was barely eight o'clock. "You must have been out and about awfully early this morning."

"One of my deputies had some personal business to take care of today, so I'm covering the early patrol for him. To be honest, it feels good to get out of the office for a little while."

Abby piled all the muffins on a large plate and passed them to Tripp. As he took one, Gage gave both her and Tripp stern looks. "I know you've got questions and want to talk about the status of my investigation. Can we at least hold off on that until after I finish my first muffin?"

Neither she nor Tripp bothered to deny his assumption that there had been an ulterior motive behind the invitation to share pastries and coffee with them. Tripp gave his friend a quick nod. "It's a deal."

Neither of them was in a big hurry to make Gage mad, so they actually waited until they were all finishing up their second muffin before turning the conversation back to what they'd learned.

Tripp drained the last of his coffee and then refilled his cup from the pot Abby had started just as he'd arrived. He held up the carafe, asking without words if either of them wanted more. After topping off Abby's, he rejoined them at the table. Meanwhile, Gage pulled out his all-too-familiar spiral notebook to jot down any useful information they might have to offer. Abby had lost count of the number of conversations the two of them had conducted accompanied by the sound of his pencil scratching across the paper.

"Start talking. What have you guys been up to this

time? Don't forget to include the brawl at Beer last night."

Abby was more than willing to let Tripp take the lead, but he just sat there waiting for her to jump in. Fine, it wouldn't be the first time she'd dipped her toes in an investigation.

"I . . . no, actually Tripp and I both decided to talk to some friends about Bryce Cadigan and what happened between him and Denny Moller back in high school. We met them at the bar."

The lead in Gage's mechanical pencil suddenly snapped off. After a heavy sigh, he clicked out a new piece and said, "And so?"

"Seems there was an incident during a football practice that involved the two of them. Our source didn't see what happened, but it resulted in Denny getting badly hurt. He didn't just miss a lot of school because of the resulting surgeries, he lost any chance of getting the athletic scholarship he was counting on. Bryce wasn't at school for a few days afterward. He came back after the investigation ruled that the incident was an accident. Oh, and the coach ordered his players to not talk about anything they'd seen or risk being kicked off the team. That might have been him simply wanting to keep rumors from starting, but it sounds like it could've been part of a cover-up to me."

There was a long silence while Gage continued to take notes. As far as she could tell from the blank expression on his face, he might have been writing his weekly grocery list. Finally, he set the pencil down and leaned back in his chair.

"I would point out that I already warned you that I had a cell with your name on it if I caught you doing anything like this. Clearly that failed to make any kind of impression on you at all."

She really didn't want to spend the foreseeable future living behind bars. On the other hand, as long as she was in jail, at least she wouldn't have to share her quarters with the barnacle. Well, unless Gage tossed the woman into the adjoining cell. It would be better if he put Tripp in between them. That image made her snicker, probably not the smartest thing to do under the circumstances.

"You really think this is funny?"

Whoa, an irritated Gage was scary enough, but the sudden cold chill in his voice was so much worse. "Sorry, Gage. I promise I'm not taking the situation lightly. I don't want to end up in jail, and neither does Valerie. The thing is, we don't exactly get along all that well. I was wondering if it would be too much to ask for you to put Tripp in the middle cell to act as a buffer."

Now both men were glaring at her, especially Tripp. "Not funny, Abs."

Gage evidently agreed with that assessment, but he wasn't any happier with Tripp. "What were you thinking? She stumbles into enough danger on her own without you encouraging her. I swear, I should throw all three of you in one cell and lose the key."

He was already mad, so she might as well tell him the rest of it. "While we're still confessing our sins, I figured out that it was for sure Gil Pratt I saw at the auction."

Before Gage could choke out a response, she hurried to finish her explanation. "I promised you I wouldn't go looking for either of the Pratts, and I didn't. Tripp and I were out on the dance floor when I spotted Gil in the bar. I did not go near him or try to talk to him. The only reason I found out his name at all is I asked a friend if he knew him."

Gage grabbed another muffin off the plate and slowly peeled off the wrapper. Then he methodically broke the pastry into bite-sized pieces. He glared at Tripp the whole time. Finally, he said, "Let me get this straight. You've somehow decided I can't actually do my job without your interference. So, for the sole purpose of poking your nose in my investigation, you decided to take Abby to that biker bar even knowing the type of crowd that hangs out there at night."

It wasn't exactly a question, so that was probably why Tripp didn't respond. After a few seconds, Gage took a bite of the muffin and washed it down with some coffee. "I'm pretty sure you knew I didn't want Abby near the Pratts or any of their friends."

This time both Abby and Tripp nodded.

"I'm guessing the friends you met there were most likely Spence and his buddies."

Abby's mood brightened instantly. "And their wives, too. We had a great time."

Tripp grimaced. "You're not helping, Abby. But she's right, Gage. We played a little pool, ate a few burgers, and hit the dance floor. It was just a nice time out on the town right up until the fight broke out. We immediately stashed the women behind some tables and waited it out."

"So Deputy Chapin told me. It was also one of the biggest brawls in recent history. At least ten idiots were arrested, and three others besides Gil Pratt ended up in the emergency room."

They all sat and pondered how close they'd skated to disaster last night. At least Gage hadn't brought up the threat of jail time again. That didn't mean they were out of the woods yet.

Despite all of that, it was the best adventure Abby had been on in ages. Maybe ever. She supposed now wasn't the time to ask Tripp when they could go back again.

She thought of another question. "Did Deputy Chapin also tell you that Gil didn't start the fight?"

"Yeah, he did, although that might've been a first for Gil. As promised, we didn't include your name in the report, though. If anyone asks why he didn't get locked up with the others, it's because he ended up with some cracked ribs and a possible concussion. The doctor wanted to keep him awhile to make sure there weren't any complications. Most of the others will make bail long before Gil gets out of the hospital. We're still investigating what started the fight in the first place, but he's free to go home."

That was good. Now, on to the next touchy subject. "So, Valerie mentioned you stopped by again."

"I did." Gage looked up at the ceiling before continuing. "I assume she's still staying here for the time being."

"Yes, she is."

Abby didn't bother to point out that could change at any moment if the barnacle didn't learn how to control her mouth. Something in the quick look Tripp gave her made it clear that he was thinking along the same lines.

"I'll tell you what little I can. Bryce died from an overdose. What that involved is being kept confidential for now. As far as why I was talking to Ms. Brunn again, she hasn't been exactly forthcoming on what happened that night or her relationship with Bryce Cadigan."

Tripp frowned big-time. "What relationship? She swore she'd never been near the man before the night of the auction."

Gage suddenly looked pretty tired. "Maybe that much is true, but she knew him all right. We have the e-mails and texts to prove it. While I won't reveal the content of those messages, you can take my word for it that they were pretty inflammatory."

Abby had a bad feeling about this. "But why would she lie about something like that? She has to know that only makes her look more guilty."

Another voice joined the discussion to answer. "Well, isn't this cozy?"

All three of them turned to face Valerie, who stood in the hall just outside of the kitchen glaring at each of them in turn. As usual, she was dressed fit to kill, although under the circumstances that probably wasn't the most appropriate way to describe her. And why put on that much makeup just to hang around in Abby's dining room all day? Then it occurred to her that the clothes and makeup might be the barnacle's armor against a world that might not feel all that welcoming right now.

Valerie finally ventured all the way into the room. After helping herself to a cup of coffee, she sat down at the table across from Abby and next to Tripp. Her calm demeanor in the aftermath of being caught out in such a massive lie was impressive. She made a pretense of choosing the best muffin from the few left on the plate before speaking again.

As she peeled off the wrapper, she ignored both Abby and Gage to speak directly to Tripp. "I came here to Snowberry Creek to see if you could help me convince Bryce to return something to me. Something very personal. I'd been watching for a chance to confront him at a public appearance because he refused to meet with me privately. When I found out about the auction, I figured it was as good a time as any. That you were also going to be there was just icing on the cake."

Tripp looked skeptical. "If you didn't know him, what did he have that belonged to you?"

Her composure slipped a little, making it clear she was nowhere as calm as she was pretending to be. "Actually, it belonged to Becca. She dated him for a short time. Seems Bryce liked to film certain, uh, shall we say 'activities.' Once she broke off with him, he threatened to post the videos online if she didn't start making regular payments."

Tripp looked shocked. "That jerk was blackmailing her?"

She shook her head. "Me, actually. My sister isn't the one with deep pockets, and he knew I'd do whatever it took to protect her."

At that comment, Gage went on point. "Ms. Brunn, before you say another word, I would suggest you contact an attorney."

Then he stood up, grabbed his hat off the counter, and stalked out the door.

Chapter Seventeen

Stunned didn't even come close to describing how both Tripp and Valerie looked after Gage's grim suggestion and abrupt departure. Abby suspected she looked much the same as the other two. Yeah, on some level she'd known that Valerie was right in the middle of the crosshairs when it came to the investigation into Bryce's death, but it hadn't really hit home that she could actually be charged with the crime.

Abby might not like the woman, but she couldn't quite picture her as a murderer. On the other hand, it was clear that she was protective of her sister. Maybe she really had meant that she would do anything to protect Becca. But did her determination extend to murder?

Tripp wasn't happy with his ex-wife's behavior, but Abby knew him well enough that he would stand by the woman as long as she was being threatened. It didn't surprise her one bit that he left his chair to kneel in front of Valerie, who was doing her best to maintain a brave front even as she blinked back an onslaught of tears. He grabbed a tissue out of the box on the counter and pressed it into her hand.

Valerie dabbed at her eyes. "I didn't kill him, Tripp. I swear I didn't."

"I know, babe, but Gage is right. It's time we get you a lawyer. If you can't afford one, I can help with that."

His offer clearly surprised Valerie, but she was already shaking her head. "I can handle the expense as long as this doesn't drag on forever. I'll call an attorney friend of mine who works in Seattle and see if she can recommend someone for me."

It took her two attempts to stand up, another sign of how badly shaken she was by the morning's events. Tripp had stood up and moved back to give her room but immediately reached out to steady her. "Let me know when you've set up an appointment. I'll go with you if it would help."

She sniffed again. "I don't want to take up any more of your time."

Abby almost choked on the sip of coffee she'd just taken. As lies went, that one was a whopper. If Valerie wasn't interested in spending time with Tripp, she wouldn't have reacted with so much anger over him going out with Abby yesterday evening. Her original reason for reaching out to her ex-husband really might have been to elicit his help in dealing with the threat to her sister, but that wasn't the only driving force behind Valerie's interest in Tripp. Yeah, for now she needed his help dealing with Gage and the investigation. However, whether either of them realized it or not, Valerie wanted more from Tripp than that.

That was his problem, not Abby's. She took another sip of her coffee only to realize it had gotten cold. Evidently she'd been so lost in thought that she'd missed out on more of the conversation. Valerie was on her cell phone talking to someone, presumably her lawyer friend. Tripp looked on as she disconnected the call and immediately started dialing again.

Rather than just sitting there listening, Abby cleared the dishes and wiped down the table. It didn't take long for Valerie to set up an appointment with the defense attorney for early that afternoon.

As soon as she hung up, Tripp said, "Allowing for traffic, we should leave here no later than eleven thirty. If we end up getting there too early, we can always grab a cup of coffee somewhere beforehand."

Valerie was already looking more composed. Abby didn't know about her, but in her own life just having a plan of action in place made any situation, no matter how dire, easier to face. Abby folded the dish towel and hung it to dry on the oven door handle. "Let me know if you need me to do anything."

Valerie actually gave the matter some thought before finally shaking her head. "Thank you, Abby, but I don't know what that would be. I wouldn't expect us back for dinner, either. I don't know how long this meeting will last, but traffic could be awful by the time we get out of the attorney's office."

Tripp nodded in agreement. "We'll grab a burger on the way back."

Valerie's expression brightened. "Dinner will be my treat, Tripp. I'm sure we can manage something better than a burger."

"As long as it doesn't take too long. I have homework I can't put off forever. In fact, I'm going to head back over to my place and see how much I can get done before we have to leave."

He'd started for the door when Valerie spoke again. "No insult intended, Tripp, but can you wear something nicer than jeans and a T-shirt to the appointment? From what my friend said, this guy is a full partner in one of the top firms in the area."

Tripp just nodded and continued on his way out. While he didn't seem to take offense at the suggestion that he didn't know how to dress for the occasion, Abby was insulted on his behalf. Rather than comment, though, she reached for Zeke's leash. Before leaving, she dug a spare house key out of the drawer and laid it on the counter.

"That's for you. I'll be back in an hour or so. I've got my own keys, so lock up if you decide to go somewhere while we're gone."

Valerie acknowledged she'd heard her with a vague wave of her hand. Abby gathered up the few things she and Zeke needed and left. Rather than drive to the park, she led her buddy down the sidewalk several blocks to where one of the trails through the national forest began. It was one of Zeke's favorite places to explore, and they could walk a long loop without having to backtrack.

Being out in the fresh air helped banish all the frustrations of dealing with her unwanted guest and everything else that had happened. She was also well aware that her few days of freedom were almost over. Starting Monday, she'd be at a dead run right up until the big dance next weekend.

While everything was on schedule so far, she was actually dreading the actual event. Too many people had suspected she'd hoped to attend the dance with Tripp. Now he'd be there with Valerie, while Abby would be going solo. Well, unless Gage actually arrested the barnacle for Bryce's death. No matter how disappointed she was in how things had turned out, Abby wasn't petty enough to want that to happen just so she'd have a date for the evening.

It was time to stop stewing about the whole mess. She'd done everything she could to find out what had happened. Gage was well aware of the people who had interacted with Bryce at the auction, and she really did trust him to do his job. Well, mostly, anyway. He'd never told her and Tripp if he'd already known about the old football incident between Bryce and Denny. The man certainly liked to play his cop cards close to the vest.

At the halfway point in the trail, Abby poured Zeke a bowl of water. He slurped it up in a hurry and then tried to rub his face on her leg, but she danced back out of reach just in time. Whether by accident or design, he often stored some of his water in his jowls, which then ended up slurped all over her pants if she wasn't careful.

"No, you don't, boy. I'm on to your tricks."

His efforts thwarted, he resorted to plan B and gave his head a hard shake. That sent the water flying through the air right at her. She tried to brush some of the droplets off her clothes with only marginal success. There was no winning sometimes.

Deciding she was in no hurry to go home, she tugged on his leash and resumed their walk. The longer they were gone, the less time she'd have to spend watching Valerie get ready for her long afternoon and evening in Tripp's company.

As it turned out, Valerie and Tripp were about to leave when she and Zeke walked up the driveway. Valerie was decked out in a navy-blue pantsuit with a cream silk blouse. The colors suited her blond hair and coloring. Once again, Abby couldn't help but applaud the barnacle's fashion sense, which was stylish without being flashy. It was the perfect outfit for visiting a high-end attorney regarding a possible murder charge.

Tripp had also chosen his clothes well. He was wearing dark gray slacks and a white knit shirt with a blue sports coat. She couldn't help but grin at him. "Boy, I've said it before. You sure do clean up nice."

His cheeks flushed a little red. "The occasion seemed to call for it."

She got that. Turning her attention back to Valerie, she said, "I really hope the attorney can help you."

Valerie tightened her grip on her purse. "Thanks. I'll be really glad when this is all over. I've got the key you gave me, so don't feel like you need to leave the door unlocked if you go to bed before we get back."

Seriously? How long was she expecting her appointment with the lawyer to take? Not that it was any of Abby's business. Tripp had made it clear he needed to get back home in time to finish his classwork, although he didn't contradict Valerie on the subject. Zeke chose that moment to decide he really wanted attention from the other two humans. Abby tugged him back out of reach. Contrary to what the dog thought, neither Tripp nor Valerie would appreciate being festooned with dog hair right now.

"Stay back, Zeke. They've got places to go and people to see."

The two of them watched Valerie carefully back her car down the driveway and out to the road before going inside. What should she do to fill the empty hours stretching out in front of her? Maybe it was time to spend more time working on the quilt her aunt had started right before she died.

She'd only made it to the second floor when the doorbell rang. Zeke charged back down the steps to

stand at the front door. As she joined him, she tried to
interpret his reaction to whomever stood out on the
porch. It wasn't someone he knew, but he wasn't growling, either.

She peeked out the window and caught a glimpse
of a black leather vest and scraggly ponytail. That was
all she needed to see. Her first instinct was to hustle back
upstairs and hide. That might be cowardly, but it was
probably also smart. She seriously considered whether to
call Gage and request backup, but then she spotted the
bouquet of flowers in Gil Pratt's hand. Curiosity won out
over caution.

After grabbing Zeke's collar to keep him from bolting outside, she opened the door far enough to reveal
the dog before letting herself be seen. Gil's black eye
looked worse than it had last night, and the deep lines
bracketing his mouth hinted that his ribs were hurting
something fierce. His one good eye widened and his
eyebrows shot up in surprise as soon as he got a good
look at the mastiff mix. Then his mouth kicked up in
a quick grin. "Whoa, boy, aren't you a big one?"

When Gil held out the back of his hand for Zeke to
sniff, the big dog dragged Abby out onto the porch.
She tried to act like it had been her idea, but the hint
of a twinkle in Gil's eyes made it clear she hadn't quite
pulled it off.

"That's a handsome dog you've got there, Ms.
McCree."

Zeke took the compliment as his due and gave Gil's
hand a quick lick. The biker scratched the dog's ears
before turning his hard-eyed gaze back in Abby's direction. Then he held out the flowers. "These are for you.
I'm sorry for dropping by with no notice, but I wanted
to thank you for speaking up for me last night."

She accepted the bouquet of yellow alstroemeria.

The small lilies were one of her favorite flowers. "This wasn't necessary, Mr. Pratt, but thank you. I love them. They're so pretty and last a real long time."

He looked pleased with her reaction. "I'm glad you like them. Now, I'll let you get back to whatever you were doing."

Maybe it was the surprising gift of flowers or the fact that Zeke obviously liked the man, but she gave in to the impulse to ask him to stay for a few minutes. She had questions only he could answer.

"Mr. Pratt, can I ask you about Bryce Cadigan?"

Some of the hard edge she'd seen in him last night came flooding back, but he finally nodded. "You can ask. I might not answer. I have one or two I wouldn't mind asking you in return."

"Fair enough."

She pointed toward the two chairs at the far end of the porch. "Have a seat. Talking is thirsty work. I'll get us something cold to drink and some munchies and be right back. Is it okay if I leave Zeke with you?"

"Sure thing. He and I can get better acquainted while you're gone."

She liked that he didn't hesitate. "Do you want iced tea, beer, or a soft drink?"

"I'd love a beer, but you'd better make it iced tea. I'm on pain meds for my ribs, and the doc said not to mix them with alcohol."

Abby waited until he'd slowly eased himself down in a chair before ducking back into the house. When she returned a few minutes later, Zeke had his head in Gil's lap, his eyes closed as the man slowly stroked his fur.

"Looks like you made a friend, Mr. Pratt."

He nodded. "I like dogs of all kinds, but Zeke here is pretty special. Where did you get him?"

"My aunt found him at a local shelter. From what she said, they thought he'd been abused and abandoned. It took some time for him to start trusting people again. I inherited him along with this house when Aunt Sybil passed away a while back."

"Sorry for your loss."

Most of the time people said something like that because it was expected. Somehow she thought he really meant it.

She set a trayful of drinks and cookies down on the small table between the two chairs. After sitting down herself, she handed Gil a plastic bag with a few of Zeke's favorite treats in it. "I'll let you dole those out to your buddy there. I'll warn you that he'll gobble them all down at once if you let him and then beg for your share of the people cookies. He has mooching down to an art form."

Gil laughed and slipped Zeke a treat before tucking the rest into his shirt pocket. He reached for his glass of tea and took a long drink. "That hits the spot."

Hoping to encourage him to answer her questions, she said, "Why don't you tell me what you want to know, Mr. Pratt?"

"Call me Gil. When people call me Mr. Pratt, it usually means I'm in trouble of some kind." He softened the comment with a small smile. "I noticed you watching me at the bar last night when you and Tripp Blackston were out on the dance floor. You looked a bit . . . let's say, scared. If our paths crossed before then, I don't remember it."

She sighed. "The answer to that question ties into my questions about Bryce. I saw you talking to him the night he died. There seemed to be a lot of tension between you at the time."

Gil slowly ate one of the cookies and reached for a

second. "I'm guessing that's why Gage Logan got all up in my face about that night."

"Sorry, but yeah. He asked me for the names of everyone I saw talking to Bryce that night. I didn't know your name, but some friends of mine did. I'm sorry if I caused you problems with Gage, but he talked to a whole bunch of people about that night."

He shrugged. "Gage and I manage to get along most of the time. It's not the first time he's shown up on my doorstep. It won't be the last. I'll tell you the same thing I told him. I didn't kill Bryce and don't know who did. But if you made a list of people who had reason to hate that guy, it would likely be a long one."

"It sure seems that way."

As she pondered what to say next, Gil asked another question. "So if you thought I might have killed Bryce, why would you go out of your way to tell the police I didn't start the fight last night?"

"Actually, I wasn't the one who told them."

He snorted. "You were watching me as you walked out into the parking lot and then said something to Blackston. He made a beeline over to talk to one of the deputies. Next thing I knew, they took the zip tie off my wrists, stuck me in a squad car, and then drove me to the hospital. Gage said no charges would be filed because a witness stated someone else threw the first punch."

She couldn't argue with his logic. "How did you get my name? Gage told me this morning that they didn't include it in the police reports."

"Same way you got mine. I asked around to see who the pretty lady was who'd been dancing with Tripp."

She blushed just a little at his description of her. "I told them because it wouldn't have been right not to. I saw how those guys kept crowding you at the bar.

When you tried to step away, they wouldn't let you. Are they going to come after you again?"

"I'll be fine. My brother took care of the problem." Then he gave her a hard look out of his swollen eye. "You really don't want to draw their attention in your direction, by the way. It's best if you don't ask a lot of questions where they're not welcome. Things might not turn out the way you would like."

That was an understatement. Sitting on her front porch sipping tea with a badass biker was a prime example. Still, she smiled. "I'm glad you're in the clear, but message received and understood. It's actually something I hear pretty often from Tripp and Gage."

"Maybe you should listen better if they have to keep telling you that." Gil finished the last of his tea. "So what questions did you have about Bryce?"

Trying to choose her words carefully, she stated the obvious. "I can't say that I knew him at all, but I do know he could turn his charm off and on like a faucet."

The biker looked thoroughly disgusted. "That's putting it mildly. I'm guessing you know Bryce grew up next door to us, although he was quite a bit younger than me. By the time he reached high school, my brother and I had both enlisted, not that it had been our intention to do any such thing."

She held off asking him what he meant, figuring this was his story and he had the right to tell it any way he wanted to. She nibbled on a cookie while she waited.

"Someone in our neighborhood vandalized a bunch of houses over a period of a few weeks. The cops tried to catch whoever it was, but they didn't have any luck. Back then my old man owned the motorcycle repair shop, but Gary and I both worked there. We all had uniform shirts with our names on them. The police conveniently found one of my shirts at one of the crime scenes. Luckily, I had an ironclad alibi for that night. They tried to pin it on my brother next, but they couldn't make it stick."

He offered Zeke another treat and went back to stroking the dog's fur. "Not saying we were angels, mind you, but we weren't guilty that time. In the end, the old chief of police made it clear to us that he'd had enough of us to last a lifetime. He offered us a deal: either we enlisted and let the military make something of us, or the next time we stepped out of line he'd throw the book at us."

"How does Bryce play into this?"

"The first time I came home on leave, I caught him about to use a can of spray paint on a neighbor's car. When I cornered the jerk, he laughed about me ending up in the navy for something he did. I wanted to wring his scrawny neck for him, but that would've only caused my folks more problems, not to mention me."

"So he had a history of causing trouble."

"Yeah, he did, not that any of it ever stuck. I never could understand how he managed to fool so many people. Then, while Gary and I were away, someone broke into the folks' place several times and stole stuff. It's not like our family had much to begin with, but my mom had a few pieces of silver that had been handed down in the family. The cops couldn't figure out who was behind the break-in, but a couple of the items eventually turned up in a pawn shop up in Tacoma. The person who hocked them fit Bryce's description, or at least it sure seemed that way to me. Nothing ever came of the investigation, though."

"Did your mom get her silver back?"

"Yeah, Gary and I bought it back for her. The

homeowner's insurance had paid off on the claim, but she'd already used the money to pay Dad's medical bills."

Well, Abby had gotten her answers. She was quite sure that Gil could be every bit as scary as she'd thought he'd been last night, but he was also a man who had clearly loved his parents. Even though she'd only heard his version of how things had played out between his family and Bryce all those years ago, she found herself believing Gil's account of the events.

"Thank you for trusting me with your story. I appreciate it."

He patted Zeke's head one last time and offered him the last of the treats Abby had given him. "Well, I need to get back to the shop. Thanks for the tea and cookies."

"You're welcome, and thank you again for the lovely flowers. I put them in a vase on my kitchen table, where I can enjoy them."

They both stood up. When he winced, she asked, "Should you be working with your ribs still hurting like that?"

"I'll be fine. Gary is already there working on the bikes. I'm going to spend a few hours catching up on paperwork, which we both hate. He figures he got the better end of the deal."

"Before you go, would you like some cookies to take with you? You don't even have to share them with your brother if he gives you too much grief."

"I like the way you think, Ms. McCree." Gil's laughter had him wincing in pain. "And I'd never turn down a chance at some homemade cookies, especially if I can lord them over Gary."

"Give me a second to grab you a container of them. I always have a supply in the freezer. I like to bake when things are bothering me, and that seems to happen all too often lately."

"Sorry to hear that, but I'll be glad to take some off your hands."

She was in and out in a flash with the promised goodies. "Here you go. I hope you feel better soon."

"Thanks, I'll be fine."

He took the container and started down the front steps, still moving pretty gingerly. When he reached the bottom, he turned back to face her. "I should also thank you for organizing the auction and the dance to help out veterans. That was real generous of you. I'm just sorry things went off the rails at the auction like they did."

"It's me who should thank you for your service, Gil."

He shifted from one foot to the other and back again, clearly uncomfortable with her comment. Finally, he jerked his head in a quick nod. "Do me a favor, show your gratitude by letting Gage Logan figure out who murdered Bryce. If someone was desperate enough to kill him, they won't think twice about coming after you, too."

Then he walked away.

Chapter Eighteen

After watching Gil drive away in a beat-up pickup truck, Abby spent the afternoon working on her aunt's quilt. She finished stitching the last two strips together and set the quilt top aside. It took several attempts to work the kinks out of her back after spending so much time sitting in one position. It was well past time to head downstairs to fix something to eat.

Zeke followed her into the kitchen to stand by his food bowl, a less than subtle hint that it was well past their normal dinnertime. When she didn't immediately spring into action, he sighed and nosed the bowl a couple of inches in her direction before lifting his mournful gaze to meet hers.

"Okay, okay, don't nag. It's not like you're starving."

He clearly didn't agree with that assessment. Rather than continue to disappoint him, she quickly filled his bowl and then set about fixing her own dinner. She heated up a bowl of the soup left over from two days before and made a sandwich to go with it. When everything was ready, she carried it down the hall to the living room. She often ate by herself in the kitchen, but tonight she couldn't face sitting alone at the big oak table.

Instead, her plan was to park herself in her favorite chair and watch a movie as she ate. Torn between several options, she finally chose a romantic comedy. It would be nice to enjoy a few laughs and see at least someone's love life work out for them.

With Zeke curled up at her feet and a glass of wine sitting close by, she settled in for a long evening of waiting to see just how late it would be before Valerie and Tripp came back home.

As it turned out, she didn't have to wait all that long. The movie was only about half over when Zeke announced he needed to go outside. Abby followed him to the kitchen and let him out the back door. Deciding a breath of fresh air would be welcome, she walked out onto the porch to watch the dog make his evening rounds. He'd made it only halfway around the perimeter of the yard when he suddenly jerked his head up from the ground to watch the driveway.

Although she didn't hear or see anything that would've caught his attention, Abby didn't doubt for a second that someone was headed their way. Sure enough, a few seconds later headlights lit up the driveway as the barnacle's rental car pulled into sight. Zeke made a beeline for Tripp as he climbed out of the passenger side. Valerie was a little slower to leave the confines of the car, but she finally stepped out.

Even from where Abby stood, it wasn't hard to interpret the body language between her tenant and her houseguest. The tension was almost palpable, leaving her wondering what was wrong. Had the meeting with the attorney gone badly? Or was Valerie not happy that they'd gotten back far earlier than she'd hoped.

Telling herself it wasn't really any of her business, Abby decided to head back inside. If either Tripp or Valerie wanted her to know how their afternoon had gone, they knew where to find her. On her way to let Zeke out, she'd carried her dinner dishes back in from the living room. She gave them a quick rinse before putting them in the dishwasher. Valerie walked in just as Abby was closing the dishwasher door.

"Welcome back."

Clearly Abby's innocuous greeting didn't go over well, because Valerie didn't slow down from the second she came through the door until she started up the stairs at the other end of the hall. As she exited the kitchen, she called back over her shoulder, "I'm going up to my room for the night."

Well, at least that eliminated the need for Abby to try to make conversation. She'd lost interest in her movie, and it was too early to go to bed. Besides, she also needed to wait until Zeke was ready to come back inside. When she peeked out the kitchen window toward Tripp's house, he was sitting on his front porch step petting his furry friend.

She grabbed a couple of beers out of the refrigerator and headed their way. He kept his focus on the dog until she drifted to a stop a few feet shy of where he sat. If he didn't want company, he could say so.

Finally, he looked up. "Are you going to drink both of those yourself?"

"I wasn't planning on it."

He immediately scooted over to make room on the step for her. She handed him his drink and made herself comfortable. The three of them sat for several minutes, letting the sounds of the night surround them. When Tripp remained silent, Abby tried priming the pump.

"I had an interesting visitor right after you guys left today."

Tripp gave her a sideways glance but didn't say anything. Taking that as her cue to continue, she braced herself for a possible explosion and said, "Gil Pratt stopped by while you were gone."

To her surprise, Tripp took the news remarkably well. "What did he have to say for himself?"

"He wanted to thank me for letting the deputies know that he didn't start the fight last night. He even brought me flowers."

Okay, that clearly surprised Tripp almost as much as it had her. "Seriously? He doesn't seem like the type."

She nodded. "Yep, he did. I hesitated to answer the door when I realized who it was, but then I saw the bouquet. Maybe I'm crazy, but I couldn't imagine him taking the time to buy flowers if he meant me any harm."

"Well, unless that's exactly what he was hoping you'd think."

"True, but I also made sure Zeke was the first thing Gil saw when I opened the door." She huffed a small laugh. "I've always trusted Zeke's taste in people, and he took an instant liking to Gil."

Tripp frowned big-time. "That deputy promised to keep your name out of the report, so how did he figure out you were the one who talked to the cops?"

The answer to that question had her smiling. "Gil asked around to see who the 'pretty lady' was who'd been dancing with you at the bar."

Tripp's tension faded as quickly as it had appeared. "The joys of living in a small town."

"True enough. Anyway, I invited him to sit out on the porch and offered him iced tea and cookies. Then we took turns asking each other questions."

"Learn anything interesting?"

"Yeah, I did." She paused long enough to sip her beer and then gave him a brief rundown of what Gil had told her. "Everything he said fits with the picture I'm getting of what kind of man Bryce Cadigan was. A lot of glitz hiding a dark nature."

Tripp set his empty bottle down on the porch. "So, I only have one question about Gil. After all this time, was he still angry enough to want to kill Bryce for the trouble he caused his family back in the day?"

That was a question she'd been mulling over herself, finally deciding all she could do was go with her gut feeling. "I'm pretty sure Gil is capable of violence, but I don't think he killed Bryce. It wasn't as if he hadn't known where to find Bryce all this time. If he'd wanted to take revenge on him, there would've been plenty of other opportunities where Gil wouldn't have painted a target on himself as a possible suspect."

Tripp considered that for several seconds. "That makes sense. We'll leave him on the list but consider him a low probability."

"Good. I'd hate to think I sent a killer home with three dozen of my best oatmeal raisin cookies."

It felt like a long time since she'd heard Tripp really laugh. Too bad they still had something else to talk about. She waited for him to move on to Valerie's visit with the attorney. When he lapsed back into silence, she decided to force the issue. "I take it that it didn't go well with the attorney."

He shook his head. "She asked me to sit in on their meeting. The guy was impressive and very experienced in dealing with felony cases. God knows he'd have to be good to charge as much as he does. He thinks the evidence against her is circumstantial at best, but he made a point of saying people have been convicted on a lot less."

Tripp leaned back to stare up at the night sky. "He wasn't sure her moving in with the prosecution's star witness was the smartest thing she could've done."

Abby tried not to sound too hopeful when she asked, "Did he tell her to move out?"

"He said the damage was already done and left it up to her."

He turned his gaze back in Abby's direction. "I will ask her to leave, though, if you want me to. She's my problem, not yours. I should never have suggested she move into your house instead of mine."

There was no way Abby would admit that she'd rather have the barnacle holed up in her third-floor guest room than sharing the rather close quarters of Tripp's place.

"It's fine, Tripp. This isn't easy for any of us."

It was time to go. She picked up the empty beer bottles. "Now, Zeke and I will head home and let you get started on your homework."

Tripp stood up at the same time she did. To her surprise, he gave her a quick hug. "Thanks for . . . well, everything. Maybe I'll give Gage a call in the morning to see how things are going."

"And I'll give some thought on how we can approach Denny Moller. He's the only one of the suspects on our list we haven't made a connection with as yet."

"Okay, but don't go doing anything crazy on your own. You've managed to survive encounters with two murderers since you moved here. I'm not sure 'third time's a charm' comes into play when it comes to killers."

His dire assessment of the situation hung there in the air between them, sending chills skittering right up her spine.

"I'll be careful."

Because he was right. Everybody's luck ran out eventually. Unfortunately, Valerie learned that lesson the hard way when Gage came knocking at the front door bright and early the next morning. One look at his grim expression made it clear he wasn't there for coffee and cookies. Instead, he'd come to read the barnacle her rights.

Chapter Nineteen

Abby had dealt with Gage in his professional capacity before and so had Tripp, but having previous experience didn't make it any easier. That Ben Earle, the homicide detective from the county sheriff's office, had accompanied him only made things worse. Both Abby and Tripp had had their issues with him a few months back when he'd arrested Tripp for withholding evidence in a homicide case. His only concession at the time was to let Gage hold Tripp in the Snowberry Creek jail instead of taking him to the county jail.

Near as Abby could figure, Tripp had spotted the police cars as soon as they pulled up in front of the house, and immediately charged across the yard to warn Valerie. Without bothering to knock, he'd charged through Abby's back door and bolted down the hallway to plant his stubborn feet right in the entryway and do his best to prevent Gage and Ben from entering the house.

For her part, Valerie hovered just out of sight on the staircase. Her face was pale and her eyes wide with fear. She had good reason to be scared, but there wasn't much anyone could do right now to help her. In fact, if he didn't back down, Tripp would end up in the back of a police cruiser right along with his ex-wife.

It wouldn't be the first time he'd spent time in jail in defense of someone he cared about. If it happened again, Abby somehow doubted Gage would be as understanding as he'd been last time. She was also convinced that it hadn't been an idle threat when he'd promised to toss them both into a cell if they interfered in another one of his investigations.

She squeezed between Tripp and the open door, keeping her back toward the men on the porch. Ignoring both the cops and the accused criminal, Abby focused all of her attention on the one person who really mattered to her. Keeping her voice low and calm, she tried to get through to Tripp. "Come on, please step back. You know you can't keep them out forever."

He barely spared her a glance. "It's working so far."

Praying for patience, she tried again. "You're not going to be any help to Valerie if you're behind bars, too."

It was hard not to go into full retreat when he turned his furious gaze in her direction. "For the last time, Abby, she didn't kill that guy. She shouldn't get arrested for something she didn't do."

"If she's innocent, then she has nothing to worry about."

There was no amusement in Tripp's bitter laughter. "Yeah, right. Like no innocent person has ever gone to prison for a crime they didn't commit. Do you really think they'll keep looking for the real culprit once they arrest her?"

At his assessment of her chances, Valerie whimpered and plunked down on the steps as if her legs would no longer support her. At least she hadn't fainted, al-

though that would have at least broken the impasse between Tripp and Gage. Abby wished she could say he was
wrong. She settled for saying, "Regardless, this isn't helping her at all. You'd do better by calling Valerie's attorney
to tell him what's happened. He can find out what's
changed that suddenly they've decided to make an arrest."

She took his hand in hers and gave him a gentle
tug. Considering the difference in their relative sizes,
there was no way she could move Tripp unless he co-
operated. At first he remained rooted to the spot, but
then he gave her hand a quick squeeze before retreat-
ing to stand in front of the staircase, continuing to
block access to Valerie. Still not helpful, but at least it
was an improvement.

Abby was uncomfortably aware that she was still in
her pajamas with her hair uncombed and teeth not yet
brushed. Definitely feeling at a disadvantage to the
two lawmen with their freshly shaved faces and crisp
uniforms, she motioned for the two men to come in.

"Have a seat in the living room, and we'll be right
with you."

Gage stepped inside but made no effort to move
beyond the entryway. "Abby, this isn't a social call."

She was so tempted to roll her eyes at that observation. "Yes, Chief Logan, I realize that. However, since
you didn't bother to call first, neither Ms. Brunn nor I
are exactly dressed to greet visitors. If you don't want
to sit in my living room while we take care of that
problem, then go to the kitchen and help yourself to
some coffee. Tripp knows where everything is and can
make a fresh pot."

Without giving him a chance to respond, she shoved
her way past Tripp and climbed the few steps to where
Valerie was still sitting. "Come on, Valerie. We'll both

feel better after we're dressed and ready to face the day."

It took the other woman two tries to stand up, but she finally managed to find her balance. Abby put her arm around Valerie's waist and gently led her up to her room on the third floor. When they got there, she said, "Are you up to taking a quick shower and getting dressed on your own?"

Valerie slowly straightened to her full height, shoulders back, cool pride firmly back in place. "I'll be fine. I just didn't expect them to come pounding on the door with no warning."

"Me either. While you get dressed, I'll go do the same. If you get done before I do, come wait in my room. We'll go back downstairs together."

Valerie headed into her bedroom. "It won't take me long."

Abby made it halfway down the first flight of steps when Valerie reappeared at the top of the stairs. "I should've said thanks, Abby. I know you never wanted to get tangled up in this mess in the first place, and that you're only doing this because of Tripp. Even so, I appreciate that you made the effort."

There wasn't much Abby could say to that, so she nodded and kept going. Gage and Ben might be willing to give them a little time to regroup, but she knew from past experience there was a limit to their patience.

Twenty minutes later, Abby stepped out of her bathroom to find Valerie sitting in the easy chair by the bedroom window. It was amazing how much more the other woman had managed to accomplish in the same amount of time. After taking an extra fast shower, Abby had pulled her still-damp hair back in a neat ponytail, brushed her teeth, and put on the first clean jeans and shirt she found in her closet.

The barnacle, on the other hand, was decked out in one of her pantsuits, her hair perfectly styled, and just enough makeup on to erase the haggard look she'd worn after the unexpected arrival of the police. Amazing. Maybe someday she'd share the secret of how she managed to pull that off.

Abby slipped on her shoes. "Are you ready?"

Valerie shook her head. "Not really, but I guess I don't have any choice."

She stood and picked up a small travel bag. Holding it out, she said, "I wasn't sure if they'd let me bring anything with me, but I packed a few things just in case."

Abby doubted they'd let her bring anything into jail with her, but she could be wrong. Regardless, she would let Gage and Ben be the ones to deliver any bad news. "Let's go."

The two of them arrived in the kitchen to find Tripp and the two police officers seated at the table and engaged in a three-way staring contest. Would there be some kind of prize for whomever held out the longest? While this was clearly no time for joking around, Abby had to do something to break the tension before things got out of hand. She grabbed a handful of cookies out of the jar and circled the table to drop two in front of each of the contestants.

Gage was the first to respond. "I told you this wasn't a social occasion, Abby."

When he tried to give back the cookies, she refused to take them. "I know what you said, but it looked like you guys decided to kill time indulging in some kind of manly competition involving glaring until someone broke. Since I couldn't pick a clear winner, I decided to hand out prizes to everyone."

From the look Valerie gave her, the woman was seriously questioning Abby's sanity. On the other hand, both Ben and Tripp blinked and then slowly reached for their cookies. They all might think she was crazy, but at least the tension level in the room was down to a more reasonable level.

As he munched one of his cookies, Tripp noticed Valerie hovering near the doorway and immediately offered her his seat at the table. She drew a slow breath and kept her eyes focused solely on him as she ventured far enough into the room to sit down. Abby wasn't at all surprised when he positioned himself behind the barnacle, making it clear whose play he was backing in this early-morning drama.

Aware that neither she nor Valerie had had a chance to eat breakfast, Abby's innate need to feed people when they sat down at her kitchen table roared to life. Or maybe it was only that she needed to do something with the surge of hyper energy zinging up and down her nerves. Either way, she quickly filled Zeke's bowl and then stepped closer to the table.

"Valerie, I'm guessing you probably don't have much of an appetite right now, but you really should eat something. You might be in for a long day and will need your strength. Can I get you a tub of yogurt or something?"

Tripp offered Abby an appreciative smile when Valerie slowly nodded. "I could eat some toast and maybe a cup of tea."

After filling the kettle and putting it on to heat, Abby asked, "While I'm at it, do any of the rest of you want something?"

"Nothing for me, Abby." Ben Earle stifled a small

smile as he leaned back in his chair, legs stretched out in front of him. "Gage, you weren't kidding about Abby's compulsion to play the good hostess."

Gage's grim demeanor softened just a little. "She's good about things like that."

While she waited for Valerie's toast to pop up, Abby poured cups of coffee for the three men and herself. Gage and Ben had probably eaten breakfast somewhere around zero dark thirty. Tripp was another early bird, usually taking his morning run before the sun rose very high in the sky. With that in mind, she fished some muffins out of the freezer and zapped them in the microwave.

If Gage wanted to stick to his guns that this wasn't a social occasion, fine. At least she would've made a token effort to make her guests feel welcome even if they were both uninvited and unwanted. When the tea and toast were ready, Abby set them in front of Valerie and then carried the muffins over to the table and took the seat next to Gage.

She chose a muffin for herself and then held the plate out to him. He stared at the stack of pastries long and hard before finally accepting one. He passed them over to the homicide detective, who didn't even hesitate. When Tripp reached for a muffin, Abby stopped him. "Sit down and eat that. It's hard to enjoy my breakfast, such as it is, with you standing there frowning at everybody."

Valerie's eyes flared wide when he followed Abby's orders without protest. To be truthful, Abby was as surprised as she was that he'd listened to her, but she hadn't been kidding. Just having everyone sitting down and eating something put a whole different spin on the mood in the room. It was likely only a temporary reprieve, but at least everyone was getting a chance to slow down and deal with the rush of emotions Valerie's imminent incarceration had stirred up.

After a few bites, Valerie set her toast down and pushed her plate away. Her hand trembled when she picked up her tea and took a sip, but that was the only visible sign of her inner turmoil. Then she put the mug back down on the table but kept her hands wrapped around it, no doubt taking comfort from its warmth.

Valerie then met Gage's and Ben's gazes in turn. "Okay, gentleman, where do we go from here?"

The barnacle would never be her favorite person, but once again Abby admired the woman's cool poise. Ben nodded to Gage, indicating he should take the lead. "Well, Ms. Brunn, after reviewing all the evidence, the district attorney has decided to press charges. Although the murder happened within my jurisdiction, this type of case is prosecuted at the county level, which is why Detective Earle is here."

Mount St. Helens had nothing on the eruption Abby could sense brewing in Tripp. His fists were clenched so tightly that his knuckles stood out in stark relief. One wrong word at this point, and she had no doubt he would go ballistic. In an effort to deflect the impending explosion, she reached over to touch his arm.

"Tripp, I know you're upset about the situation, but we both understand that Gage and Ben have no choice but to do this. If you stop and think things through, you know these officers both know they can't interrogate Ms. Brunn without her attorney present. The best thing you can do for her right now is to call his office and let him know what's happening."

Before releasing her hold on him, she turned to Gage. "Where will she be held?"

He'd been watching Tripp, but he slowly shifted his gaze to her. "The D.A. has agreed to let us keep her here in Snowberry Creek for the short term. I can't promise how long that will continue, but that's where we're headed. Let her attorney know that we're aware she has obtained representation and will act accordingly."

Abby wasn't sure how she'd been elected spokesperson for the non-cop members of the crowd, but someone had to say something. "I'm sure Valerie and Tripp join me in being grateful that you were able to do that for her. Once the dust settles, will you let us know when and if we can visit her?"

For some reason Ben Earle found that funny. He wadded up the wrapper from his muffin and tossed it down on the table. "Abby, we both know if you show up with a box of cookies or muffins, Gage's people will trip all over themselves to let you in to see whoever you want. If I wasn't guilty of enjoying a few of those goodies myself in the past, I might feel compelled to report his department for accepting bribes."

Tripp finally joined the conversation. "That's what I told Gage when I was behind bars there. The problem is proving it since they always destroy the evidence."

Valerie was the only one who wasn't enjoying the joke. "Can you all please take this seriously?"

All three men immediately put on their grim game faces. Gage carried his empty cup over to the counter. "Sorry, Ms. Brunn. You're right, of course. We should get going."

Valerie rose to her feet but stopped Tripp from doing the same. "Abby's right, Tripp. All you can do right now to help me is call the attorney."

"I will. Do you want me to notify Becca, too?"

Valerie immediately shook her head. "No, not yet. I've had a hard enough time getting her to stay put in Los Angeles. I don't want her to freak out until I know more. She feels bad enough already."

"Okay, but have your attorney or Gage let me know if I need to make that call."

She managed a small smile. "I will. Please don't worry about me, Tripp. I'll be fine."

Abby wasn't sure anyone really believed that was true, especially Valerie herself. This time Tripp wouldn't be denied when he surged up to his feet. Between one second and the next, he had enfolded Valerie in a tight hug. "We'll clear your name. Don't doubt that for a minute."

When he released her, she managed a nod, her eyes shiny with tears. Ben gripped her arm in gentle support and led her out of the room. At least he hadn't broken out the zip ties or handcuffs.

Gage hung back until they heard the front door open and close. Then he gave both Abby and Tripp a hard look. "When you said, 'We'll clear your name,' I would like to assume that you're talking about the police investigating Cadigan's murder. However, I know both of you better than that. I will say this one last time—stay out of this case. If you don't, I'll ship Ms. Brunn off to the county lockup and let you two cool your heels in my jail."

Then he took a single step closer to Tripp. "Got that?"

Abby wasn't at all happy about once again having to intercede between the two men. They were seriously at risk of doing some permanent damage to their friendship. Bracing herself for the worst, she parked herself right between them. "Okay, guys. Enough is enough. I think we can all agree that we're on the same page here. We all want the right person to go down for Bryce Cadigan's murder, and Gage has no choice but to follow where the evidence leads him."

She gave each man a gentle shove, pushing Gage toward the hallway and her angry tenant back toward the table. "Tripp, you know Gage wouldn't be doing this without good reason, whatever it might be. So let him do his job, and you do what you can to help Valerie, which is call her attorney. The sooner you do that, the faster he can find out what's going on."

At least Gage took her cue and walked away. If the front door slammed shut with a little more force than necessary, she wasn't going to complain. At least he was gone. Tripp started to follow, but she planted herself in front of him again. "Don't go watch, Tripp. It will only upset you and embarrass Valerie more than she already is."

He didn't step around her, but neither did he retreat. This time, she put her hands on his chest and gave him another gentle shove. "Please sit down and call her attorney. Meanwhile I'll fix us something to eat."

At the same time, Zeke bumped his buddy's leg with his big head, adding his own considerable weight to the discussion. She didn't know if it was the dog's efforts or her own that made the difference, but Tripp finally sat back down at the table. He stared off into the distance and ran his fingers through his hair before finally reaching for his phone. While he made the call, she got out her favorite cast-iron skillet to make them bacon and eggs.

The conversation with the attorney lasted longer than Abby would've expected. Trusting Tripp would fill her in after he hung up, she didn't bother trying to follow the discussion. He finally hung up just as she set their food on the table. Before digging in, Tripp studied his heaping plate and then grinned just a little.

"Gage is right, you know. All it takes is someone walking in the door for you to start offering up food of some kind. You just can't help yourself."

Maybe the worst of the crisis had passed if he was up to teasing her. "Well, considering how often you benefit from that compulsion, I wouldn't complain if I were you."

He immediately loaded up his fork with a huge bite of the scrambled eggs. "Not complaining. Just making an observation."

She gave him a mock glare. "Just eat your breakfast before it gets cold. Then we've got work to do."

"And what's that?"

"We've pretty much eliminated Gil Pratt from our suspect list, but the jury is still out on Denny Moller and maybe even Mrs. Alstead. Who knows, if we play our cards right, we might even figure out if there's someone else out there who wanted Bryce dead."

"And what about Gage's threat to toss you in jail for messing with his case?"

She shrugged. "As long as you're in the next cell, at least we'll both have someone to play chess with."

Tripp reached for his coffee. "But who'll bring me treats if you're right there in the next cell?"

Abby pretended to give the matter some serious thought. "Well, considering how mad Gage would be, I'm betting he'll recruit Jean to make us one of her special tuna casseroles. Maybe a combo with all your unfavorite ingredients. Yum! Anchovies, jalapeño peppers, and crushed barbecue chips."

Tripp shuddered. "That idea alone is enough to give me both nightmares and heartburn."

"So you're saying we should stay out of the investigation?"

He didn't even hesitate. "No, I'm saying we'd better not get caught."

Chapter Twenty

Worry over what they were about to do made it impossible for Abby to finish her breakfast. Well, and then there was the muffin she'd eaten earlier when Ben and Gage had still been there. Either way, she gave Zeke a rare treat of scrambled eggs and a crumbled-up piece of bacon. The dog wolfed down the unexpected bounty and then resumed his hopeful stance next to Tripp. He should've known better, but dreams die hard.

"Sorry, boy, but seems I worked up quite an appetite myself."

Despite his words, Tripp broke a piece off his last strip of bacon and slipped it to his furry friend. "I know we've got plans to make, but you're not the only one who didn't get a chance to shower today. I was up until after midnight doing homework, so I got a later than usual start on my run this morning. I had just gotten back when Gage and Ben pulled up out front."

That explained how he'd managed to spot them so quickly. "Go do whatever you need to do. I've got a couple of chores that need my attention. I'll meet you out on the back porch"—she paused to glance at the clock—"say, in about thirty minutes. If you need more time than that, just text me."

When Tripp carried his dishes over to the sink and reached to turn on the faucet, she stopped him. "Leave those for me this time."

He didn't argue but remained right where he was, his hands clamped down on the edge of the counter and his eyes tightly closed. "I hate this for her, Abby, because I know what it's like to be on the inside of those bars looking out. I thought I'd go crazy locked in that cell like a caged animal even if it was my own fault that I was there. I know you've figured out that I patrol the yard at night because I don't always do well with enclosed places anymore. All that kept me going from day to day for the short time I was locked up was knowing that eventually they'd have to let me out."

She hated the pain in his voice as he kept talking. "As jail time goes, I get that I had it easy. I had Gage to play chess with and then there was you. Stubborn woman that you are, you kept shoving your way past any barriers they tried to put in your way to make sure I was okay. That helped more than you know."

He drew a shuddering breath as he finally turned to face her. "But unless we figure out what really happened that night, Valerie could end up doing hard time. I'm not sure I can live with that."

Earlier, Tripp had hugged his ex-wife, saying without words that she wasn't alone in this mess. Now, Abby offered him the same bit of comfort, slipping her arms around his waist and laying her head against his chest. "She's not alone in this, Tripp, and neither are you."

He responded by resting his chin on her head and

wrapping his arms around her shoulders. They stood in silence for several seconds. Then Tripp leaned back and smiled down at her. "Thanks, that helps."

Then he did something totally unexpected. He kissed her, and it wasn't one of those hit-and-run cheek kisses he gave her sometimes. No, he took his time and did it right. When at last he released his hold on her, Abby staggered back a step to lean against the kitchen table.

She wasn't sure she could've put together a coherent sentence even if she'd known what to say. He knew it, too, judging from the rather smug grin he offered her right before heading toward the door. He pointed toward the clock on his way out.

"See you in half an hour. Let's not be late."

Thirty minutes passed in a blur. After washing the few breakfast dishes, she started a load of laundry before doing a quick sweep of the tiled kitchen floor as well as the hardwood floors in the hall. One of the few downsides of having Zeke for a roommate was his unfortunate habit of leaving a dust cloud of dog hair behind wherever he went. Considering how much she appreciated his company, having to run the dust mop several times a week was a small price to pay.

Besides, she did her most creative thinking while her hands were busy doing something else. As she did one last loop around the edge of the kitchen, she reviewed everything that had happened since the night of the auction. It all played out in her head as if she were watching one of those TV mysteries where the murder happens right at the beginning of the show so the viewers know who the killer is and watch as the homicide detective figures it all out in less than an hour. Deductive thinking always proved that the bad guys were never as smart as the cops.

Too bad real life didn't work that way, no offense intended to either Gage or Ben Earle. Even though she trusted and respected both men, she didn't know a darn thing about the district attorney who had evidently now taken control over the case. Again, on television it always seemed like the D.A. was ambitious and wanted to use a high-profile murder trial as a stepping-stone to further his career. What if that was true in this case? After all, Bryce had been a locally known celebrity of sorts. A beautiful woman like Valerie Brunn made a much more captivating villain than the other people on Abby's list of suspects: a small-town plumber, a retired school teacher, and a biker.

After putting away the dust mop, she gathered up the notes she'd been making and poured two glasses of iced tea. Before carrying them out onto the porch, she considered making up a plate of fresh fruit for her and Tripp to munch on. She had apples, strawberries, and some blueberries she could use. However tempting, she'd been teased enough about her habit of feeding everyone in sight. A movement in the backyard caught her attention. Tripp was right on schedule, so she let Zeke out to greet their guest.

Once the dog was out of the way, she stepped out onto the porch. As usual, Zeke had already convinced Tripp to stop and play fetch for a few minutes. It was a good way for both man and dog to burn off a little energy before it was time to settle down and get to work.

After half a dozen or so tosses of Zeke's ball, Tripp gave the ecstatic dog a thorough scratching and then a belly rub before throwing the ball one last time. As he made his way to where she waited on the porch,

Abby noted his hair was still damp, and his face was now clean shaven. Although she didn't mind a little scruff, he looked better. Definitely calmer. That was good, because cool heads were imperative when trying to solve a murder.

Her partner in crime dropped down in the other Adirondack chair with a heavy sigh. "I definitely feel more human. Did you have time to get everything done that you needed to?"

"Enough. I'll have to go change loads here in a little while, but otherwise everything is under control."

"Good."

He picked up his tea but frowned as he looked around. "What? No snacks? It's been half an hour since you shoved food in my direction. Are you feeling okay?"

"Jerk."

She'd put up with a little razzing as long it meant he was smiling again. "I thought I'd hold off until you had time to digest the huge breakfast I made for you."

"Good idea." Then he grinned and rubbed his hands together. "So I'm pretty new to this detective business. What do we do now?"

She opened her file. "We review the facts as we know them, think about the people involved, and go from there."

"That makes sense. Should we start with the victim himself? You'd think if we can figure out what he did to get himself killed it would lead us straight to his killer."

"Sounds good to me."

She pulled out the page with Bryce's name at the top and quickly skimmed biographical information she knew about him. When she was done, she handed it to Tripp. "See if I forgot anything."

It didn't take him long to read over it. "No, that

pretty much paints the picture I have of him, which is basically an egotistical jerk with a stunted conscience."

Then he held out his hand for her pen. "Now, let's list everything he did that either speaks to his rotten character or to motive for his murder."

Abby bit her lower lip while she decided which person they should start with. Finally, she said, "If we believe what Gil Pratt told me, Bryce was a juvenile delinquent who never got caught or if he did, no one has mentioned it."

As Tripp took notes, he added, "We also know for a fact he wasn't above a little blackmail if the opportunity presented itself."

Hindsight was always perfect, but Abby found herself saying, "Although I understand why they made the decision they did, it's really too bad Valerie and her sister didn't go straight to the police as soon as Bryce threatened Becca. It would've been embarrassing if the video had come out, but at least Valerie wouldn't have gotten caught up in a murder investigation. Now, even though she's innocent, her name is going to be dragged through the muck and at least the existence of the video could still become public knowledge."

Tripp didn't disagree with her. "They'll both survive the embarrassment. A life sentence for murder is a whole different matter."

True enough. "Now let's review our suspects and what we know about them."

It didn't take long to read over their meager findings and the few facts they knew weren't all that impressive. Tripp did a quick recap.

"Gil Pratt's family didn't like Bryce because of the trouble he caused both brothers with the local police. They also suspected him of stealing their family silver, but it seems unlikely they would've waited this long to get their revenge. Let's leave him on the list for now but as a low-probability suspect."

"Agreed."

Who should they discuss next? For no particular reason, she picked the school teacher. There was just something about that woman that bothered her even if she couldn't quite put her finger on what it was.

"I included Robin Alstead on the list. I swear she wasn't at all happy to see Bryce at the auction, but she insisted otherwise. That she was glad to see him and proud of his accomplishments. I thought she sounded far more sincere when she said similar things about Denny Moller. Regardless, she clearly took the news of Bryce's death hard that night, making it difficult to picture her as a killer."

Tripp frowned. "I'm pretty sure killers don't all look alike."

"True enough. I don't mean to sound judgmental, but you wouldn't believe how much that woman has changed since the beginning of her teaching career. She looked so happy and really pretty in the faculty section of the yearbooks I looked at. Honestly, I was surprised when Melanie said Mrs. Alstead was barely twenty when she started teaching. That would make her somewhere in her early forties now."

That news clearly shocked Tripp. "Seriously? I would've guessed she was another ten, maybe even fifteen years older than that."

"You've got to wonder what happened to make her change that much."

"There's no telling. It could be any number of things. You mentioned she's a widow. Losing her husband at such a young age would definitely have its effect on her."

There didn't seem to be anything Abby could have

said to that. She'd lost her own husband, but then a divorce was a completely different thing. It was a relief when Tripp moved on to the next suspect, even if this one was particularly difficult for him to consider. "Bryce blackmailing Valerie's little sister seems a whole lot worse than what he did to the Pratts back in the day. Add in the fact that Valerie had words with the man on the night in question, things clearly don't look good for her. I still say that while she's ambitious and maybe even ruthless when it comes to her career or protecting Becca, I don't believe she's capable of murder."

Abby hesitated before commenting. Deciding this process wasn't going to work unless they looked at everything from both sides, she jumped into the deep end. "So let me play devil's advocate here, Tripp. Believe me when I tell you Valerie was really angry when she confronted Bryce at the auction. She was clearly darned determined to end the threat to her sister, which was why she decided to reach out to you in the first place."

Then it dawned on her to ask something she'd been wondering about from the beginning. "Did she ever tell you what she expected you to do about it?"

He shifted as if he suddenly found his chair uncomfortable. "Yeah, she wanted to see if me threatening to beat the daylights out of him would convince him to stop."

Abby was instantly outraged on his behalf. Yeah, he was a highly trained soldier with all kinds of mad fighting skills. That didn't mean he was some kind of weapon that Valerie could point at a target like Bryce Cadigan and simply pull the trigger. "Are you kidding me? Did she really think you'd do something like that? Clearly she doesn't know you as well as she thought she did."

Tripp frowned as if he couldn't understand why Abby was so angry. Seriously? After years without any contact, that woman had been willing to use her ex-husband in a way that could've hurt him. If Tripp had gone after Bryce, he might've ended up in trouble with the law and right back in jail.

What was it about Valerie that prevented him from seeing how she was using him? Since he didn't want to hear what Abby was trying to tell him, let him figure it out for himself. Right now, they needed a plan.

She fished a fragment of ice out of her glass of tea and stuck it in her mouth in the hope it would cool her throat as well as her temper. As it melted, she considered their options. "So, we need to figure out a way to talk to Denny Moller about his relationship with Bryce. The problem is how to approach him without being obvious about what our real motive is."

"He's a plumber, right?"

"Yeah, he is, and from what I've heard, he's done all right for himself."

Tripp nodded. "Even if he built a good life, it wasn't the one he'd envisioned for himself. The damage Bryce caused Moller was as far back in the past as the trouble he caused the Pratt brothers. The only difference is that each day Moller picks up a wrench to fix a pipe, he's reminded of what might have been."

"Exactly." She set her tea aside. "There's something else about him. Leif and the guys were at the auction for the same reason you were—to support the veterans group. You're all members because you spent time in the service. The same was true for most of the people there. Some others, like the mayor, for instance, were there because it's expected that people in her position will show up at community events."

"Yeah, I guess that's true."

"So why was Denny Moller there? He isn't a veteran. Mrs. Alstead said her late husband was in the service at some point. It would make sense that she might want to show her support, but Denny never served."

"So you're wondering if Denny only came because he heard Bryce Cadigan was going to be there."

Before she could respond, he shook his head. "I wouldn't put too much stock in that thought. I'm sure a lot of people were there just to support our group. I know some of Pastor Jack's parishioners came for that reason."

Darn, she'd thought she'd been onto something there. Sighing, she said, "Yeah, you're right. We're not exactly back at square one, but we still don't have a plan for how to approach Denny Moller."

"Why not make him come to us instead? You've got an old house with old pipes. You can legitimately get an estimate to update some of the plumbing."

Not a bad idea but potentially expensive if he charged for making a house call. On the other hand, she did have some improvements that would eventually need to be done in both her house and the one Tripp lived in.

"Maybe I can come up with a small job for him to come out and fix. To make it worth his time, I could also tell him I need some firm prices on some future jobs so I can see how far my budget will stretch toward getting things up to current code."

Her co-conspirator looked a bit worried. "I could always crack one of the pipes under the kitchen sink. Something that wouldn't be a hard fix. It would be easy to make it look as if I tried to do the work myself and managed to screw it up. I'd pay the bill, of course, since we're doing this to help out Valerie."

Personally, Abby thought Valerie should be the one to pony up the money, but she knew Tripp better than to even suggest it. She offered her co-conspirator a grin. "And am I supposed to tell him that you didn't know your own strength when you twisted on that old piece of pipe?"

Tripp immediately raised both arms and flexed his biceps. "Yeah, that's me. Too strong for my own good."

Abby laughed and pressed the back of her hand to her forehead. "Warn a girl if you're going to flaunt your muscles like that, mister. You could give a lady a fit of the vapors if you're not careful." Then to pull his chain a bit, she added, "But if you do that in front of Jean sometime, I bet you'd earn a lifetime supply of tuna casseroles."

He looked horrified by that prospect. "Sometimes you're just mean, Abby McCree."

Then he stood up. "I've got to get going. In the meantime, think about which pipe you think you can live without for a few days."

"That sounds ominous."

She wasn't kidding, but Tripp didn't look too concerned. He started down off the porch but paused on the bottom step. "I'd be more worried that he's already too booked up to take on a small job. If he can't come out, then we'll have to go to plan B."

"And what's that, exactly?"

"I'll let you know when I think of one."

There wasn't much she could say to that, so she picked up their glasses and headed back inside to study her plumbing.

Chapter Twenty-One

Abby smiled at Denny Moller as she opened the door. While not as flashy as Bryce Cadigan had been, he was a good-looking man with a friendly smile, the kind that made people want to trust him on sight. If she didn't have reason to suspect him of murder, she might have felt that way herself. Once again, she kept Zeke close by as she invited the man into her home. "Thanks for coming out so quickly, Mr. Moller."

"No problem, Ms. McCree. I was in the area and finished up a job earlier than expected. Why don't you show me the toilet that needs fixing?"

After careful consideration, she decided a chronic problem with a toilet that really didn't always shut off made more sense than breaking a pipe and risk causing more damage than they meant to.

"It's just down the hall here. The problem isn't exactly new, but I had a houseguest for a few days, and it got worse while she was here. Jiggling the handle works some of the time, but that gets old. I also worry that it will keep running all night or while I'm gone."

Denny looked around as he followed her to the half

bath located on the main floor. He stopped to study their surroundings. "I love these old houses, but there's always something that needs replacing or upgrading."

"True enough. My aunt did her best to keep up with things, but it got harder for her as she got older. She had the upstairs bathroom completely redone, but she never got around to this one or the one on the third floor. I want to keep everything as original as possible, but I know some upgrades are definitely in order."

She stopped outside of the small bathroom to let him go in first. It didn't take him long to diagnose the problem. "It won't take me long to replace the guts of this toilet with a more modern version. That'll fix it right up."

"That's great. I really appreciate it. I'll be down the hall in the kitchen when you're done."

As soon as she left him, she texted Tripp that their quarry had arrived. He responded that he'd be back home from class in a few minutes. Neither of them had expected Denny would be able to come over as soon as Abby called. Not only had they yet to finalize a workable plan to pry the truth out of the plumber while they had his attention, but Tripp hadn't wanted her to be alone with the man. After all, if somehow he figured out they'd drawn him there on the off chance he'd killed Bryce, things could go very badly for her.

Luckily, Denny was still banging around in the bathroom when she heard Tripp's truck in the driveway. A few seconds later, he knocked at the back door. She waved to tell him to come in while she jotted down a few more notes about the future work she'd like to have done, if not by Denny Moller, then by some other plumber.

"How was class?"

Tripp helped himself to a bottled water out of the

fridge and joined her at the table. "It was fine, but my biology professor sure does love to hear himself talk. I noticed there's a truck parked out front. Did something happen while I was gone?"

"Nothing major. I told you that I needed someone to fix the toilet in the hall bathroom. I lucked out, and the plumber I called had a last-minute opening in his schedule. He took one look at it and knew exactly what needed to be done. Maybe I could've figured it out myself, but even my dad always said that plumbing was one area where it was smarter to hire a pro."

Tripp followed her lead. "I'm surprised he got here so fast. You just mentioned you might call someone this morning. I was going to tell you that I could probably fix it for you. I've done simple repairs like that before."

She kept an eye on the hall that led toward the bathroom. "That's okay, you do enough around here, not to mention you've got a full class load to deal with."

It was hard to tell if Denny could hear any of their conversation, but they'd both felt it was important to have a reason why neither of them had made an effort to do the work themselves. A few minutes later, Denny appeared in the doorway.

"All done."

Abby set down her pen and smiled. "Boy, that didn't take long."

Denny grinned at her. "When you've done as many as I have, you'd be that fast, too. Let me show you how it works before I do my paperwork."

Abby dutifully admired the mysteries of the new float and then invited Denny to follow her down the hall to the kitchen. He stood by the table. "Mind if I sit down while I write out the bill?"

"Not at all. Would you like a cold drink while you work?"

"Sure, if it's not too much trouble."

Abby introduced the two men and did her best to ignore Tripp's smirk as she fixed Denny a glass of iced tea and set out a plate of pecan bars. It was tempting to smack his hand when he reached for one of the cookies, but then she'd have to explain to Denny what the two of them were squabbling about. Okay, fine. She did like to offer refreshments to guests. However, having a quick snack and a drink would also ensure that Denny stuck around a little longer.

He bit into one of the bars and smiled. "This is delicious, Ms. McCree, and really hits the spot."

While he set up his laptop, he said, "I always like to know how a customer came to call me to do the work. Did you see my ad in the paper or online?"

Again, it was better to go with the truth. "Actually, I thought of you because of your support of the local veterans at the auction the other night."

Denny looked up in surprise. "You were there, too?" Then he answered his own question. "Of course you were. I thought your name sounded familiar. You were in charge of the whole thing."

He also glanced at Tripp. After studying him for a second, he grinned. "And you're the guy who got sold for the big bucks."

Tripp glared at her as he nodded. Then he bit into a cookie, no doubt using that as an excuse to not say anything more on that particular subject. She had to wonder if he was ever going to forgive her for putting him in that position in the first place.

Rather than dwell on that, she refocused her attention on the plumber. "We appreciated everyone who turned out in support of the veterans. It's a bit tardy, but thanks for being there that night. Were you there to support a specific veteran or just the group as a whole?"

Looking up from whatever he was typing, Denny said, "Several members of the group are friends of mine, and my dad served in the marines with Clarence Reed."

Tripp rejoined the conversation. "Clarence is a great guy. He's really involved in our outreach programs."

Denny nodded. "I'm familiar with some of what he does. He occasionally asks me to let one of the guys just out of the service shadow me for a few days to see if they'd like a career in one of the trades."

He went back to typing again. "Ms. McCree, if you can give me your e-mail address, I can send you the invoice right now."

She spelled it out for him and nodded when he read it back to her. "I'll get my credit card."

She wished she'd thought about getting it out right after he got there. Unfortunately, she'd left her purse upstairs. As she ran up the steps, she could hear the two men talking but couldn't make out what was being said. Tripp would no doubt fill her in later if he learned anything important, but she hated missing out on the chance to ask a few pointed questions if the opportunity presented itself.

By the time she returned, they were discussing a few other acquaintances they had in common, including Gage Logan. She hesitated in the hallway, not wanting to interrupt whatever Denny was telling Tripp. "Yeah, he talked to me that night and again since then. Actually, twice. Evidently he and that detective from the county somehow caught wind of the fact that Bryce and I have had our problems."

Tripp looked sympathetic. "I never actually met the man, but Cadigan seemed to be a bit full of himself. Did you do some work for him that he wasn't happy with?"

She had to give Tripp credit for finding a way to bring the conversation around to the source of trouble between Denny and Bryce without revealing what they already knew. She halfway expected the man to dodge the subject, but he didn't.

"No, Bryce didn't live in this area, and I doubt he would've called me even if he did. The problem started back in high school when we were on the football team together."

Tripp asked, "I played on the offensive line in high school myself. What position did you play?"

"Wide receiver." Denny reached for another cookie as he continued. "Not to brag, but several colleges sent scouts to watch me play. My dad and I even visited a few of the schools."

He stared off into the distance. "Those road trips were fun. Dad was so proud of me and the possibility that I'd be the first one in the family to go to college."

"What happened?"

Denny's smile disappeared, his attention now focused on the leg he had stretched out in front of him. "We were at practice. I went up to the parking lot to get a piece of equipment I'd left in the car."

He held out his hands, the palms parallel to the tabletop, one higher than the other. "The practice field was on one level and the parking lot was up two flights of stairs. Just as I started back down, I took a header down the steps and tore the heck out of my knee in the process. Several surgeries and a nasty infection followed. Trying to play again would've put me at risk of further damage."

The pain in his voice sounded fresh, not just a
echo of something he'd suffered through in the pas
Unlike Gil Pratt, Denny's problem with Bryce clearl
continued to haunt him. Abby held out her cred
card. "That's terrible. I'm so sorry."

Denny took the card and entered the number o
his computer. "Don't be. It wasn't your fault. Beside
it was a long time ago."

Tripp looked puzzled. "So was the problem wit
Bryce that he took your spot on the team or something?

"No, although that happened, too. The problem
was that I've always believed someone shoved m
down those steps. I never got a clear look at the gu
but Bryce was the only one who would benefit if I wa
off the team."

Abby wondered if Denny even realized that he wa
rubbing his knee as he talked. "That's terrible. Wha
did they do about it?"

Denny shrugged. "There was a brief investigatior
but only because my dad raised such a stink abou
what happened. But without witnesses, nothing eve
came of it. Bryce even came to visit me in the hospita
I might have been drugged to the gills, but I hated th
way he smiled at me."

Denny's cell phone rang, jarring all of them out o
the story. He checked the number and said, "Sorr
I've got to take this. It's the boss. My wife is the on
that keeps our business running smoothly."

After swiping his finger across the screen, he lef
the table and disappeared down the hall. "Hi, hone
what's up?"

While he talked to his wife, she and Tripp ex
changed glances. Now clearly wasn't the time to discus
what they'd learned, but she really wondered wha
Tripp was thinking. If she had to guess, he was furiou

bout what Bryce might have done to Denny all those
ears ago. That didn't necessarily translate into him
1inking Denny was the kind of man who would've
aited this long to exact his revenge.

Speak of the devil, the man in question was back.
Sorry about that. Jaycee schedules most of my ap-
ointments, so I don't like to ignore her calls."

"Not a problem."

He sat back down. "So back to Bryce. I almost didn't
o to the auction at all when I found out he was going
) be there. I ended up going because my friends de-
erved my support. Besides, it happened a long time
go."

Denny finished typing her invoice. "Regardless, I
gured it wouldn't be hard to avoid him considering
1e size of the crowd that was expected to turn up that
ight, but he actually sought me out."

Abby didn't confess that she'd seen them talking.
Really? All things considered, you'd have thought he
ould've wanted to avoid you, too."

"I agree, but I think he was having a good time play-
1g the role of the hometown boy who did well. From
hat I heard, he made a point of bragging about his
ccomplishments to anyone who would listen."

To keep the conversation going, Abby said, "I hap-
ened to run into Mrs. Alstead at the store where she
/orks. She pretty much said the same thing. She ad-
hired Bryce's accomplishments, but she was just as
roud of yours."

That seemed to please Denny. "She's a nice lady.
Ve were her first class, you know."

"That's what she said. She also said she tutored you
/hile you recuperated from your surgery."

"And wouldn't accept a dime for it." Denny laughed.
My dad had a hard time believing she was actually my

teacher when she first approached him. She looked to
young to be teaching high school. Heck, she w
barely older than I was. A lot of the guys were jealo
that I got to spend extra time with her, because sh
was so hot."

His face flushed a little red. "Don't get me wron
though. She was always very professional, at least wit
me. I wouldn't want to give you the wrong idea abo
the time the two of us spent together."

Interesting that he'd felt compelled to qualify h
comment with that "at least with" him. Had the
been rumors that she'd acted differently with som
one else? Abby really wanted to know more but su
pected he'd shut down completely if she pressed hi
on it. Instead, she went back to their conversatio
about Bryce. "I take it he bragged to you, too."

Denny shrugged. "Yeah, although he made a toke
effort to ask how my business was doing. I told him th
truth. My family and I have a good life together. Whe
Bryce started to rehash his glory days on the footba
team, I really didn't want to listen to it. He wasn
happy when I tried to excuse myself, but I didn't car
I ended up simply walking away. That's the last I saw
him."

Abby wished she could say the same, but she hadn
been that lucky. Evidently Denny knew that, too. "I'
sorry you were the one to find him, Ms. McCree. Th
had to be hard for you."

Then he frowned and gave Tripp a long look.
heard they arrested a woman for his murder. Wasn
she the one who bid so much to buy you at the au
tion?"

He sat up straighter, no longer looking quite s
friendly. "In fact, she's your wife, isn't she?"

Tripp folded his arms across his chest, still looking remarkably calm. "Actually, Valerie is my ex-wife."

Denny gave each of them a hard look. "I'm betting she's the houseguest you mentioned earlier, and you two don't think she did it."

Before either of them could respond, he slammed his hand down on the table. "So that's the real reason you called me out here on a piddling little job that could've waited weeks, if not months. You're looking for a scapegoat to get your lady friend off the hook."

He lurched to his feet. "No matter what you think, I didn't kill Bryce. I have too many good things in my life I would never put at risk just to get some kind of stupid payback after all these years. My wife and kids are worth so much more to me than what I lost back then."

When he stalked off down the hall, Abby trailed after him with Zeke hot on her heels. Denny probably didn't want to hear anything she had to say, but she at least had to try to apologize. "Mr. Moller, I'm sorry."

"For what? For thinking I'm a murderer? For leading me on about the possibility of doing more work for you?"

Darn it, he had every right to be angry, but she and Tripp weren't wrong to want the truth to come out. Drawing comfort from Zeke's warm presence against her leg, she did her best to calm the waters. She held out the list of jobs she'd written down earlier. "First of all, I do need to have these upgrades done if you'd still consider doing the work. Secondly, I'm really sorry if we brought back bad memories. We both are, actually, but Valerie means a lot to Tripp. You can understand why we both want to know what really happened that night."

Denny stopped short of walking out the door. "I get that it's a problem for the lady, but that doesn't mean I want people thinking I did it. It's bad enough the cops have been talking to me about that night. I don't need anyone else getting involved. I have to live in this town, and I can't afford rumors flying around that could hurt either my family or my business."

At least she could reassure him on that point. "I promise we won't repeat anything you told us."

Although he had no reason to believe her, she really hoped he'd take her at her word. He studied her list for several seconds before slowly nodding. "I'll hold you to that. Once things settle down, maybe I'll call you to set up a time to discuss your plumbing."

"Please do."

When he was gone, she sagged against the door frame and petted Zeke. Tripp wandered into the entry silently watching Denny get into his truck and then drive away.

"I wish I could believe he was guilty, but I don't."

She couldn't disagree with his assessment. Tripp looked down at her, his expression bleak. "I'm actually surprised he told us as much as he did, considering he didn't know either one of us before today."

Her stomach hurt a little from the confrontation with Denny and also knowing how all of this was affecting Tripp. She wanted to hug him but wasn't sure he'd let her right now. "Yeah, it was likely on his mind anyway. I know he said we were the ones to stir up all those ugly memories, but I think it was Bryce who did that just by coming to town. Regardless, I think Denny might have a few 'what might have been' regrets going on, but he strikes me as a man who is happy with the life he built and wouldn't change how things turned out even if he could."

Tripp mirrored her stance, leaning against the other side of the doorway. "Lucky him, but where does that leave us? More importantly, where does that leave Valerie?"

They both knew the answer to that last question. It left her in a cell facing a charge of first-degree murder.

Chapter Twenty-Two

In the aftermath of their discussion with Denny Moller, neither Abby nor Tripp was in the mood to discuss the case anymore. He went outside to work off some of his frustration on the blackberries that were staging a comeback in the backyard. Zeke decided to hang out with him for a while, probably sensing that Tripp was the one who could use his undemanding company.

Meanwhile, Abby had a major meeting to prepare for, something she should have already been working on. The executive board for the veterans group was meeting in the morning to go over the final plans back at the hall where the dance would be held. Afterward, a group of volunteers were going to start decorating the place, transforming the room to look like a World War II–era USO. While she hadn't exactly forgotten about the meeting or the dance, neither of those things seemed all that important right now.

No, she couldn't afford to think that way. Regardless of Valerie's problems, it wouldn't do to forget the reason they were holding the dance in the first place.

The veterans group was depending on the proceeds from the auction and dance to fund a lot of great programs.

Abby booted up her laptop. Luckily, she'd already done a rough draft of the agenda for the meeting, so it needed only a quick polish. After that, she needed to write up the to-do lists for the various committee chairs to make sure they were all on the same page about what was left to be done before the night of the dance rolled around. She was just finalizing the agenda when Tripp reappeared in the doorway. "Hi, what's up?"

He gave her a hopeful look. "I got a call from Valerie's attorney. They're transferring her to the county jail either tonight or early in the morning because they've scheduled a bail hearing at the courthouse. He wanted to know if she can still stay here if he convinces them to let her out. Evidently that's questionable since the D.A.'s office is making noise about her being a flight risk since she lives in California."

For Tripp's sake, Abby didn't hesitate. "Sure thing. I don't see why not. Will they need me to be there? Because that would be a problem. The dance committee is meeting tomorrow, and I have some errands I really need to run."

"I'll call him back and ask. Maybe it's enough that I'll be there for her."

Abby ignored the small twinge of what she was afraid was jealousy. Of course Tripp would want to be there for Valerie. It would've been more shocking if he didn't. At least Abby could make it as easy for him as possible. "Give the attorney my number in case he has questions. If it turns out I need to sign something, have him let me know the particulars. I'll do my best to get it taken care of as fast as possible."

"Thanks, Abs. I knew I could count on you."

He disappeared back down the hall toward the kitchen, and Abby forced herself to get right back to work. It wasn't long before Tripp was back still talking on the phone. "Okay, I'll let her know, and I'll see you at the courthouse in the morning."

He hung up and shoved the phone in his pocket. "He said the prosecutor's office may call you to verify that it's all right if Valerie comes back here to stay. They also might put one of those stupid ankle bracelets on her, the kind that keep track of someone's movements."

Abby could imagine just how much Valerie would love that. On the other hand, it would be a vast improvement over staying behind bars. "I'll keep my fingers crossed that they decide to be reasonable about things."

She half expected him to leave again, but he remained standing in front of her, shifting his weight from one foot to the other and back again. "Was there something else, Tripp?"

"Look, I know you're busy and everything. Heck, I should be back at the house doing laundry and homework myself, but I'm too restless right now to do anything useful. I was wondering if you'd like to go shoot pool or something. I'll understand if you've got things to do."

Her own mood immediately brightened. "Will you buy me another burger at the bar?"

He grinned. "I'll even throw in a beer and some onion rings, too."

She didn't hesitate. "It's a deal, but I need to finish up here and do a couple of other things. Give me an hour."

"You got it."

Looking much happier, he headed for the door.

Glad she was able to do something to help him out, she called after him, "Just so you know, the loser buys."

He snickered. "Bring lots of money then."

She could still hear him laughing after he walked out the door.

Abby picked up her last French fry and offered it to Tripp. He ate it and washed it down with the last of his beer. Then he nodded toward the other side of the room.

"Looks like a table is opening up."

She glanced over to where a couple of guys were putting their cues back up on the rack behind the pool table. Without waiting for her to respond, Tripp was already out of the booth and heading over to stake their claim, leaving her to follow after him. He quickly had the table set and ready to go.

Chalking the tip of his cue, he asked, "Let's play eight ball. Do I need to explain the rules?"

When she shook her head, he asked, "Do you want to go first? I'll even spot you a couple of balls."

She checked several cues before deciding on one and then offered him an innocent smile. "I wouldn't want to take advantage of you like that. Why don't you show me how it's done?"

Abby stepped back against the wall to give him room to maneuver. Explaining what he was doing as he moved around the table, he managed to put three solid colored balls away before missing a shot. "Your turn. Let me know if you want any advice on how to line up a shot."

She ignored him as she studied her choices. Okay,

this was going to be fun. After walking around to the other side, she sent one ball after another flying across the table to disappear into the pockets. After clearing the last striped ball, she calmly took her last shot, dropping the nine ball in the corner pocket. Without saying a word, she racked the balls. Tripp stood there watching with his mouth hanging open while she lined up the cue ball to break. "Want to go best two out of three to decide who buys the next round?"

He nodded and muttered something unflattering about pool sharks. She laughed and took her shot. When she finally missed and surrendered control of the table back to him, she couldn't help but feel a bit smug. "Did you think big bad soldier boys were the only ones who knew how to play?"

He tossed the chalk at her. "How many poor guys have you fleeced out of their beer money over the years?"

"Enough that eventually I had trouble finding someone willing to play me. I haven't actually picked up a cue since college, so I'm a bit rusty."

He snorted at that statement. "If that's true, I'm not sure I'll be able to afford playing against you when you're back in top form."

She patted him on the arm. "Don't worry, big guy. I can always spot you a few points."

"There goes that mean streak of yours again, Abby. I don't know how you keep your reputation for being all nice and helpful."

"Remember I'm sneaky, too."

"You are that."

Then he made a bank shot to sink his first ball in the side pocket. Looking pretty proud of himself, he moved around to the other side of the table to line up another shot. Experience had taught her that some men, her ex-husband included, didn't like losing to a woman. Tripp, on the other hand, clearly enjoyed the challenge of playing someone who was as good or maybe even better than he was. For her part, Abby didn't care if she ended up buying every round of drinks if it meant Tripp could shed his worries about Valerie long enough to enjoy himself.

They were about to start another round of games when she spotted a familiar face in the crowd. "Tripp, Gage is headed this way."

He kept his attention on the table as he asked, "Is he in uniform?"

"Yeah."

"Does he look ticked off?"

She risked another quick look in Gage's direction. "It's hard to tell. Why? Do you think Denny ratted us out to him?"

"It's a possibility."

Any concerns Tripp had over Gage's mood or reason for being there didn't affect his shot. He quickly sank the nine ball, winning the game. She decided to wait until Gage reached them before heading over to the bar to order the next round.

Gage stopped to talk to a couple of people on his way through the crowd. By the time he finally reached them, she was on pins and needles. Tripp nudged her. "Try not to look so guilty. Even if Denny didn't snitch on us, Gage will suspect you've been up to something. If you need something to do, set up our next game."

She promptly dropped the first ball she picked up, sending it rolling across the floor. Tripp chased it down and brought it back to her. "Calm down, Abby. What's the worst that could happen?"

She muttered, "We could end up in the slammer and living on Jean's tuna casseroles."

"Look on the bright side. They're better than eating roasted rats."

Before she could decide if Tripp was teasing or speaking from experience, Gage finally reached their little corner of the bar. She pasted a smile on her face. "Hi, Gage. I was just heading over to buy our next round. Can I get you anything?"

"Sorry, I'm on duty."

"I've already switched to soft drinks since beer adversely affects my game. Tripp, on the other hand, mysteriously gets better after a few cold ones."

Gage didn't look surprised. "He's had years of practice. But I'll take a cola if you're buying. While you're at it, can you put in an order for a burger and fries for me?"

"Will do."

The bartender saw her coming and already had Tripp's beer waiting. She showed him her empty glass and held up two fingers. By the time she reached the bar, he had her order ready for her. She had him add the drinks and Gage's meal to their bar tab and then paid the bill. Although she and Tripp were still having fun, she had a feeling they'd be leaving soon. The only question was if they would be headed for home or that jail cell that had been haunting her dreams lately.

When she turned back toward where she'd left the two men, they were nowhere in sight, and someone else had taken over the pool table. She finally spotted Tripp standing near a booth along the back wall. As soon as he knew she'd seen him, he sat down across from Gage. She set the drinks down on the table and slid in next to Tripp. "So, Gage, is this where you usually eat when you're on duty?"

"Sometimes. I like to check in with the owner once

in a while to see if there's been any trouble I should know about. Tonight, though, I spotted Tripp's truck out in the lot and thought I'd see if he and the guys had a game going."

He gave her a long look. "He was just warning me about your mad pool skills. Seems you've taken him for a few drinks tonight. He suggested I bring extra cash if I ever pit my skills against yours."

She was feeling pretty proud of herself. "Don't worry, Gage. I'd go easy on you for the first round. After that, it's everybody for themselves."

"Good to know."

Then his smile faded as he looked at Tripp. "I hear Ms. Brunn's bail hearing is tomorrow morning."

"Yeah, I'm meeting her attorney there. Abby has already said that Valerie can come back to the house once all the paperwork is signed."

If anything, Gage looked even more grim. Had something happened that made it unlikely that Valerie would be getting out anytime soon? Abby tightened her grip on her glass, hoping against hope she was wrong. She wasn't the only one who was sensing a storm on the horizon. Tripp set his beer back down on the table with exaggerated care. "What's happened now?"

"It's not good, Tripp. We just learned Bryce Cadigan had applied for a restraining order against not just Becca Brunn, but Valerie as well. Becca allegedly vandalized Bryce's car, and Valerie made a bunch of threatening calls when he reported her sister to the police."

Tripp slammed his beer down on the table. "But he was the one blackmailing—"

Gage cut him off. "I know, Tripp, and so does the D.A. Here's the thing, though. Bryce also recorded his phone calls. Your ex-wife didn't sound exactly sane when she was screaming at him, and she made some pretty ugly threats while she was at it."

Abby wrapped her hand around Tripp's arm and leaned her head against his shoulder, hoping the connection would help him control his temper. While she was at it, she drew Gage's attention back in her direction. "So if you've figured out that Bryce was a sleezy jerk, you have to figure Becca wasn't the first one he's blackmailed. Surely there are other people who had strong motives for wanting him dead."

"We're looking into that, but we haven't found anyone else who was at the auction that night who had a recent grudge against him. Considering Valerie came all the way from California that night to confront Bryce, she was pretty strongly motivated to end the threat to her sister."

Now Abby was the one getting mad. "We both know there are other people right here in town who had problems with him—Gil Pratt and his brother, Denny Moller, and maybe even Robin Alstead."

Gage sighed. "We've already talked to Gil and Denny, but what do you know about Robin Alstead that I don't?"

She felt bad about trying to throw both Denny and Gil under the bus, but her first loyalty was to Tripp. As far as the former teacher went, she'd yet to learn anything concrete about the woman's past relationship with Bryce other than he'd been in her class.

She settled for simply saying, "I just think there was something off about the way she acted when he talked to her at the auction. She was the only person in the whole place who broke down and cried when she learned he was dead; but when I talked to her, she acted as if he was just one of all the hundreds of students she'd had over the years."

"I can't arrest someone for crying, Abby." Gage leaned forward, elbows on the table to stare right into her eyes. "For the last time, I'm telling you to stay out of my case. You know Ben and I won't stop looking until we get to the truth. Hopefully Valerie will make bail and stay with the two of you until we do."

He met Tripp's gaze head-on. "The only reason I told you about the restraining order and recordings is that I didn't want you to get blindsided tomorrow if the judge denies bail. I know you'll take that hard, and it won't be easy for Valerie, either. I can't swear that my word that you and Abby here will keep an eye on Valerie will carry any weight, but I plan to be there to tell them that."

Tripp relaxed just a little. His voice was rough, but there was no mistaking his sincerity when he spoke. "That means a lot, Gage. All you can do is try."

At that point, the bartender delivered Gage's meal. When he reached for his wallet, the bartender waved him off. "The lady already took care of it."

Gage waited until the man left once again before responding. "I don't suppose you'll let me pay you back."

She did her best to lighten their mood. "No way. You know how I like to make sure my friends are well fed."

Both men laughed and shook their heads, the tension between them gone for the moment. Abby figured the cost of a burger and fries was worth every penny if it meant Tripp and Gage could make it through another day with their friendship intact. Of course, that could all change tomorrow if things didn't go well for Valerie.

However, if she did make bail and came back to the house, Abby planned on having a long and ugly conversation with the woman. She'd deliberately misled both her and Tripp about how bad things were between her, her sister, and Bryce Cadigan. If she'd lied about phone calls and threats, had she also lied about not killing him?

For Tripp's sake, Abby hoped not.

Chapter Twenty-Three

As expected, Abby's meeting with the veterans group went smoothly. Although she had no intention of getting caught up in any more committees, she had to admit that Pastor Jack and the others had been amazing to work with. She hadn't had to nag about anyone's assigned duties, nor was she going to have to step in at the last minute to pick up the slack for someone who had made promises he or she couldn't keep. They'd even applauded when she and Zoe summarized how much they'd made at the auction. That they'd sold out of tickets for the dance was icing on the cake.

She was also grateful that no one brought up the murder. It was never far from her mind, but that didn't mean she wanted to rehash it over and over again. At least the meeting kept her busy while she waited to find out how things had played out in Valerie's court hearing that morning.

For now, she smiled at everyone at the table. "Thanks again for coming today and for all your hard work. I don't know about the rest of you, but I'm thrilled with how well all of this is turning out, and I can't wait to see the hall all decorated for the dance. I've heard from a lot of people how much fun they've had getting their costumes, too."

As soon as the meeting broke up, those involved in the decorating moved to another table in the corner to get organized. Abby picked up her files, planning to head back home, only to realize the pastor was waiting to speak to her. At least he'd brought both of them a fresh cup of coffee. "Was there something else we needed to discuss?"

"Don't worry, I'm not going to bring up the subject of you heading up my church's fund drive again." His eyes twinkled just a little as he added, "Until after the dance is over, anyway."

She was sure he was only teasing about the whole idea. Mostly, anyway. "That's very considerate of you."

His expression turned more sober. "Seriously, I wanted to touch base with you to see how you're holding up after what happened at the auction. You handled everything so well that night, but the effects of something like that have a habit of popping back up when we least expect it. If you find yourself needing someone to talk to, twenty-four/seven, you know you can call me."

The sympathy in his voice was almost her undoing. "I really appreciate the offer, Jack. While I won't say it's been easy, I'm doing okay. I've been keeping busy, which helps."

Jack didn't look as if he quite believed her, but he didn't push it. Instead, he asked, "And how about Tripp? From what I've heard, his ex-wife's reappearance in his life came as a bit of a shock to him, and now she's been arrested. I'm betting that's got him wound up pretty tight."

She debated how much to say. Tripp and the pastor were friends, but that didn't mean he'd appreciate her confessing everything to Jack. For sure, she wasn't going to admit that the two of them had been doing a bit of sleuthing themselves.

"He's understandably worried about Valerie. They might not have remained close since the divorce, but he's doing whatever he can to help her. In fact, he went to her bail hearing today. If everything goes well, he'll bring her back to stay at my house until her case is resolved one way or the other."

Jack always saw more than other people did. "You seem to have some doubt that she'll make bail. Is it because of money issues or something else?"

Having such mixed feelings about the whole situation made it hard for her to answer. "I have no idea what kind of bail the D.A. will recommend or anything. But since she lives out of state, I'm worried they'll want to hold her until the trial. I can't imagine how Tripp will react to that."

"Yeah, I can see why that would bother him." Jack stirred his coffee. "I take it you don't think she did it."

Although it wasn't really a question, she responded anyway. "I think there's a lot of room for doubt. I never met Bryce Cadigan before that night, and I certainly have no complaints about how he handled the auction itself. Having said that, if I could go back in time, I would never have hired him. It's not nice to speak ill of the dead, but I've learned a lot about him since the auction that makes it clear he wasn't a very nice man."

Jack patted her hand. "I've heard a few things myself. Don't blame yourself for how things turned out, Abby. We did our due diligence before we offered him the job, and he did come highly recommended."

That much was true. "Yes, he did. I have to think that the reason behind what happened to him had its roots somewhere in his past here in Snowberry Creek. I'm sure Gage and Detective Earle are both checking into stuff like that."

"That doesn't mean it's easy to sit by and wait for them to figure it all out. For you or for Tripp."

He was right about that. "Yeah, it's been hard, especially on him. I'm betting some of the local folks were relieved to learn that Valerie was arrested. They might not appreciate it if the cops keep asking questions that might lead back to someone here in Snowberry Creek. Far better to blame a stranger whenever something goes wrong."

The pastor sighed. "Sadly, that's true. I won't mention any names, but a new visitor to my church mentioned that very subject just yesterday. She said she left her previous congregation because of how judgmental they'd become."

He checked his watch and set his coffee back down on the table. "Well, I should be going. I have another meeting to get to. I meant what I said, Abby. If there's anything I can do to help either you or Tripp, let me know."

"I will. On another subject, I'm expecting a couple of invoices to arrive in the mail either today or tomorrow. When they come, I'll drop them by the church if that's okay."

"That'll be fine. I'll approve them and pass them along to the treasurer to pay."

She walked outside with Jack. It was time to head home and find out if her houseguest was back.

As it turned out, Tripp had come back home alone. According to Valerie's attorney, there was a chance she would be able to post bail, but it would be at least tomorrow before they found out for sure. Tripp wasn't happy, but all Abby could do was remind him that it was only a matter of time.

After filling her in on what happened, he'd taken his bad mood back over to his place and slammed the door shut behind him. She was pretty sure he'd been mumbling something about needing to go to class. Although Zeke had been following Tripp, he either didn't notice or didn't want company. The dog had stared at Tripp's door for several minutes before giving up and returning to her side. On the way back to her own house, she pondered what she could do to help Tripp but didn't come up with anything. Maybe it wouldn't hurt for the two of them to spend a little time apart.

The next morning, the invoices she'd been waiting for arrived, which gave her the perfect excuse to leave for a while. After picking up her dry cleaning, she would stop at the church to drop off the paperwork with Pastor Jack and then take Zeke for a walk at the park.

Grabbing Zeke's leash, she called him to come. "Come on, boy. We'll go see Pastor Jack and then stop by Something's Brewing to grab us a couple of snacks and a latte. After that, we'll hang out in the park for a while and then go for a walk in the national forest. That sounds like fun, doesn't it?"

Zeke came running at the mention of several of his favorite words—snacks, park, and walk. As soon as she opened the back door, he bolted outside and made a beeline for the car. Before he got there, though, Tripp stepped out on his porch. Zeke immediately veered off in his direction, his tongue hanging out and his tail wagging a mile a minute. It was as if he hadn't seen his friend in days.

As soon as he reached Tripp, he skidded to a halt and then jumped up to put his front paws on Tripp's chest, putting his head at his buddy's eye level. The impact forced Tripp back a step, but then he managed to hold his ground.

"You're sure excited, Zeke. I see you're wearing your leash, so you must be taking Abby somewhere fun." As he spoke, he ran his fingers through Zeke's fur and put up with a couple of slobbery licks on his face. Abby finally caught up with her exuberant pet and grabbed his leash. She gave it a sharp tug, dragging the dog back down to stand on all fours.

"That's enough, Zeke. Tripp doesn't need doggy kisses making his face all sticky."

Tripp grinned. "Don't worry. Doggy love washes off."

"Yeah, but you can't say that about those paw prints he just put on your shirt."

Tripp glanced down and then frowned at the dog. "I swear, Zeke, you always manage to do that at the worst times. I got all the way to class last week without realizing I had muddy prints on both my shirt and pants."

He made a halfhearted effort to brush the dirt off his shirt. "I told him he was a dead dog if he did this to me again."

Cute. "Sorry, Tripp. He got away before I could grab his leash. It's my fault he's so excited. I promised him a treat from Bridey's place, a trip to the park, and then a walk in the woods."

He patted Zeke's broad back. "Wow, the trifecta of his favorite things."

"How about you? Any more word on what's going on with Valerie's case?"

"The attorney is supposed to call as soon he knows anything. I'm hoping it's soon. I'd like to pick her up and get back here before rush hour. This standing around and waiting for word drives me crazy." He shuffled his feet and added, "Sorry if I was kind of a jerk yesterday."

"That's okay. I know you're worried about Valerie. You'd be welcome to ride along with me and Zeke. If the lawyer calls while we're out, I can drive you back here to get your truck quickly enough."

"That sounds good, actually. Let me lock up and I'll—"

He stopped midsentence and pulled out his cell phone. "Oops, give me a second, Abby. It's Val's attorney."

The call didn't last long, and Tripp looked a lot happier by the time he hung up. "I'll have to take a rain check, Abby. They're finalizing the paperwork now. In theory she should be ready to go about the time I get there."

When he headed straight for his truck, Abby called after him, "Doggy prints, Tripp."

"Right. Thanks for the reminder."

He did an immediate about-face and headed back into his house. Zeke tried to follow him, but she headed him off at the pass. "Come on, dog. We've got places to go and treats to eat."

After a quick stop at the dry cleaners to pick up her dress for the dance, it was a short drive to the church. Rather than leave her furry friend in the car while she ran inside, she clipped on Zeke's leash and took him with her. Jack wouldn't mind, and it wasn't as if they would be there for more than a couple of minutes.

That had been the plan anyway, but unfortunately the door to his office was closed, and the church secretary was nowhere to be seen. Abby could hear the muffled sound of voices, so clearly Jack was with someone. At least there was a small sign on the counter that said the secretary would be back in another fifteen minutes.

"Zeke, looks like we're going to hang out here for a while. I'd rather wait a few minutes now than make a second trip."

She settled into one of the two visitor chairs by the window. Meanwhile, Zeke sighed and sat on the floor next to her and rested his head in her lap. She stroked his wrinkly forehead and thanked him for his patience. While they waited, she found herself trying without success to figure out what else she and Tripp could do to help clear Valerie's name. They'd run out of viable suspects, so she really hoped Gage was having more luck than they were. The only person she still had questions about was Mrs. Alstead, but it was hard to picture the rather dowdy woman doing anything so horrible to a former student.

The sound of Jack's door opening startled her out of her reverie. She sat up straighter and prepared to let the pastor know she was there to see him. He stepped into sight still talking to the woman who walked out right behind him. "Thanks again for stopping by, Mrs. Alstead. As I said, I'm really sorry to hear that you'll be leaving Snowberry Creek soon. If I can do anything to help, let me know."

Meanwhile, Abby struggled to make sense of what she was seeing. If that really was Mrs. Alstead standing there, the former teacher had undergone an amazing transformation since the last time their paths had crossed. The drastic changes in her appearance had taken years off her appearance, and she looked far more like her old yearbook picture. Was she the person Jack mentioned had walked away from a more conservative church recently? It seemed likely, and Abby could only imagine what Mrs. Alstead's friends there would have to say if they ever saw her sporting skinny jeans and blond highlights in her hair.

As soon as Jack spotted her, he said, "Hi, Abby. I hope you haven't been waiting long. I'll be right with you."

Then he looked a bit chagrined as he turned his attention back to Mrs. Alstead. "I'm sorry, where are my manners? Abby, do you know Mrs. Alstead?"

All things considered, she realized she didn't know the woman at all. "Yes, we met a few days ago when she was kind enough to help me at the store where she works. I'm sure the manager there really appreciates how helpful she is."

From Mrs. Alstead's response, that might have been laying it on a bit thick. It was even more surprising when she said, "That was actually my last day working there."

Abby wasn't sure what to say to that. She could be wrong, but all the major changes in the woman's life seemed suspicious to her. She somehow doubted the woman would welcome any questions on the subject, though.

Meanwhile, Zeke, who had been curled up behind the front of the counter, picked that moment to make his presence known. He stood up and approached Jack, maybe hoping he had some doggy treats. Luckily, the dog froze in place when Mrs. Alstead gasped and quickly retreated back into Jack's office.

"Get that animal away from me!"

Abby hauled back on Zeke's leash. He gave her a re-proachful look but dutifully returned to her side. "I'm sorry he startled you, Mrs. Alstead. I promise Zeke's a gentle giant."

Her claim might have been more believable if the dog apparently hadn't taken a delayed dislike to the woman. While he didn't growl—much anyway—he stood at attention and watched Mrs. Alstead's every move as if he expected her to go on the attack any second.

Looking confused, Jack quickly stepped in between his guest and Zeke. "Why don't I walk you out, Mrs. Alstead? Abby, I'll be right back."

Then he walked out of the office right behind the other woman, leaving Abby staring at the empty door-way.

By the time Jack returned, both the church secretary and Jack's next appointment had arrived. With any chance of quizzing the pastor about Mrs. Alstead's future plans gone, Abby apologized for Zeke's questionable behavior and handed over the invoices before beating a hasty retreat.

To her surprise, Robin Alstead hadn't actually gone far. Instead, she stood watching the front of the church from the far edge of the parking lot. It was too much to be hoped that she was waiting for Pastor Jack or maybe her ride. But no, she went on point the minute Abby stepped out of the church.

"Come on, Zeke. Let's see if we can reach the car before that woman catches up with us." He dutifully broke into a slow trot, dragging Abby along in his wake. She'd just managed to let him into the back seat and close the door before Mrs. Alstead planted herself behind Abby's car. Short of running her over, there was no way to avoid hearing whatever the woman had to say.

"Was there something you needed, Mrs. Alstead?"

"Yes, I need you to stop spreading rumors about me."

"I haven't been." Not really. She'd just told Gage about the woman's behavior the night of the auction.

"You've been talking to the police. I know that for a fact since they came to my house to grill me about the night Bryce was killed."

Feeling seriously defensive now, Abby sputtered, "I wouldn't take it personally. They're talking to everyone who spoke to Mr. Cadigan that night."

The woman drew herself up to her full height. "Of course I take it personally. We both know they've already arrested the woman who poisoned poor Bryce. She came all the way from California just to kill him with that lethal cocktail of drugs she had tucked into that fancy silver purse she was flashing all over the place at the auction."

She took a step closer to Abby. "Valerie Brunn is a cold-blooded killer, but I don't expect you to believe me since she's friends with both you and that man you live with. Not only that, I've learned you're both good buddies of Chief Logan. It's no surprise he's trying so hard to find someone else to take the blame. Well, that's not going to happen, not if I can help it."

How many people had Robin Alstead just insulted? Abby didn't even know where to begin to straighten out that much wrong thinking. Still, she gave it her best try.

"First of all, Valerie Brunn is not my friend, although she is Tripp's ex-wife. Second, he doesn't live with me. He rented the house behind mine from my late aunt, so he was already living there before I ever moved to Snowberry Creek. That makes him my tenant, not whatever you were trying to imply. And finally, if you actually knew Gage Logan at all, you'd never accuse him of being anything but an honorable man. He won't be satisfied until he finds the truth."

Forcing herself to take a deep breath, Abby walked away. She opened her car door and glanced back at the still-fuming woman. Mrs. Alstead's body was rigid with pure rage as she snarled, "You're right, Ms. McCree. The truth will come out. Eventually the cops will find the evidence, and that woman will pay for Bryce's death. She'll rot in that jail cell for the rest of her life."

Abby was so done with this conversation. "Actually, she's getting out on bail even as we speak. Now, I would suggest you move out of the way. Zeke and I have somewhere we need to be."

Thank goodness by the time she was inside the car with the engine running, Mrs. Alstead had already stalked away so Abby could leave. She waited until she was several blocks away to pull over to the side of the road and sat there until her hands stopped shaking. Putting the car back in gear, she glanced at Zeke in the rearview mirror. "That is one scary woman, Zeke. The trouble is I think I'm the only one who knows that."

He woofed in sympathy, which made her feel a little better. "We're not going to let her spoil the rest of our afternoon. Let's go see Bridey and then stop at the park."

That earned her a sloppy kiss, but at least she was smiling again.

Chapter Twenty-Four

After getting their treats at Something's Brewing, Abby and Zeke spent some quality time lazing in the sun at one of the picnic tables at the park before taking their walk along the river. It had taken her a while to shake off the tension from her unexpected confrontation with Robin Alstead, but Zeke's undemanding company helped a lot. Her improved mood lasted right up until she turned onto her street and spotted Tripp's truck pulling into the driveway.

Even from a block away it was clear that he wasn't alone. As Abby followed them into the driveway, she told herself it was a good thing that Valerie's attorney had been able to arrange bail. Tripp had taken her arrest hard and having her back out on the street should go a long way to improving his mood. She didn't know what would happen if the police didn't find the real killer soon.

But that was a worry for another day.

Plastering a smile on her face, she parked the car and let Zeke out of the back seat. As usual, the dog charged across the grass to where Tripp and Valerie stood on his front porch. His smile looked far more genuine than did the barnacle's, but Abby didn't hold it against the woman. She'd had a tough few days, and her future wasn't looking that much brighter.

"I'm glad you're here."

Valerie didn't look convinced of that, but she managed a small smile. "Thanks for letting me come back. My attorney said your offer of a place to stay and Chief Logan showing up at court made all the difference in how things played out."

Tripp unlocked his front door, but then turned back to join the conversation. "Val and I were headed inside to update Becca on what's happening. Later, I thought I'd drive over to the diner and pick up dinner for all three of us. How does that sound?"

"Great, actually. I'll have whatever the special is and a piece of chocolate cream pie. If they're out, then coconut cream will be fine."

"Got it. I'll let you know when we're ready to eat."

Then he followed Valerie inside and closed the door. Abby stared at the empty porch for a few seconds before calling Zeke to her side and heading back to her own place, feeling more alone than she had in a long time.

Two long hours later, she finally got a text from Tripp that he'd gotten back with dinner and to head on over to his house. She thought about offering to have them eat at her place, which had far more room. However, this was the first time he'd ever invited her over. She wasn't going to miss the opportunity.

Even though his house was small and might feel a bit cramped with three people and a big dog, she wasn't going to leave Zeke behind. It would hurt his feelings, and she knew Tripp wouldn't care. She grabbed the bottle of wine she'd chosen as her contribution to the night's festivities.

Tripp opened the door as soon as she stepped onto his porch. "Come on in. Valerie will be out in a minute. She didn't sleep much the whole time she was in jail, so she took a nap after we talked to her sister."

"I'm sure she'll sleep better tonight."

Valerie walked out of the bedroom. "I hope so. I'm still feeling pretty ragged. I have to say that my cell here in Snowberry Creek was a luxury resort compared to the one at the county jail."

She shuddered, but then laughed a little. "I never thought I'd see the day that I could do a personal comparison of two different jails."

"Well, we don't need to think about that tonight." Tripp motioned them to have a seat at his tiny kitchen table. "Let's treat Frannie's cooking with the respect it deserves."

Abby smiled at Valerie. "He's right. Her pot roast is to die for, and her pie is perfection."

Valerie must have agreed with their assessment of Frannie's pot roast because she finished every bite on her plate. They had to wait for Tripp to finish his double order of pot roast before he'd let them have dessert. He was just passing out the individual cartons containing their pie when Valerie frowned and pointed toward the front window. "What's that flickering red light?"

By that point, Zeke stood at the door, his deep growl filling the silence. Abby didn't answer even though she had her suspicions about what was going on outside. They were confirmed as soon as she crossed the short distance to the window and pulled the curtain aside.

There were at least three police cruisers in the driveway and maybe a couple more out on the street in
front of the house.

"What's going on, Abby?"

She glanced back over her shoulder to look at Tripp.
He was standing next to Valerie, his hand on the
woman's shoulder, his protective instincts clearly on the
rise. Doing her best to sound far calmer than she was,
she said, "There's a whole bunch of cops here. You two
stay here and keep Zeke with you while I go see what
they want."

Tripp started to protest, but she cut him off. "No,
it's my house, my responsibility. I've got my phone. As
soon as I know what's going, I'll let you know."

She drew a deep breath and stepped outside. Several
officers stood on her back porch while one pounded
on the door. Rather than charge into the middle of
whatever they were doing, she stayed where she was and
called out to get their attention.

"If you're looking for me, I'm over here."

When no one responded, she tried again but louder
this time. Finally, one of the officers tapped the man
knocking on her door on the shoulder. She hadn't left
the porch light on, so it was hard to make out any details, but she recognized Ben Earle's voice when he finally answered her. "Ms. McCree, I need you to come
here. I regret to tell you that we're here to execute a
search warrant on these premises."

"I'll be right there."

After telling Tripp what was happening, she stepped
down off the porch. Her stomach did a slow roll, and
she struggled not to lose her dinner right there in the
backyard. It was with some relief that she reached her
back porch with her dignity intact.

All of the deputies seemed to tower over her, including Ben himself. That didn't mean she was going to be intimidated by either their superior height or numbers. Deliberately using his first name to remind him that he'd been a guest in her home more than once, she asked, "What's this all about, Ben?"

Even in the shadows, she could see the sympathy in his eyes. "We just received new information that leads us to believe that there is evidence hidden in your house regarding the murder of Bryce Cadigan."

There was no way to prevent them from doing what they had to do. Rather than defend her territory, she stepped back out of the way. "The door's unlocked. Do what you have to. Should I go back over to Tripp's house to wait, or do you need me to be here while you go rampaging through my home?"

Okay, that was probably out of line, but having them root through her possessions just because she'd been nice to Valerie left her feeling violated.

Ben knew it, too. "I'm sorry about this, Abby, but we have no choice but to follow up on any credible lead. Gage and his men are here, too. I promise we'll take care with your home. Even so, it might be easier for you if you wait with your friends. Gage and I will come talk to you when we're finished."

She didn't trust herself to say another word. It was bad enough that she was having trouble seeing clearly through a thick sheen of tears. After giving him a quick nod, she walked away.

Tripp paced his small living room like a caged animal while Valerie sat at the kitchen table with her arms wrapped tightly across her chest. "What's taking them so long?"

Abby prayed for patience. "It hasn't been even fifteen minutes, and I have a big house. It could take hours for them to go through everything. I'd just like to know what they're looking for."

She gave Valerie a questioning look, but the woman only shrugged. "I have no idea. All I have with me is a few changes of clothing, my laptop, and some toiletries. Nothing incriminating if that's what you're wondering."

"Actually, I believe you. Detective Earle said they'd received information that there was evidence hidden in my house. He didn't say where they got the information, but you have to think the real killer is trying to make sure they have good reason to focus all of their attention on you."

Tripp stopped pacing. "Do you have any idea who that might be?"

When the doorbell rang, it brought their conversation to a screeching halt. Tripp jerked the door open to reveal both Ben Earle and Gage Logan standing on the porch. At least this time he made no effort to prevent the pair from coming inside. If the small house had felt crowded before, the addition of two more big men made it so much worse. The tension ratcheted up so high that it was hard to draw a full breath.

Ben looked past Tripp toward Valerie. He held up a silver clutch that was wrapped in a plastic bag sealed shut with duct tape. "Ms. Brunn, do you recognize this purse?"

She left the table to get a closer look. "It looks like mine, but I haven't seen it since the night of the auction."

Turning her attention to Gage, she said, "I told you then it was missing, and Abby said her people didn't find it when they cleaned up the hall after the auction."

Ben glanced at Gage, who nodded in confirmation. "That was her story at the time. I didn't put it in my official report. All things considered, I should have."

Valerie's worried gaze bounced back and forth between the two men. "It's the truth. Tell them, Tripp. We looked all over for it that night."

He crossed his arms over his chest, his feet planted wide apart. "We did look. She said she left it on the table when she went to confront Bryce. It wasn't there when she got back."

Gage didn't look convinced. "An eye witness insists you had it with you when you followed Bryce outside."

Valerie shook her head. "That's a lie! Besides, what kind of idiot would hide something incriminating where it could be easily found. Wouldn't it have been smarter to throw the darn thing in the trash if there was something in it that would tie me to the murder?"

Abby couldn't argue with the logic of that. She closed her eyes and let her memory of that night play out in her head. "I watched her talking to Bryce right up until they walked out to the parking lot. I don't remember seeing her holding anything in her hands. Does it have an over-the-shoulder strap or chain?"

Ben held the purse up to examine it through the plastic. "I don't see one. But don't some women's purses have a chain that tucks inside when they don't want to use it?"

Valerie sounded a little calmer when she answered. "They do, but not that one. You have to carry it in your hand."

Abby had a question of her own. "It didn't take you very long to find it. Did the person you talked to tell you where to look or something?"

"No, they didn't. We split up. Some of the officers

went upstairs to search. The rest of us started on the main floor. We found it in the downstairs bathroom."

Well, that didn't make any sense. Why would Valerie have hidden something in a room that everyone used? Besides, Abby had been in and out of that room herself and hadn't seen it. "Where was it hidden? It's such a small room. Something like that would've been hard to miss."

Gage answered this time. "I found it at the bottom of the toilet tank."

Tripp blinked and shook his head as if to clear it. "Wait a minute. You're talking about the downstairs bathroom, right? The one in the hall between the entry and the kitchen?"

When both men nodded, Tripp smiled and gave Abby an expectant look. It took her a few seconds to realize why. As soon as it hit her, she grinned back at him and then turned to face Gage and Ben. "Gentlemen, I know for a fact that Valerie didn't put that purse there. She couldn't have."

"Why not?"

"For two reasons. First, she hasn't set foot in my house since Tripp picked her up today. She's been over here the whole time. But more importantly, you both know where she was yesterday. She was in your custody, and that's when Denny Moller came over to replace the float and everything in that toilet. If the purse had been in there then, he would've said something, and I know he didn't put it there afterward. When he was done, he called me into the room to show me how the new style of float worked. I will cheerfully sign a statement that there was nothing in the tank besides the new stuff he put in and water."

Ben's stance relaxed as his attitude shifted from suspicious to curious. "So how do you think it could have gotten there?"

"I was gone most of the afternoon, and Tripp was gone picking up Valerie. I'm pretty sure I locked the doors when I left to run errands, but I honestly can't swear to that. Regardless, I know I didn't lock it when I came over here."

She gave them a little time to digest that much before asking, "When did you receive the tip about the evidence?"

Gage waited until Ben nodded before answering. "An anonymous e-mail came in to our office just over an hour ago. We're still trying to trace the source, but it could take some time."

Tripp was back to frowning big-time. "So this helpful person doesn't want you to know his or her identity. Doesn't that seem a bit suspicious, not to mention a little convenient, considering Valerie just got back here a few hours ago?"

Neither policeman denied that. Ben said, "That doesn't change the fact we had to investigate."

Valerie looked far less haggard than when the conversation started. "Of course you did. My only question is what happens next?"

Gage answered first. "We do our best to track down the author of that e-mail."

Then Ben added, "And once we know who sent it, we'll know who is trying so hard to point us in your direction, Ms. Brunn."

Both men started for the door, but Abby reached out to stop Gage. "Can I go home now, or are your people still going through it?"

Ben Earle left with the purse, but Gage stopped to answer her. "We called them off as soon as we found the purse, so you can head back over anytime you want. If you want to go now, I'll walk you over."

The realization that someone had been sneaking around in her house creeped Abby out big-time. She'd definitely feel safer with a police and mastiff escort. "I'd like that. Valerie, are you coming?"

The barnacle stepped closer to her ex-husband and said, "If it's okay with you, Tripp, I'd rather stay here tonight."

He didn't look happy, but he also didn't say no. That left Abby no choice but to go home alone. She carefully schooled her expression and said, "Well, I'll be going. Come over for breakfast in the morning if you want to, Tripp."

Faking a smile, she added, "Of course you would be welcome, too, Valerie."

Then she almost bolted out the door with Zeke and Gage right behind her. For a second she thought Tripp called her name, but she didn't slow down to find out.

Her escort didn't say anything until they reached her back porch. "After we get this mess cleared up, she'll be heading back to California."

She didn't want to talk about it, but she appreciated Gage's heavy-handed effort at offering comfort. "I know."

"Not to mention our boy is too busy watching you to notice that she wants more from him than a chance to sleep on his couch. She's pretty fragile right now. Hanging on to him helps."

"Yeah, the barnacle has a pretty firm grip on him right now."

Gage's laughter rang out across the yard. "Seriously, you call her the barnacle?"

Abby slapped her hand over her mouth. Good

grief, she couldn't believe she'd let that slip. She must be more tired than she thought. "Yeah, I do, but just in my head. Please don't say anything to Tripp. He wouldn't appreciate it."

Still chuckling, Gage held up his hand as if swearing an oath. "My lips are sealed. Just remind me never to get on your bad side."

It was well past time to change the subject. "So what comes next?"

"We'll check in with Denny to verify what you told us. Hopefully the D.A. will believe Ben when he tells him that Valerie couldn't have hidden the purse herself, and that neither you nor Tripp would've been that stupid."

She managed a small laugh. "Thanks—I think."

He followed her into the house to make sure everything was locked and secure. "I'd better hit the road. I'm headed home, but call if you need me."

He was out on the front porch headed for his cruiser when she finally figured out what was bothering her about the whole situation. "Gage, can I tell you a couple of quick things before you go?"

He hesitated, but then finally said, "Sure."

"I'm ninety percent sure Valerie didn't have her purse with her when she went outside with Bryce. In fact, she never had it with her anytime I was around her."

"Okay, we'll take that into consideration."

"That's not what I'm saying. Have you seen Robin Alstead lately?"

"Not since a day or so after the auction. Why?"

"She made a big show of crying that night as if Bryce's death hit her harder than it did anyone else. But since then, she's gone through this amazing transformation, to the point I almost didn't recognize her.

She's also quit her job at the discount store, and I overheard her and Pastor Jack talking about her leaving Snowberry Creek for good."

By that point Gage was reaching for his notepad and pencil. "Go on."

"When I left his office, she was waiting for me out in the parking lot. She went on a total rant, blaming me because you talked to her about Bryce's death. She made a point of claiming Valerie had been flashing that fancy silver purse all over the place the night of the auction and no doubt it held the cocktail of poisons she'd used to kill Bryce."

Gage looked up from his notes, his gaze intense. "You're sure that's how she described it? As a 'cocktail of poisons'?"

"Yes, that's what she said. Why? Is that important?"

"We've never released the details on what killed him, just that he was poisoned. Only the killer would know for sure that it was a mix of drugs, not just one."

He dropped down into one of the chairs. "But why would she kill him, though? As far as I can tell, it's been years since their paths have crossed."

Abby paced the length of the porch as she tried to piece together everything she'd heard about the woman. "She started teaching the year Bryce and Denny were juniors. I've heard that she was only about three years older than they were at the time since she graduated from college way early. Someone said she taught for two years and then took a year off for some reason. What if that had something to do with Bryce? Maybe Valerie's sister wasn't the only person he's been blackmailing."

Gage stood up. "Well, looks like this day is about to get a whole lot longer."

"I'm sorry."

"Don't be. Go inside and lock the doors. I'm going to call Ben, and then we'll go pay Mrs. Alstead a little visit."

"Be careful, Gage. She scared me at the church today. I think maybe she's more than a little crazy."

"Thanks for the warning."

As he headed back down off the porch, she called after him. "I'm sorry I got in the middle of your case again. I did it for Tripp."

He waved his hand. "We'll let it slide this time considering you may have given us the last few pieces to solve this puzzle."

Then he was gone.

Chapter Twenty-Five

A huge mug of dark roast was the only thing that made being awake at six in the morning tolerable. Even Zeke had refused to abandon his bed at that ungodly hour, and Abby didn't blame him. Not even the sound of her making breakfast had convinced him to come downstairs. After eating a bowl of cereal, she'd taken her coffee outside onto the porch, where the morning air was damp and cool, and the scent of Aunt Sybil's roses hung heavy in the air. She cuddled under a quilt and sipped her coffee while the sun slowly peeked over the horizon.

She'd checked the local morning news shows, but there'd been no mention of any new developments in the Bryce Cadigan case. At least the search of her house hadn't made any headlines, but it was worrisome that there was also no mention of any new arrests being made. Had Robin Alstead been able to explain away her comments about Valerie's purse or the poisons to Gage's satisfaction? It was too early to call Gage considering he'd probably been out to all hours last night. If she didn't hear from him or

Ben by midmorning, though, she'd make a couple of calls.

The sound of approaching footsteps had her sitting up straighter. It was about the time that Tripp usually got back from his morning run. She tried not to think about where—or how—he'd spent the night. It was none of her business, or at least that was what she kept telling herself. After tossing her quilt on the porch railing, she stepped down off the porch to wait for him to appear.

Unfortunately, the last person she wanted to see stepped out of the shadows. Robin Alstead stalked toward her, that same wild-eyed look on her face that had scared Abby at the church. "You just had to go shooting your mouth off to the police about me, didn't you?"

Abby jumped back. "Mrs. Alstead, what are you doing here?"

The woman's smile was even more terrifying. "I'm here to snip off one more loose end before I leave town. Luckily for me, I wasn't home when your good buddies from the police department decided to pay me a late-night visit. I have one of those apps on my phone where I can monitor my front porch from anywhere. Soon as I saw them prowling around, I made a U-turn and holed up somewhere else for the rest of the night."

Abby backed up a step and then another. "What's that got to do with me?"

Mrs. Alstead followed her step for step. "Don't play coy, Ms. McCree. At first I couldn't figure out why the police didn't drag that Brunn woman right back to jail if they found that purse stashed in your bathroom. The only answer I could come up with is that it was something I said to you at the church yesterday. No matter. Once I shut you up permanently, the cops won't be able to prove anything since you won't be around to testify."

As she spoke, she pulled her hand out of her jacket pocket; it was clutching a syringe full of a murky liquid. "The bad news for you, Ms. McCree, is that this stuff is lethal. The good news is that heroin combined with fentanyl is surprisingly fast acting. Just ask Bryce. Lucky him. I really wanted him to suffer for ruining my life, but I couldn't risk someone finding him too soon."

When she suddenly lunged toward Abby, she threw her hot coffee, mug and all, right at Mrs. Alstead's face. The woman howled as she tried to scrub the scalding liquid off her skin. Abby used the distraction to shove her into the large climbing rose by the porch before bolting across the yard, screaming as she ran. Tripp's door slammed open and Valerie stepped out on the porch. Abby shouted at her, "She's crazy! Get back inside and call nine-one-one!"

She'd never make it to Tripp's house before Mrs. Alstead caught up with her, so she headed around the back of the house toward the driveway, hoping to follow it down to the street out front. As she rounded the corner of the house, she could hear Zeke inside barking like crazy. At least he was safe. It was tempting to look back over her shoulder, but that would only slow her down. Regardless, with Mrs. Alstead shouting threats each step of the way, it was clear she was coming on fast. Either a good dose of adrenaline or insanity was giving the woman an unexpected boost of speed.

Approaching the sidewalk out front, Abby had but a second to decide which way to turn. Going right would lead her closer to Main Street and the possibility of more people, but going left increased the likeli-

hood she'd run into Tripp. She didn't hesitate. Left, it
was. She pelted down the sidewalk, struggling to keep
up the killer pace. Then her foot caught on a crack in
the sidewalk, sending her plunging to the ground. Ignoring the pain in her knees and hands from hitting
the concrete hard, she struggled back to her feet.

It was too late. The slight delay gave Mrs. Alstead
just enough time to catch up with her. She grabbed
Abby's ponytail and give it a hard jerk, nearly dragging
her back down to the ground. "This would all be so
much easier for both of us if you'd just stop fighting."

"Not happening."

She kicked out, hitting the woman's knee hard,
which sent her flailing backward. Abby scrambled
backward and took off running again. The pain in her
legs made it hard to keep moving, but she'd die if she
slowed down. Then, miracle of miracles, her own personal hero stepped into sight where the trail into the
national forest ended at the sidewalk. It was enough to
give her one last burst of both hope and speed.

"Tripp!"

He spotted her immediately and kicked it into high
gear. "Abby, run to me!"

Thanks to his long legs, he closed the distance between them incredibly fast. He shoved Abby aside,
putting himself directly between her and her attacker.
She struggled to draw in enough air to pant out a
warning, hoping he'd understand what she was trying
to say. "Syringe. Poison."

"Got it."

Mrs. Alstead had to know she didn't stand a chance
against a man Tripp's size, but that didn't stop her
from trying to do an end run around him to get to
Abby. In a lightning-fast move, he grabbed her wrist
and twisted it, the sound of bone breaking nauseating

to hear. At least it forced the woman to release her weapon. When the syringe dropped to the ground, Abby picked it up and jumped back out of the way as Tripp took the woman down on the sidewalk and kept her there.

Abby fought to catch her breath as the sound of her pounding heart gave way to the roar of sirens and screeching tires.

For once, Abby wasn't the one handing out munchies and drinks. Gage made the coffee while Valerie set out plates and cups. Tripp dug several kinds of cookies out of the freezer and arranged them haphazardly on a platter. Even Zeke was fretting up a storm and acting all apologetic that he hadn't been out there to help Tripp save the day.

Tightening the quilt Tripp had draped around her shoulders, Abby endured all the fussing as best she could. When they all finally joined her at the table, she realized someone was missing. "Where's Ben Earle? I'm sure I saw him out there, too."

Gage stirred his coffee. "He followed the ambulance to the hospital. Once they take care of Mrs. Alstead's wrist, he'll escort her to the county jail for processing."

That was good news. There was no way that woman should be running around loose armed with syringes and threatening people. Abby nibbled a cookie and patted Zeke's head. "Do we know for sure why she killed Bryce?"

Tripp ignored her question. Instead he pulled his chair close enough to hers that he could put his arm around her shoulders. With his other hand, he pushed her coffee cup closer to the edge of the table. "Drink that. It will warm you right up."

"Fine, but I still want to know what drove her over the edge." She dutifully picked the coffee up and took a sip. Yep, just as she expected. He'd laced it with brandy. Considering how badly shaken up they'd all been by her near brush with death, she wouldn't be surprised to learn everyone's cup contained equal parts alcohol and caffeine.

Maybe if she waited long enough, the brandy would loosen Gage's tongue, and he'd fill her in on what had transpired after Tripp turned Mrs. Alstead over to the police. Abby had been too busy getting patched up by the EMTs—again—to keep track of what was going on. Once they'd cleaned and bandaged her knees, Tripp had reluctantly allowed her to limp back into the house. He'd wanted to carry her, but she insisted on making it that far on her own. A woman had to have some pride. Back inside, she'd wanted to stay in the living room, where she could watch what was happening out on the street, but he'd nixed that idea and settled her at the kitchen table instead.

The brandy slowly eased the sting of her scrapes and took the edge off the lingering fear from knowing how close to dying she'd come. Tripp, too. It was a miracle that neither of them had been stuck with that syringe filled with death. She leaned in closer to him, the direct contact a nice reminder that they were both safe and sound.

When he tightened his hold on her, she tilted her face up to look at him. "Things are still a bit foggy. Did I thank you for charging to the rescue?"

Valerie rolled her eyes and set her mug down on the table. "At least four times so far."

For the first time Abby noticed the lines of tension bracketing Valerie's mouth as she stared at her ex-husband sitting with his arm around Abby. Maybe it was time to put a little room between the two of them, but Tripp only tightened his hold on her when she tried to shift away. Before the moment became even more awkward, Valerie's phone rang.

"It's my attorney."

She immediately left the table and headed down the hallway to take the call. The conversation with her lawyer must have been brief and to the point because she was back a short time later. "Good news, everybody. The charges have been dropped, and I can go home."

Gage smiled. "That's really great, Ms. Brunn. It was bound to happen, but Detective Earle must have nudged the D.A.'s office into putting through the paperwork extra fast."

Tripp stood up and moved as if to hug her, but she backed away. "I'm going to go call my sister and let her know this nightmare is finally over. Then I'll see if I can get a flight out later today."

No one said a word when Valerie bolted back down the hallway. Abby was happy for Valerie, although she wouldn't miss having her underfoot. Then she remembered the bad news. The dance was only a few days away, so the barnacle would be back for her big night out with Tripp.

With that unhappy thought, she held her cup out to the man in question and said, "Can I have more brandy?"

Gage left not long after that, but Ben returned two hours later to take everybody's official statement on the morning's events. Tripp sat on the other end of the couch from the detective, while Valerie took the chair next to Abby's, positioning herself to face the two men. Her luggage was already sitting by the front door, but she'd had to delay leaving for the airport long enough to answer Ben's questions. Now that they were done, Abby decided to ask one of her own. "So did Mrs. Alstead say why she killed Bryce?"

Ben put his paperwork aside and leaned back in his seat. "You had it right, Abby. She and Bryce were briefly involved right after he graduated from high school. He was nineteen and evidently just killing time until he left for college, and she was barely twenty-two. The age difference wasn't all that much, and I guess she took the affair pretty seriously. One thing led to another, and she ended up pregnant. That he would refuse to marry her came as a real shock. Evidently, he made it clear that he had plans for his future and wouldn't give them up for her. Back then, she must have thought the district wouldn't keep an unwed mother on staff, so she took a leave of absence ostensibly to work on a graduate degree."

He looked pretty disgusted by that point. "If Bryce hadn't decided to try his hand at blackmail a few years later when she got married, she might have done all right. When she finally refused to pay him another dime, he made good on his threat to tell her husband. Mr. Alstead didn't believe in divorce, but she said things were never the same between them. She used the money from her job at the store just to ensure Bryce didn't tell anyone else. I suspect it was her husband's prolonged illness and death that caused her to snap, but we'll never know for sure. Regardless, for some reason she clearly decided to put an end to Bryce screwing up her life once and for all. She might fill in a few more of the blanks if the case goes to court, but I hear her attorney is pushing hard for a psych evaluation and a plea agreement."

Abby almost hoped the lawyer was successful. After all, Bryce had caused a lot of people pain, not that his bad choices justified cold-blooded murder. She didn't know about the others, but she was still wondering about a few things that had happened the night of the auction. The detective wasn't there to satisfy her curiosity, but surely it wouldn't hurt to ask.

"So, Ben, do you know why Mrs. Alstead tried to frame Valerie? That couldn't have been part of her original plan since no one knew she would be there that night." She glanced in the other woman's direction. "Not even Tripp."

Ben sipped his coffee and set the cup aside. "Near as I can tell it was a spur-of-the-moment thing, and Ms. Brunn here had the bad luck of being in the wrong place at the wrong time."

Well, that was putting it mildly considering Valerie had come darn close to taking the fall for the murder. If Abby and Tripp hadn't lured the plumber over to fix the toilet under false pretenses, Mrs. Alstead might have even gotten away with it.

The detective was still talking. "Mrs. Alstead admitted she came to the auction with the specific intent of killing Bryce. She tracked his movements after the actual auction ended, hoping for an opportunity to catch him alone, preferably in the parking lot."

Then he nodded in Valerie's direction. "My best guess is that she noticed the two of you arguing and saw Bryce insisting on taking the discussion outside. Who knows, maybe he'd even told her he was about to leave since the main event of the auction was over."

Ben paused to look at Abby. "I meant to ask, was he

under any obligation to stay for any specific length of time after his official duties ended?"

"No, the contract only specified that he'd act as master of ceremonies to emcee the auction. He was free to leave after that, but he obviously decided to hang around to catch up with old acquaintances."

Pausing to make a couple of notes on his report, Ben picked up the story where he'd left off. "Regardless, Mrs. Alstead didn't want to miss what might have been her best chance. She exited the building through a side door in the hallway by the restrooms and waited to see what happened next. When Ms. Brunn went back inside, Mrs. Alstead followed Bryce over to his car. After he got in, she knocked on the driver's window and asked him to roll it down so she could tell him something. As soon as he did, she stabbed him in the neck with a syringe."

"Rather than risking being seen, she immediately retreated back inside the building through the side door, which she'd left propped open. From there, she eventually rejoined her friends without anyone noticing she'd been gone."

Abby was puzzled. "Bryce's car door was open when I found him. Do you think he tried to go after her?"

Ben frowned. "More likely he was trying to get help. Either way, he wouldn't have gotten far. From what I understand, death would have taken minutes at best."

Valerie joined the conversation. "All things considered, I'm surprised he would have let that woman get anywhere near him. He had to know how much she hated him."

Tripp looked disgusted. "Apparently that guy had been getting away with all kinds of bad stuff his entire life without any consequences. I doubt he thought anyone would ever get the best of him, especially a woman."

Ben agreed with Tripp's assessment. "Which just shows you what an idiot he was."

There was one more thing Abby wondered about. "So Mrs. Alstead managing to get her hands on Valerie's purse was just the icing on the cake when it came to pointing the police in her direction."

"Yeah, Mrs. Alstead saw Valerie lay it down on the table before joining Tripp at the door to watch what was going on outside. She picked it up with a tissue to avoid getting her fingerprints on it and then slipped it inside her own purse. It's doubtful anyone would have noticed with everything that was going on right then."

Valerie rubbed her arms as if she were cold. "That's what I get for leaving the stupid thing just sitting there while I wandered around the room. There wasn't anything of value in it, so I wasn't concerned about leaving it undefended. That's the last time I make that mistake."

Meanwhile, Ben closed his notebook and stood up. "Well, I need to get back to the office. Feel free to call me if you have any more questions, Ms. Brunn. I'm really glad things worked out for you."

"Me too, Detective."

Then he grinned at Abby. "Do me a favor and try to stay out of trouble for a while. As much as Gage and I enjoy your cookies, we could use a little less excitement around here."

She almost choked on her coffee. Did he think she really wanted to get caught up in murder investigations? She was still trying to come up with a scathing reply as he started toward the door. Meanwhile, Valerie stood up, too. "Since we're done here, I'm going to leave for the airport. My reservation isn't for several hours yet, but there's a chance they can get me on an earlier flight if I arrive in time."

Tripp headed for her luggage. "Give me your keys, and I'll take these out to the car for you."

Instead of following the men outside, Valerie lingered nearby to stare out the window as Tripp stowed her bags in the trunk of her rental car. Finally, she glanced back at Abby. "I know I really blew it with Tripp all those years ago. Yeah, he was gone too much, and we were both too young to be married. But looking back, I wish I'd stuck it out a while longer. Maybe we could have gotten through the bad times and come out okay in the end."

Turning back to the window, she sighed. "Seeing him again has stirred up all kinds of emotions, both good and bad. I've dated other men over the years, but none ever lived up to my memories of Tripp. I thought maybe I'd romanticized him all out of proportion, but as it turns out, I didn't."

Finally there was something Abby and the barnacle could agree on. "He is a good man, Valerie. One of the best."

There was something really sad about Valerie's answering smile. She pulled two pieces of paper out of her purse and dropped them on the table next to Abby's chair. "Those are the tickets to the dance. I won't be coming back for it."

Abby picked them up. "You paid a lot of money for these, Valerie. I'm not sure the veterans group is set up to offer refunds, but I can ask."

"Don't worry about it. The money is going to a good cause." Her expression turned a bit wistful. "Take Tripp to the dance, my treat."

She started for the door, stopping long enough to say one more thing. "I know you probably don't want any advice from me, Abby. But as you said, Tripp's a good man, and he obviously cares about you. If you get the same chance I had back in the day, don't blow it like I did."

Then Valerie walked away, leaving Abby sitting in stunned silence. She started to follow her outside but changed her mind. All things considered, the barnacle deserved to say goodbye to Tripp one last time without an audience.

Epilogue

The night of the dance arrived at long last. Abby had met the other committee members at the hall two hours before the dance was due to begin in order to finish up a few last-minute details and get the refreshments organized. Meanwhile, the photographer they'd hired to take portraits set up in a small room off to the side. And although a live band might have been more realistic for a World War II dance, they'd decided a deejay was far more practical, not to mention economical. It took a little longer than expected to get his sound system set up, and people were already arriving by the time everything was done.

Abby stopped to look around the hall and was amazed by the transformation. She'd studied pictures of dances from back during the war years, and the committee had done an amazing job of bringing that world to life. She couldn't wait for the festivities to get underway.

Slipping into the ladies' room, she traded her work clothes for her dress and then touched up her makeup. Finally, she took a deep breath and stepped in front of the full-length mirror on the wall. Wow. Between the old-fashioned dress and her hair done up in victory rolls, she barely recognized herself. Even if she said so herself, she was really rocking the look.

After the stressful events of the past two weeks, she suspected the whole town was ready to have a little fun. It was time to go find her escort for the evening. Tripp hadn't let her see the uniform he'd rented for the night, so she had no idea what he'd be wearing.

She could only hope it wouldn't be hard to pick him out of the crowd of soldiers and sailors out there. Taking a deep breath to steady her nerves, she opened the door out into the narrow passage that led back toward the hall, where the music had already started playing. As it turned out, she needn't have worried.

A tall, handsome soldier, looking extra sharp in his army uniform, stood leaning against the wall a short distance away. As soon as she appeared, he straightened up and sauntered toward her, an appreciative smile on his face that she felt all the way from her head to her toes.

Then Tripp offered her his arm. "Miss McCree, I do believe this next dance is mine."

Connect with Us

Visit us online at
KensingtonBooks.com
to read more from your favorite authors, see books
by series, view reading group guides, and more.

for sneak peeks, chances to win books and prize packs,
and to share your thoughts with other readers.

facebook.com/kensingtonpublishing
twitter.com/kensingtonbooks

Tell us what you think!

To share your thoughts, submit a review,
or sign up for our eNewsletters, please visit:
KensingtonBooks.com/TellUs.

Grab These Cozy Mysteries
from
Kensington Books